Veil of the Phoenix

ERIKA GIFFORD

ISBN-10:0-9992659-0-3
ISBN-13:978-0-9992659-0-1

Published by Teragram, ink,
www.teragram.ink

Edited by Sandra Peoples, Next Step Editing,
www.nextstepediting.com

Cover art by Grace Bohlen

Cover design by Megan Jarosz

DEDICATION

To the softly falling light of day...
and those who shared it with me.

CONTENTS

Veil of the Phoenix

PROLOGUE

I n the quiet after the storm, a figure slipped through the afternoon shadows of the castle garden. Falkerstone Castle had been built many years ago when the Davia kingdom was still young. The king at the time knew that his people needed a stronghold to gather in when times got rough. He knew a strong structure would make sure his people felt secure, and that they would acknowledge him as protective leader of the people. Falkerstone's strong, gray walls did make the people love their leader more, but in the cool, rain-bathed afternoon light, the dark, glistening stones were foreboding and the figure that slipped out from under the shadow felt the same. Those walls were a prison rather than a sanctuary, the walls harboring enemies far worse than anything it had ever encountered.

The figure slipped through the gate in the garden and silently closed the latch. A great weight seemed to fall from the figure's shoulders. It stood more erect and threw back its hooded head in premature jubilation. But in another minute, nothing was further from its mind.

Behind the figure arrows flew from the walls and stones ricocheted off the cobblestone path. The gate to the castle was lifted, unleashing a patrol of soldiers and knights bearing the insignia of a phoenix.

The figure ran down the hill that led beyond the river, to the woods that would offer it asylum. Its cloak slipped off and fell behind. The soldiers closed in, swords drawn and spear tips gleaming.

An arrow from the castle met its mark and the figure stumbled and slid down the rest of the hill.

The patrol slowed and came to a halt. They sent a half of the men down to check the body. It wasn't moving. Its breath was shallow and blood poured out of the wounds in its arm and head.

The soldiers took a good look. The figure's black hair fell down over its pale forehead and closed eyes. He seemed frail for the small boy that the soldiers saw: the brown shapeless tunic was big and unmarked, and his boots came all the way up to his thighs, making it harder to run away.

The false alarm was over and the soldiers had better things to do than save a young boy from dying. They were needed back at the castle to finishing executing the remaining royalty. These soldiers were a part of the Phoenix Followers and had the sole responsibility of finishing off the old king's descendants.

An ancient prophecy foretold this year as bringing a change in the bloodline of the rulers. The Phoenix Followers thought they were the ones chosen to bring about this change by force, and that's just what they were trying to do.

The soldiers were certain the boy had been on the list to execute—his face looked familiar though they couldn't put their finger on it—but it didn't matter now that he would be dead in a few hours.

They reported back to their captain and returned to the castle.

Back at the bottom of the hill, the dark-haired boy's chest heaved and the arrow quivered. His eyes fluttered open. Sweat beaded on his brow as he stood up and stumbled into the river. His pale, bloodied fingers clutched at his arm where the arrow entered and he squinted as he searched the other shore.

The water reached past his knees but didn't get any deeper. The boy's breath was short and he coughed. Blood streamed down from the cut in his forehead and dribbled down to his tunic, mingling with the blood from his arm. He reached the other shore and fell down on his side as he clutched at his arm.

His eyes fluttered and pain coursed through his body and into his head, overpowering his senses and leaving him in a death-like sleep.

The shadows lengthened and the cool breeze from the storm that had moved east chilled the boy to his bones. His breath slowed, his heart faltered, his pale hands chilled and clenched at the arrow in a death-like grip.

The boy did not move.

CHAPTER ONE

T he morning outside the manor walls sang with beautiful anticipation. Lord Lucas and his son Philip had been staying at their manor house in Southland for the summer, and almost nothing could have taken them away from the beautiful peace they enjoyed together.

Philip's eyes fluttered open, their blue pupils matching the blue sky outside his window. How could anything go wrong on a day like this? It was the kind of day one would look back on and would feel sad because such beauty is fleeting, but in the moment, nothing could be further from their minds, except for the great evils that the day would indeed thrust upon them.

Philip leaped out of bed, eager to be ready for when his father called him. His shirt slid over his head and settled in around his frame in the perfectly tailored manner he was accustomed to.

He made his way downstairs, greeting servants until he arrived at the dining room.

He entered, his shoulder brushing against the doorframe in his clumsy manner, and greeted his father with a smile as he sat down to eat.

"Good morning," he smiled at him.

His father, Lord Lucas of Southland, looked up from his food and book and repeated the formality.

Philip was given a plate already laden with food, and he fell to demolishing it.

They were still at table when a messenger came through with a letter for the lord of the manor.

"Lord," the messenger began, his heart thumping loud enough for Lucas to look up from his food in alarm, his whole being now bent on hearing him out.

"Yes?" he replied, his voice strained. The book fell closed like the chapter of his life that he had previously enjoyed.

"Sir, Falkerstone Castle has been taken over by a group of men who claim they fulfill the year of the Phoenix and call themselves Phoenix Followers. Your lives are in danger if you stay here any longer," the messenger bowed, knowing full well he had risked his life to bring this message to this man who had saved his life years ago. But if Lucas had saved his life then, he was saving Lucas and his son's life now.

"Philip?" Lucas began, ignoring his food, his book, and the servant. He spoke in a voice that told his son he had been expecting something like this for a while. "We must finish up here quickly. Then we will head down past Falkerstone to Farvel Forest. We will be needed. If there are any other nobles left, or others who are against this new order, they will convene there. It is the perfect place to train an army as it is still close to the castle—just north of it—and no one would suspect it," he sighed. "I have seen this coming for years. With the new unrest in the country it was bound to happen that someone would take that old poem literally and use it as an excuse to become ruler. However, I have informed the other nobles that if such a thing like this were to happen, we would gather in Farvel Forest and create a resistance."

"Father?" Philip asked, strangely courageous for his eighteen years. "Would you like me to head down to the other villages to see if anyone else will join us?"

"No. We had better not," Lucas replied, thinking carefully. "We don't want the information getting into the wrong hands."

Philip stared down at his plate and bit his lip. He knew that his father didn't want to lose him the way he had lost his wife.

Many years ago, when Philip was still very young, she had gone out into the village when the plague came through, and she never come back. After that, Lucas had been as protective of his son as of a mother cat to its kitten. Philip had been taught how to fight with a sword and shoot with a bow, but his father knew those skills couldn't defend him from everything.

"Father," Philip pressed on. "If we'll be fighting, we'll want everyone we can get!"

"I know that!" Lucas reminded him. "I've been in more wars than you have, thankfully. Don't worry, they'll come of their own. Now, hurry up and finish breakfast. We need to be off as soon as possible."

Philip dashed up to the room he had lived in since the day he was born, that room which had earlier told him not to worry because today could only be the best day he had ever lived. His curly blond hair bobbed back at him in the mirror as he bent over the chest of drawers, gathering the few items he would be able to take with him.

He changed from the fancier tunic to something more practical for being an outlaw.

"Outlaw," he whispered the word to himself. "Something in its ring speaks of adventure. And of loss."

He turned to the small bundle he had ready. His sword, bow and arrows, cloak, and the dagger he always carried on his person made the few things he had to take seem light in comparison. He left his armor behind knowing he would soon get leather armor that wouldn't be so heavy to carry.

He slung his pack over his shoulder and took one last look at his old room: His small bed with the cotton covers, the handmade rug on the floor that he had sat on when he was a child, the window to the east that had always woken him up in the mornings, the window he would look out of and daydream about having adventures and saving people from enemies. That window meant so much to him. At night he could see the stars in the sky, glittering orbs of light he could wish upon when no one was listening.

Philip turned from the room and closed the door behind him as he trudged down the stairs. He passed through the huge dining hall and out through the main gate. His father was waiting with the horses.

"We have enough money to get to Falkerstone Castle before continuing north to Farvel Forest. From there, we will be shooting our own food!" Lucas smiled. "Come on, it is an adventure. Don't look like you're going to your own funeral."

Philip attempted to put a smile on his face, if only for his father, but those words hardly instilled any hope within him.

They headed out past the last gate in their town and turned to the north. It would take them three days to get to the castle, and another day to reach Farvel Forest. Philip knew the way well. He had traveled it only once to the ball for the queen's niece. But after they had passed the castle, it would be up to Lucas as to what needed to be done and where they would go. Philip's knowledge of the outside world only went so far.

The days were still warm for early spring, but once they got to the forest, they would be thankful for the warmth. Otherwise the shade would be too cool for the clothes they had brought.

Father and son walked their horses slowly as they made their way up to where they would spend the night.

CHAPTER TWO

L ucas didn't sleep that first night on the road, fearful that someone had heard of their leaving and would come after them. Perhaps the next night they shouldn't stop to sleep, but rather pull forward to make sure they weren't being followed. He sighed—that would make for two nights in a row when he wouldn't sleep. Getting ahead would have to wait, and Lucas had to make sure he took care of himself first.

The soft, spring night caressed their faces. Philip stirred in his sleep, his hands on the hilt of his sword in readiness. The starlight illuminated the trees around them and the stars themselves could be seen hanging over the small village that was nestled below them.

To the north he could see the constellation of a tree. Everyone knew the mythology behind it, though it was just that: myth.

The stars seemed to shine just a bit brighter though there was no reason for them to. The trunk of the tree was made up of many stars, but what made it different from other constellations was the branches. They started out where the trunk ended very close together. They seemed to spread out in line from there, creating depth and reaching away from the north.

Always north they must go. How else could they reach the forest? Lucas looked out from their camp, smoke from their smoldering fire marring his view and making the features that he knew so well blurred and unfamiliar. Off to the east he knew that Lord Alonzo's powerful estate lay, and beyond that the Bucan Dynasty, the Kingdom of Davia's utmost enemy. To the west lay the great sea, the one that no one knew much about yet, the one that had beckoned to him in his youth before he had grown old and cautious, before he had fallen in love with his wife at court. To the south lay his home, the one he had lived in most of his life, the one that he had shared with his wife while she was still alive, the one that held all of his memories of her beautiful face, her loving ways, and the selfless sacrifice that had ended her life. He turned from the south, too many memories filling that place.

To the north lay his dark future. That future held the castle, so recently taken and fallen under control of an enemy they had not foreseen. But even further north than that lay his hope. The forest that would soon hold his troops, his brothers, and their sons. That forest would be their refuge, a blistering welt to the Phoenix, something to make them think twice about. Perhaps they would succeed, perhaps some royalty was yet to die, perhaps the king's bloodline would prevail and could be set back on the throne.

But perhaps wasn't enough for him. Nothing would ever come of making such optimistic expectations for the future—he had a son to worry about now. Sure he was old enough to come into his own, sure he was old enough to be introduced at court, sure he was old enough to go to battle, but how could he lose the only link he had to his wife? How could he let her son go into the kinds of danger that he had let her go into? How could he let anything happen to the boy she had left behind after she died?

He sighed and turned over, his eyes torn from the landscape he had been studying. He needed rest.

Philip woke before his father the next morning, his back stiff and aching from the stones they had been forced to make their bed upon. He opened his eyes and stretched his arms, the sword falling from his grasp where it had stayed all night. He ran his fingers through his hair, pulling it back from his face so he could soak in the morning light and air. He let the blanket fall from him, shivering in the cold that greeted him. His eyes turned from the day to his father, watching his haggard, gray face rise and fall with his breathing. His heart reached out to the man, grown old before his time. Something awakened in his heart, something heroic, something that made him want to protect his father who looked like he could protect no one.

He stood up, folded his blanket, and swiftly packed his bag. His father stirred and opened his eyes. They didn't speak, but rather packed their things and moved out without eating. They both knew they had to conserve food and if that meant skipping breakfast, they would do it. Other obstacles would keep their minds off their empty stomachs.

They silently mounted and moved down the hill toward the village they had seen last night. Their horses moved slowly, having not quite woken up themselves as they dragged their hooves through dew-soaked grass.

They reached the village without difficulty and hoped few townspeople would be awake to recognize them. They drew their cloaks further around themselves and dismounted before they reached the first house. They moved like shadows through the streets.

They had slept in too late. People were already moving about, doing their chores and going to market. As they closed in on the town square, the traffic grew more and more until they finally reached it.

In the square, there was a group of men dressed up in red cloaks and white shirts. They were heavily armed with swords, spears and arrows. The red, yellow, and orange feathers they used to set themselves apart spoke only of trouble.

"Those colors can only mean one thing," Lucas hissed to his son as he turned his face from them. "They're from the Phoenix."

Philip's heart raced. Here was the time to prove to his father that he could protect him. "Don't worry," he told him. "If they find us out, we both know how to fight."

Lucas nodded but silently prayed that no such action would be taken. After a moment he almost thought it would be impossible to pass through without a confrontation.

One of the men dashed through the crowd and stood up on the edge of the well, disrupting several women who had gathered there to fill up water jugs.

"Listen up everybody!" he called out over the ruckus. "Listen up!"

Instantly everyone hushed.

"Much better." He smiled, sinisterly. "Now, I would like to make an announcement." Everyone looked up in expectation. "As you already know, this is the year of the Phoenix, and because of that, some mystical being is supposed to rise from the ashes and overtake the king so that a new bloodline can rule our country. I am here to tell you that we are living history. Three days ago, we overtook Castle Falkerstone with the help of the Phoenix. You are all under his command and control. If you do not comply with him, you and your town will be wiped out." He paused for effect. "Your old nobles and gentry will be cast down and new ones will be put in their place. If you wish to please his royal majesty, the Phoenix, you may turn in any fleeing nobles that you may find." He pulled out a piece of paper from his pocket and unrolled it. "I have a notice for their arrest, preferably alive so they can see what their actions cause on everyone else: Lord Rodnell and his sons. As a prize, you will be given his household and estate. Lord Lucas and his son. As a prize, you will be given his household and estate." Lucas, pushed his way through the crowd, Philip following, their hearts in their mouths as they tried to pull away from the people before they would be recognized.

"I have their descriptions. They shall be posted on every street corner of this town and will not be taken down until they are found."

The other men of the Phoenix pushed through the crowd, the papers in their hands. Philip and Lucas pushed harder. In a moment, the men would catch up with them and they'd be found out. Suddenly one of the men in the crowd noticed them, his face a mask without emotion.

"My friends," he whispered to them as they passed, just loud enough for the other men around them to turn and look at them. "Willian, Kayden, I did not expect to see you here. You must come to my house for breakfast."

Philip and Lucas turned. "Friend," Lucas began, masking his voice as best he could. "I thank you for your kindness and hospitality."

"It is no problem," the man wrapped his arm around Lucas shoulder and smiled, nodding to the people around them. "I have no need to stay here any longer. I already know about those condemned nobles. They deserve what they get."

Several people around them nodded as they parted ways for them and their horses.

Lucas wasn't sure what was happening, but in that split moment he had decided to trust this man. They had been surrounded by people who were out to get them. What else could he have done?

He led the two through the crowd and in a moment they were on a deserted street. He confidently led them down it and then into a small house. Philip and Lucas tied their horses out front and followed him in a moment later.

"First of all," he silenced their questioning eyes with an upraised hand. "I would like to thank you for the confidence and trust you have just displayed to me. Secondly I would like to introduce myself, I am Murray."

The name rang a bell in Lucas's mind. "I remember you, old friend!" he exclaimed, dashing up to the man and grasping his hand. "We went to school together!" he turned back to his son. "Philip, this is my old friend Murray. We attended the same school a very long time ago." He turned back to his friend who motioned him to a chair and they both sat down.

"I see you've made some enemies," Murray smiled at his old friend.

"You could call it that," Lucas grimaced.

"I'll help you out of the town by cover of darkness tonight. Until then, you need to tell me everything you can without endangering yourself," Murray clapped his friend on the back and laughed. "Fancy finding you right in front of me after that terribly funny announcement about how you were an outlaw! Ah, you've never ceased to make me laugh." He wiped a tear from his eye as Lucas laughed with him. Philip turned from their merriment and glanced out the window, searching for any sign of the Phoenix Followers, resolute to make his father proud by standing watch for them. It was going to be a long day of waiting.

Philip had indeed seen the Phoenix several times that day, but thankfully they seemed content to go drink at the bar down the way and harass the locals as they chanced to cross their path, leaving a wake of fake merriment as they went.

Time passed slowly, but eventually it was sufficiently dark and Lucas and Murray had talked to the point that they decided it was time to go. They had been well fed and at one point Lucas had dozed off, Murray smiling and bobbing around, making sure his old friend and his son felt welcome and comfortable. But eventually the time had come. They packed up their belongings. Murray had given them more food so they wouldn't have to endanger themselves by going into a town or village to buy more and perhaps being spotted. They crept outside after making sure that the Phoenix Followers were nowhere in sight. Their horses' hooves had been wrapped by a servant to muffle their sounds as they hit the hard-stone road beneath them. The rush that they felt surpassed no other. Tonight would make or break their lives.

The horses galloped silently through the streets, their riders' eyes streaming with tears from the sheer force of the wind. Without warning, the gate of the village lay before them. It took only a moment to pass through, but it felt like forever. And when they had reached the other side of the oppressive constraints, their hearts sang with joy.

They galloped all night and all the next day. Nothing would convince them to stop for more than a few hours to rest before they would be back on the road, always and ever pushing north.

Night came upon them again, and they stopped for sleep. Both Philip and Lucas were out before they could say good night. No one stood watch over their camp that night, and thankfully no one came upon them. All night they were safe, but the next morning brought cold rain with it in the fickle way that spring has.

CHAPTER THREE

Their clothes and all their things being soaked already, they set out in a tired mood.

They had been on the road for nearly three days and the fourth would bring them within sight of the castle.

All morning they pushed on, their horses slipping in the wet grass, silent as the stone walls that they slowly gained upon.

The two slowed and became quiet as they passed the castle, making sure to stay well below the hill and out of sight of it.

Their horses plodded through the small river that ran between the hill and the woods, a precaution against dogs following them.

Drops of water dripped from the leaves and landed on their cloaks and horses. It was so cold and damp that they pulled their soaking cloaks further around their shoulders.

"Philip!" Lucas whispered, breaking the silence they had kept all day, his horse slowing to a halt.

"What, Father?" Philip asked.

Lucas pointed to a motionless figure by the side of the river.

Philip's heart went out to it. Its giant brown tunic was soaked in blood and there was a nasty cut on its head, quite visible between the shocks of black hair that lay dripping on its forehead.

Philip unmounted and dashed to the figure.

"He's alive!" he cried in hushed tones.

"Alive?" Lucas dismounted and hurried to his son's side.

Lucas knelt down beside the motionless figure and put his fingers by the boy's nose. He felt small puffs of air.

"He's alive alright," Lucas affirmed. "They must have left him for dead."

Philip moved the boy from his side and examined the arrow in his arm.

"Take him up on your horse," Lucas told Philip, making a quick decision.

The boy couldn't survive much longer and his heart reached out to him. "You're lighter than I am and your horse can take the load."

Philip grabbed the boy by his uninjured arm, slung him over his shoulder, and grabbing the boy's leg with his other, he lifted with his knees and soon the boy was situated in front of him on his horse.

"Hurry!" Lucas warned. "We have to get to Farvel Forest before we can do anything to help him. We're not safe here. He might be missed."

Philip didn't need to be reminded of that. He could feel the eyes of the castle watching him as he rode a little faster to get out of its sight.

"Don't push it, son," Lucas reminded him. "I want to get away from here as much as possible, but the horses have been carrying us with only a little rest these past few days. We can't ask much more of them."

Philip slowed down, but only a little.

"Can't we go a little faster?" he impatiently asked.

"When the sun is going down we can risk it. Until then, we'll just have to keep going. We don't want to draw any attention."

Philip sighed and adjusted to make sure that the other boy wouldn't fall off.

Slowly they closed in on the forest, and in a few hours Lucas gave the order to go faster. Philip watched as the long-awaited forest loomed into sight.

From what he could tell it was a very big forest. Tall trees, dark trees, light trees, short ones, pines, maples, oaks—nothing too strange, nothing too unfamiliar.

In the dusk, they entered the forest. Trees passing them on every side as they pushed further and further in.

Philip was glad that the journey was coming to a close, but he was concerned about the boy.

"Can't we stop and make sure that the boy is alright?" Philip asked at last. He did not want to stop till they actually got there, his concern finally won out.

"Alright," Lucas said after a long silence.

They slowed their horses and laid the boy on the ground.

"Tear that sleeve," Lucas directed, his eyes scanning the body. "I want to see that arm quickly. We should have taken that arrow out when we found him. Hopefully he hasn't bled to death by now." A note of worry shone through Lucas's tone and Philip hurried to tear the sleeve.

"Not too bad." Lucas carefully extracted the arrow and then bound the wound with the remains of the sleeve. He tore the bottom of his own cloak to wrap around the boy's head.

"Is he going to be alright?" Philip asked at last.

"Yes," Lucas sighed. "Thankfully we didn't wait too long. He should be awake in the morning and wanting food. We must be at the meeting place before that happens." Lucas stood up. "Ready to make one last stretch?"

Philip picked up the boy and placed him on his horse again. "Sure," they mounted and pressed on.

The forest quickly went from the familiar twilight to a strange and dangerous night.

They hurried on for what seemed like hours. Philip almost found himself nodding off several times, but he knew he had to stay awake and not let his father know how tired he was.

The darkness magnified the noises the two heard, and several times they thought for sure someone was following them. Night animals shuffled past in the dark, breaking twigs and howling to the moon, spring peepers were at their normal cheeping and peeping, and in between the tops of the trees you could see stars blinking in and out as bats and the birds of the night fluttered and swooped by.

Many a time the cries and howls would raise the hair on the backs of their necks. As the animals came closer or the howls grew more distant, it didn't matter: Philip had never been out at night like this and he was afraid of what was out there.

His ears picked up every sound around him, amplifying them and making the forest sound much worse than it was.

"Did you hear that?" Lucas whispered as he dropped his horse to a lower speed.

Philip nodded, something stuck in his throat. He had heard it.

The darkness pressed closer around them as they waited, holding their breaths and trying not to think about what could happen.

Suddenly, without warning, a man stepped out of the shadow. His bow was at the ready and the arrow was pointed straight at Lucas's heart. Philip reached for his bow, but he knew it was too late.

"State your business," The man demanded.

"My business is my own concern," Lucas replied with a voice like steel, trying to gauge his opponent.

"Well then, you'll have to give me a password so I can be sure that you're safe to let through."

"Fair enough," Lucas replied, "But how can I know that you're not an enemy of mine?"

"A man like you has enemies?" the fellow asked, intrigued.

"I'm afraid that in this day and age, it is a fact of life that everyone has enemies," Lucas answered, "Now, about the password?"

"Ahh, right," the man pulled his arrow back even more. "What is broken when it's not held?"

Philip could almost hear his father smile.

"A promise," he said simply. "And it's a promise I have come to fulfill."

The other man set his bow down and walked up to Lucas.

"My lord, and who do I have the honor of being acquainted with?"

"Lord Lucas the Just of Southland and his son, Philip of Southland."

"My lord," the other man knelt. "I am a simple hunter from Greengrove. I will take you to the camp."

The man gave three low whistles and took Lucas's horse by the tether to lead them on.

Slowly the lump in Philip's throat dissolved. He was safe, and they had found who they were looking for.

He followed his father's lead.

"There is another fellow with you," the hunter remarked.

"Yes. I take responsibility for him," Lucas began. "We found him on our way over. We will need to keep some things secret from him until we know that he can be trusted, but I take the responsibility on myself."

The hunter made no remark as he led them further into the forest. Now that they had a guide and knew they were close, Philip relaxed and his anticipation grew to a point where he felt like jumping out of his saddle and running ahead. He didn't do it though, if only for the fact that the other boy would probably fall.

The light from the campfire revealed itself through the trees, flickering to their left as they approached. The hunter readjusted his course to match, and in another minute the four of them were blinking in the warm light that it cast around itself.

Philip took in his surroundings quickly. There were five or six men on blankets around the fire and three more were conversing a ways off. They had a map in the middle of their circle and they seemed to be marking it with a stick.

"My Lord Wellington," the hunter quietly called out to the small group. "Sir, my Lord Lucas the Just and his son have arrived."

One of the men stood up and made his way through the men sleeping around the fire.

"My lord," Wellington bowed to Lucas. "We have been waiting for you."

Lucas dismounted and took Wellington's hand. "My lord, I am glad that my son and I have finally made it to the safe haven of the borders of Farvel Forest."

Wellington rose and bowed to Philip.

Philip, encumbered by the other boy could only nod his head and hope that Wellington didn't think him rude.

"Who are the other two?" Wellington asked.

"I am Philip," Philip introduced himself. "We found the other on our way. He was sorely injured and so we took him in."

Lucas replied, "As I said before, I will take full responsibility for him. There will be some things we have to keep a secret from him until we know if he follows the Phoenix or the old loyalties."

The other men helped Philip carry the boy and lay him on the ground.

"My lord, we'll talk in the morning," Wellington bowed to Lucas as Philip slid from his horse. Glad to have his feet on solid ground again.

The other men from the group took the horses away, and Lucas handed his son one of the blankets he had brought.

"Get some rest," Lucas told his son. "I'll make sure our guest will be comfortable."

Philip nodded and took his blanket close to the fire. The last thing he remembered was the first watch coming in and switching out with the second.

CHAPTER FOUR

Philip woke the next morning and stretched. He had gotten used to sleeping on the ground these past few days, but he still needed to stretch a few times before he felt fully awake.

Breakfast was already simmering over the fire, and the other men were working on small jobs around the place.

"Well, son," Lucas walked over to his son and embraced him. "Looks like unless the other boy stays, you'll be the youngest man here."

Philip nodded, his mind far away, and absently asked about the boy.

"He'll be awake soon. Get some breakfast and then worry about him."

Philip took the advice and it wasn't too long before he was kneeling over the boy helping his father change his wounds' dressings.

"Hopefully this won't hurt too much," Lucas took the bandage off the boy's arm and started to rub a poultice into his arm.

The boy murmured quietly and recoiled.

"It's alright," Lucas murmured. "Here," he turned to Philip. "Put this back on while I check his head."

Philip nodded and took the rag that was offered him.

Suddenly, before either one had a chance to think, the boy sat up straight.

"Hold on there!" Lucas tried to restrain the wild-eyed boy.

The boy's wide eyes darted everywhere silently.

"You're alright," Lucas began. The boy's eyes grew wider as he struggled against Philip's restraining arms.

"Did you hear me?" Lucas began again. "You're safe."

"*Mina arad!*" the boy cried. "*Lecte mina ad stele bour lu!*"

Lucas started—the boy was speaking the language of the highest nobles. Lucas had learned it as a young man when he was wooing his wife at court. She had been a beautiful child and Lucas had lived in the castle while he was courting her and it was necessary for him to learn the language to speak with anyone. Lucas had never bothered to teach it to his son after his wife had died when Philip was so young, and now the strange notes of the, truth be told, harsh language, brought back many memories that he had to push out of his mind before he could reach out to the boy.

"*Arda? Mina nin far arda,*" he managed at last.

"What did he say?" Philip asked, curiosity flooding his eyes.

"He thinks I'm his enemy and wants to fight."

Philip grinned. "And what did you say in reply?"

"I told him I'm not his enemy."

The boy still struggled against Philip's tight grip.

"Let him go," Lucas said. "I'll talk with him."

Philip reluctantly agreed, certain that the boy would fly at him the moment he let his guard down.

Strangely enough, the boy seemed to be content with just being left alone. His wild eyes regained normal size and his breathing became regular.

Lucas brought a small cup of gruel and set it down by the boy. His hungry eyes devoured it.

"You can have it," Lucas said in the language, "I'm not holding you here."

The boy reached for it and in a moment the food was gone.

"Who are you?" Lucas asked when the boy was done.

He recoiled, could he trust these people? Last thing he knew he had been shot by that arrow when he escaped from the castle. For all he knew, these people meant him harm!

"You can trust me," Lucas said at last.

The boy made up his mind. He owed it to these kind people.

"Avery," He replied.

"Alright Avery, do you remember what happened?" Lucas pried.

"Yes." Avery was curt in his reply. He still didn't trust these people.

"Can you tell me?"

"No, you'll have to answer some of my own questions before I can trust you."

Lucas shrugged, fair enough. "Alright, what do you want to know?"

"Who are you?"

"Lucas the Just, Lord of Southland."

A flash crossed the boy's face, but he didn't say anything. "And who is that? The one that was restraining me a moment ago?"

Lucas smiled. "My son, Philip."

The boy didn't seem interested. "Where are we? What are you going to do with me?"

Lucas hesitated. "We are in Farvel Forest, we picked you up outside Falkerstone Castle yesterday. You were wounded and we took you in. What we do with you is up to you."

"What do you mean?"

"You can stay with us, or if you feel up to it, you can leave."

Avery reached out his hand and Lucas helped him to his feet.

He wobbled for a few moments before Philip grabbed his shoulder and steadied him.

"Thank you." Avery watched, puzzled as Lucas translated to his son.

"Philip says you're welcome," Lucas said at last.

Avery looked lost for a moment, his eyes bulging and his head spinning as he clutched at Philip for support.

Lucas said something, and in another minute Avery was sitting on the ground again.

"You lost a lot of blood yesterday," Lucas explained. "You'll have to stay here for a few days."

"Thank you," Avery replied. "Can I ask what you are doing here in the middle of the forest?"

Lucas reasoned with himself. This boy only knew the language of the nobles, could he possibly be a Phoenix that wanted to overthrow the nobles? Did that make any sense?

"We are outlaws," he said at last.

"I am too." Avery grinned.

Lucas heaved a sigh of relief. He had told the truth, but left enough out to keep them safe. The boy could stay.

"I have to go," Lucas began as one of the other lords signaled to him. "Philip will stay with you."

Lucas turned and spoke to his son who had been silent the entire time.

"He says he's also an outlaw," Lucas told Philip. "Make sure that he stays comfortable. See if you can clean him up a bit."

Philip nodded as his father left.

"Hello," Avery smiled up at the tall boy.

Philip smiled back, not sure what the boy had said. He walked over to the blanket that he had slept on last night. He was aware that Avery's eyes followed him the whole way.

"Here," he said at last.

Avery couldn't understand what Philip said, but the clothes he was holding out in his hands spoke for themselves.

Avery took the clothes that were offered and Philip led him down to the river.

"I'll be back."

Avery clutched at Philip's sleeve.

He sighed and put his hands around his mouth to signal calling and then he pointed at himself and ran in place for a few seconds, pantomiming to get his point across.

Avery nodded and Philip left.

This is going to be harder than I thought, Philip sighed to himself as he leaned against a tree, just far enough away that he couldn't see the river, but could be there in a second if Avery called. *Why did I ever get myself into this?* he asked himself. *I only wish that the Phoenix Followers had never risen. Why did they have to read into the prophecies and say that it was up to them to put a new king on the throne?*

From the ashes of the old shall he rise
like the Phoenix of old,
the time for new has come
from the old ashes of the kingdom
Shall a ruler rise
He shall be known as the weak
But shall be made strong
He shall be known as someone
But in truth is another
He shall be hunted by hypocrites
The ones he came to save
With the lawless he will dwell
And one of them he shall be
The time has come for change
Change in the bloodline of rulers.

The poem probably doesn't mean anything! It was written a hundred years ago in preparation of the year for the Phoenix, he reminded himself, *They couldn't possibly know what could happen! That means that there is no significance to this year! Why did they have to tear me away from what I knew?* He banged his fist against the trunk of the tree and groaned. *It's a nightmare! There was nothing wrong with the king that we had, why do they think we need another ruler?*

Philip heard something from the river and his head snapped around.

"Philip?!"

He smiled. Avery must be ready.

He turned from the tree and walked back to the river. Avery was frantically climbing the bank.

"I'm here," Philip called out.

Avery's head snapped around and his eyes focused on Philip.

"Looking good," Philip smiled as he gave Avery a hand up, not sure whether or not to talk to the boy. He wouldn't understand, but walking in silence seemed strange to him.

Avery smoothed his new white tunic. He had his long boots back on and his brown leggings were baggy, but they fit as well as could be expected for a small boy wearing a taller boy's clothes.

Avery cleaned up nicely. Now that he no longer had blood covering his tunic, head and arm, his light skin and dark hair and eyes didn't seem too strange. It still looked out of place, but Philip knew he would gain some color if he decided to stay with them in the forest.

Philip led the way back to the camp and collapsed on his stomach by the fire, Avery sat straight up and looked deep into it.

"*Hele,*" he said at last.

"What?" Philip looked at him.

"*Hele!*" Avery pointed at it again.

"Oh," Philip said at last. "Fire."

Avery mouthed the word. "Uhfeer?"

Philip shook his head. "Fire."

"Vire."

Philip nodded. "Hele."

Avery smiled and pointed to the trees, "*Vacht.*"

"Trees."

Avery pointed at another thing, "*Beile.*"

"Ground."

"*Heme,*"

"Sky."

"*Mina,*"

"Me."

"*Feme,*"

"You."

Avery kept pointing at things and saying words, and Philip kept translating.

They both got so engrossed that they never noticed Lucas and the other lords watching them.

"They are a pair, aren't they?" Wellington said at last. "Are we sure we can trust the boy?"

"Yes. But perhaps there is something we could do to test him," Lucas said at last.

"We could send him with the next raiding party," someone suggested.

"It's a good idea. We could also send Philip, and if the boy gives us any trouble, Philip could take care of him while the rest of you do work," Wellington settled it.

"Could it wait till tomorrow?" Lucas asked. "We should let him rest a little bit."

"Agreed," Wellington turned back to his map. "There should be a party of new tax collectors passing through at around lunch. We should attack here," he pointed to a spot on the map far to the east. "This will keep them from guessing our campsite."

"We'll be needing a better stronghold soon. The day after we need to send out a party to find a new camp."

"But not everyone has gathered yet!" Lucas protested.

"Our instructions were to wait at the meeting place for a week if no one is there. We can send messengers here twice a week and bring in anyone that comes," Wellington explained. "We can't stay here any longer, our position will be found out."

Lucas reluctantly agreed. "It will have to do. In the meantime, we need to get our men ready to attack the caravan tomorrow."

Wellington turned back to his plans and traced the one road through the forest with his finger.

"We'll need to leave early in the morning to get there on time," he noted. "Tell the men."

One of the lords nodded and called out to the waiting men.

"We'll be attacking the tax caravan tomorrow."

"I'll tell Garret," one of the men began. "He went hunting to find some deer for dinner."

The man nodded and turned back to the map.

A tax collector's caravan? Philip asked himself. *Are we really going to be full-blown outlaws? What are we going to do with the money? We don't need it!*

"*Mata?*" Avery touched Philip's arm with a questioning look

Philip brushed the hand off and stood up to speak with his father.

Avery's eyes followed him silently and in panic as he left.

"Father," Philip began. "We don't need the money. Why are we doing this?"

"Son, we don't need the money, but we do want to keep it out of the enemy's hands. We can't let them have it. Well give it back to the people. The Phoenix is only using the poem as an excuse to take over the kingdom, and as long as we keep most of their income from them, they'll suffer. It is our job to do that." Lucas stopped and put his hand on his son's shoulder. "I asked that you be put on the list of men to go."

Philip was ecstatic. He was finally entering the world that he wanted to. Here was an adventure he would actually be allowed to go on. He could prove to his father that he was capable of protecting himself and others.

"Avery will be going too. It will be a simple little test for him, and something for you to do. Don't worry."

Philip shrugged his father's hand from his shoulder, shock flooding him. "And what am I to do about Avery? I can't understand a thing he says! I am here to help you restore the kingdom, not watch after someone else!"

Lucas looked at Avery and smiled. "It looks like you are doing a wonderful job. He's clean and he seems to like you."

Philip sighed. If he was going to have an adventure he didn't want to be stuck with a younger boy.

"Buck up, son. We'll figure something out soon."

Philip dragged his feet the entire way back to the fire. Avery was still sitting there, his brown eyes focused on every movement that Philip made.

"You don't need to look at me like that!" he cried.

Avery pulled his knees to his chest and turned his hurt eyes back to the fire.

"I'm sorry," Philip tried to sound soft. His tone was the only way he knew how to communicate him. He sat down next to Avery and put his head on his knees.

What can I do? he asked himself.

CHAPTER FIVE

T he sun streamed through the tops of the trees and woke the men from deep sleep. Lucas turned and put his arm over his eyes and fell back asleep. He had taken the midnight patrol and didn't want to wake up for another three hours.

Philip and Avery on the other hand had no choice. They ate breakfast in silence and helped the men saddle the horses. Philip went back to his things and belted his sword on and put his bow and arrows on his back. Avery watched them, not having his own weapons to bring.

Someone showed him to a horse and he mounted. Philip and the others followed suit.

"We'll reach the place an hour before the caravan should be there," the leader of the group called out. "We'll have to ride as quickly as we can to be back in time for dinner. Everyone will help with packing things up once we have the caravan under our control. Are there any questions?"

Avery had many questions, but he knew they would never understand him. He kept his thoughts to himself, repeating the few things he had been told. He was going with them on a raid—that was all he knew. He didn't know where they were going or how they would complete their mission. He just knew Lucas had told him to stay with Philip. Avery could sense the sinister undertones. Philip was his guard because no one trusted him. But as he reminded himself of what he had escaped, their lack of trust no longer bothered him. He was alive.

The group started out and the men meandered into a type of formation. Not for battle but more for talking with friends. Philip, not knowing anyone else and still trying to follow his father's orders, slid up to Avery.

"Here, I am giving this to you," As he deliberately said those words he stretched his hand out to reveal a dagger he had taken from his father's stores.

Avery looked up at him in surprise. He had no idea what Philip had said, but he understood what an outstretched hand offering him something meant. He hesitated before taking it and strapping it on. He wished he had the words to question Philip's actions, but he settled for a language anyone could understand.

"*Tolo.*" He smiled.

"Knife." Philip said back.

"*Mina frund geve mina a tolo.*"

Philip grinned, guessing words within their context. "Your friend gave you," he pointed at Avery. "A knife?"

Avery nodded. "Friend ... gave ... knife."

Philip grinned, ignoring the fact that he was there as a guard to this boy.

"Horse." Philip pointed to the beast.

"*Chatva,*"

Philip pointed to another thing and translated it.

"Here," he said at last. "Let's try this." Philip nodded his head, "Yes" and then he shook it, "No."

Avery looked at him puzzled, watching Philip repeat the actions and the words.

Philip gestured to Avery to have him do it.

"Yes," Avery slowly nodded his head. "No," he shook it hesitantly.

"Alright now," Philip began, his hopes rising. "Can you understand me?"

Avery nodded yes and then shook his head no randomly.

Philip sighed. Obviously Avery didn't understand. He wished he knew more so he could try to get across to the other boy.

"*Heourtane,*" Avery said at last.

"Heaourtane?" Philip asked.

Avery gestured to everything. Philip sighed again. He had no idea what he meant.

The sun shone through the trees and some of the men had already taken off their cloaks. Philip decided to try something else.

He purposefully put his hand in a patch of light and gestured for Avery to do the same. He could feel the sun's glow on his skin.

"Warm," He said.

Thoughts raced through his mind. What if Avery thought he meant light? Or sun? He put his hand on the dark fabric of his cloak and watched as Avery did the same on his cloak. The two had been baking in the light for the past hour and the dark fabric was quite hot.

"Warm," He said again.

He slowed down enough to touch a trunk of a tree as he passed it but Avery only watched this time.

Avery look intrigued.

Suddenly something clicked. "Warm!" Avery exclaimed excitedly. "Horse warm." He touched his horse. Sure enough, it was warm.

"Good!" Philip nodded. He almost smiled before he stopped, reminding himself that he was there to watch the boy to see if he was a spy, not teach him.

"Gud," Avery automatically repeated.

Suddenly the breeze picked up and the clouds covered the sun.

"No warm?" Avery hesitantly asked, looking at Philip.

So he had understood about the nodding and shaking. Philip smiled, "Cold."

"Cold." Avery repeated. He looked pleased with himself. Not that his vocabulary had expanded by much, but at least someone understood him.

Avery continued prodding Philip for words but he had withdrawn, remembering his responsibility.

Philip continued to give Avery words, but he watched the new boy carefully.

Avery learned a few more words like take, you, me, I, and a, among others.

When the men halted and brought out the few things for lunch, he surprised everyone by quietly joining them in preparing it.

"He wants to help," the others looked at him, aware that he couldn't be trusted.

"Help?" Avery asked looking at Philip, knowing the tone the others had said it in was not a trusting one.

Philip glanced around at the others in disgust. "This is help." Philip turned to assist Avery.

When they were finished Avery looked at Philip, unsure of how to thank him.

Philip saw the look and deciphered it. "You're welcome."

The other men looked disgusted. Philip and Avery were too young to be out there with them. Philip had only been sent to see if Avery was a spy and to them it looked like he wasn't paying attention to that. They sat back to enjoy their meal. While it irritated them to see Philip ignoring his job, it humored them to think of how much trouble he would be in if anything happened because of Avery.

"Alright men," the leader, Darren, stood up when the meal was over. "Clean everything up and get into positions. They should be here at any time."

Philip didn't even try to translate it for Avery, he was too busy cleaning things up and checking and making sure he had all of his weapons. He had learned to use them at a young age, and if Avery didn't do anything like the others expected, this would be the first time using them. He would prove to his father that he could do more than just watch a potential spy.

Philip knew where he was supposed to be and it only took him a moment to cross the path and find a bush to hide behind. Avery followed him, not sure of where to go.

"Sit," Philip sat, showing Avery.

Avery sat.

"Quiet," Philip held his finger to his lips, pulled his bow from off his back and notched an arrow.

Avery felt to make sure that his knife was still in place. He could feel fear tracing its way through his legs and up his back. It coursed through his arms and wrapped its black self around his heart.

Avery swallowed hard. He knew that the raid was about to happen.

"Listen," Philip whispered and held his hand to his ear to show Avery.

Avery listened and sure enough, the creaking of a caravan could be heard creeping toward them.

Philip raised his bow and pulled the string back to the corner of his mouth and held it there. The woods around them were silent.

Horses galloped into sight from around the bend. He waited. Darren was to give the first shot and the rest were to follow. If any of the horses got passed them, there were archers further down the road that would get them and they had horses to follow them if any part of the caravan managed to get past even them.

Philip's hands began to sweat as the horses got so close that you could see the whites of their eyes. His eyes turned from watching Avery to watching the road. This was his chance to prove himself.

One arrow loosed at the front of the caravan and a rider fell off a horse.

Philip aimed and let lose his own arrow, another following in quick succession. His whole mind was wrapped up in the battle before him. He didn't expect the weak Avery to try anything but cower in fear behind a tree.

Rider after rider fell, one dashed from his horse and led it to the forest using it as a shield. In another minute, the man had gotten free and was running toward Philip.

Philip had his eyes on the road and the caravan and didn't notice the man coming at him. Even if he had he wouldn't have shot at him. In the forest, he could have missed and hit one of his own men.

Avery was the first to notice the man running closer and closer. Fear still seized every part of him, but he forced his cold hands to reach for the knife he had been given. He flung it at the man with all his might and the man took only one more step forward before he fell. Avery looked down at his shaking hands in surprise before gathering his sense. He dashed to the man's side, carefully making sure to not give away his position. He pried the sword from the dead man's hands and retrieved his dagger.

Another man was running into the forest, dagger drawn and ready to seek his revenge. Here in the woods where his enemy was, no one would dare shoot at him for fear of killing one of their comrades.

Avery was still crouching over the other body when the man spotted him and started to run.

Philip in the meantime had shot five men from their horses and finally crept from his hiding place to dispatch the last few face to face. He never gave a second thought as to what Avery was doing. He expected that the boy was still in the woods, cowering because he didn't have anything to defend himself with except for the very close range weapon that he had been given.

After just a few minutes the last of the caravan surrendered.

Darren didn't waste a moment. "Round up the horses!" he called out. "We'll start getting everything ready to go. Our mission is almost complete. Good job men!" then he turned to Philip. "You didn't stay in the woods!" he accused him. "You put the whole mission at risk."

Philip started, his visions of grandeur falling down around his ears.

"Everyone was to stay in the woods until the whole caravan was taken down," Darren reminded him.

"They were hiding under the wagons. It was faster to engage them face to face!" Philip defended himself.

"Maybe, but everyone else had to cease fire so we wouldn't kill you!"

Only then did Philip glance around for Avery.

"Looking for something?" Darren asked him.

"No," Philip responded angrily.

"Where did you leave Avery?" Darren saw right through him.

"Have you seen him?" Philip quietly asked.

"No," Darren's face turned even angrier. "He must have left us because you couldn't follow order and watch him."

"Don't say that!" Philip retorted. "He could have been hurt! Or he could be sick! I knew we shouldn't have let him out this soon after having been injured like that."

Darren turned back to his men. No doubt Avery had been putting on a face the whole time. He did know their language; he had been gathering information because they felt free to talk around him. Obviously, he would be coming back soon with the Phoenix Followers and they would all be killed.

"Faster!" he called out.

Philip dashed back into the forest, his sword still drawn and bloodied.

Come on Avery, I told you not to run off, Philip mentally slapped himself. *Of course he wouldn't have understood me.*

He dashed back into the woods. Just a few steps away from where he had left Avery, Philip found the body of the first man and he quickened his pace, drawing an arrow in place as he jumped over logs and darted between trees.

He continued in this way for a few minutes, each one making him more afraid than the last. If he had lost Avery, his father would never trust him with anything ever again.

Suddenly he stopped in place. There he was. Avery was holding a strange sword in one hand and the dagger in the other.

"What happened?" Philip asked, still holding his bow and arrow. Of course, the boy wouldn't be able to answer him.

Philip studied Avery's reaction. He seemed shaken but not because Philip was there. There seemed to be something else on his mind.

Avery dropped the sword and wiped his knife on the grass before putting it back in his sheath. Nothing about the way he moved seemed to show that he was afraid of Philip or hiding anything from him.

"Follow me," Philip beaconed with his hand and led the way back to the path walking this time.

Avery followed him, still not acting as though he thought he should be doing anything else.

Philip burst through the tree-line back onto the path.

"You found him?" Darren looked up sounding surprised. "What was he up to?"

"I don't know," Philip answered, his voice calm. "We'll have father translate tonight."

Darren reluctantly agreed to not tie the boy up until they had real proof against him and they started off, back to camp.

Avery and Philip were silent as they rode back to camp. The fun had gone out of the game that they had played before, even if it was more than just a game. The sun had gone out of the bright day and both knew why. Philip knew that his new friend wasn't trusted, and Avery knew that he wasn't trusted. No language barrier could keep anyone from knowing that.

They had only been on the road for a few minutes when the two boys' heads pricked up and their ears strained. They had heard something.

"What is it?" Darren called to the back of the caravan.

"Our guest is making a fuss," a man called back.

"Guest?" Philip turned the head of his horse to the back of the line and charged. Avery followed him, not wanting to be left alone with people that didn't trust him.

"Come on," Philip called back realizing what Avery was doing.

"Come back at once!" Darren shouted back at them.

Philip pressed on. His horse plowing through the captured caravan as people parted before him.

"What do we have?" he asked when he finally reached the end.

"Sir!" The men turned around and exclaimed.

Two men were holding down a short little man with a faint dark beard. Philip's mind raced, who was this? His tan clothes of rough wool were like nothing he had ever seen before.

He brushed the short man's identity away and focused and what was really pressing him. The Kingdom of Davia had never dealt in slaves, much less taken them as payment for taxes. Something was very wrong about this whole thing.

"Release him," Philip commanded.

"I'm sorry?" the man exclaimed.

"Unhand him. Is that too much of an order?" Philip's voice rose a note as Avery caught up with him.

"Sir, we are only to follow orders from Darren."

Darren's horse pulled to a stop before Philip.

"What do you think you are doing?" he growled.

"My father, Lucas the Just, is the highest of the lords," Philip began, ignoring the question. "He is the leader of this group, if you wish to remain in his good favor, I suggest that you release this man."

Darren's dark eyebrows blended in with his eyes as he scowled.

"You have shown yourself untrustworthy," he growled. "You have much to answer for when you get back. Who am I to stop you from adding this to your list, your highness." His snide remark came back.

Philip pushed the man aside and watched as the small man was unhanded.

He stood on his feet and bowed as low as he could. The man came up to no higher than Darren's waist, had he been standing on the ground.

"Who are you?" Philip asked.

The man looked up at Philip and shook his head before saying something in a strange language.

Philip looked around at the others, wondering if this was some kind of joke.

Off to his left Avery pulled up having finally caught up with him.

The short man repeated the strange words again.

Avery gasped, hearing the words for the first time.

He quickly responded, dismounting his horse.

Philip and Darren glanced at each other. Neither one had been expecting this.

Avery continued speaking with the man as he walked toward him.

He walked past the two on their horses but as he neared the dwarf, hands reached out and held him back, breaking the trance.

Everything about Avery seemed to change. He called out in his language, struggling and fighting to get free.

"Avery!" Philip cried, confused. "Stop it!"

The dwarf did not understand a word that anyone said but many hands were reaching toward him and he charged forward through them.

Philip's head was reeling. "Stop it at once, all of you!" Philip shouted.

Everyone stood stock-still. Not everyone had understood the words that he had said, but his tone was unmistakable.

"We will finish this when we reach my father," His voice shook with anger. "Until then, there is nothing we can do. You guards are to treat this dwarf like the man he is. There should be nothing for him to complain about when he reaches my father. Avery," he spoke forcefully. "Horse. Sit."

Avery knew what those two words meant. "*Entschul mina.*" He shook the hands off of him and nodded to the dwarf.

"*Lon bist fel?*" The dwarf returned the bow.

"*Da.*" Avery mounted his horse and turned his eyes from the dwarf.

"Finally," Philip sighed as he led Darren and Avery back up to the front of the caravan. "I have no idea what that was about."

"Sir," Darren angrily ordered his men to resume what they were doing and turned back to the head of the line, resentful of the interference from the two boys. "Come on! We can't delay. We have to be back at the camp by nightfall!"

They slowly began moving again. Philip continuing to point to things and act out words to add to Avery's vocabulary. Philip decided to teach him the words running, walking, jumping, and others when they got back to the camp. At this point it would be too late when they got back and it would have to be put off till tomorrow.

"Hurry," Darren called back. "We're taking the road back to camp and it will take longer to get there. We have already wasted so much time uselessly trying to reason with a certain young boy who doesn't know his place," He glared back at Philip. "First you had to go back for this ragamuffin, and then you had to make matters worse with the dwarf! You are not king here, do you understand?"

Philip swallowed his pride and anger and turned back to talking with Avery. At least this boy couldn't insult him and think that he was worth less than dirt underneath his feet.

Carefully they made their way down the path. Lookouts had been sent ahead to make sure that they didn't meet up with any unwanted visitors on the way and to warn them if they actually did.

Philip and Avery's conversation slowly petered out, and they turned to watching the people around them.

Each one seemed to wear something different. One had yellow pants, one was wearing red, another had a blue tunic with expensive embroidery. Perhaps he hadn't had time to change when he heard that he had become an outlaw? Was he torn from his family, his young sons, his daughters that would never survive out here in the wilderness? Did he only save himself? What would happen to their families? Their daughters married off to men they had never met, their sons drafted into armies they would never agree with, their children sent to schools that taught them lies about their own mothers and fathers? What had happened to these men that made them so serious? Could they ever go back to the lives they had lived before?

Philip wanted to shake these thoughts from his head, he wanted to focus on teaching words to Avery, but even that reminded him of such things. Though he did not know the boy's full history, he knew Avery had been torn from his family. He had been hunted down and declared an outlaw. He could relate to these men! He had almost been killed by the enemy! He of all people knew what it was like.

Philip eventually turned his mind back to teaching things to his friend.

"Up," Philip pointed to the sky, "Down." Philip repeated the words and the actions.

"Up?" Avery mirrored Philip's actions, "Down."

"Yes," Philip smiled at his new friend. "Good."

Philip tried several more things in quick succession, but it seemed like he had lost his fines.

Philip sighed in frustration and turned back to the scenery. Everything else would have to wait till his father could explain things to Avery.

But thinking of his father reminded him that he would have to answer to him for his other actions. He had disobeyed orders—he had not paid attention to Avery and he had gotten himself involved in the dwarf. The only thing he could take comfort in was knowing that Avery had not tried running away or killing anyone when he had the chance. They could trust him; he was on their side.

The afternoon light faded and the men stopped to check the wagon. They redistributed the goods and dismantled it. There was no way that they could get it back in the woods without breaking a wheel. The trees grew so close together that Philip couldn't stretch out his arms without touching trees on either side. The wagon would be too wide.

Avery sat on his horse the entire time that they were taking things apart. He couldn't understand what was happening and he wasn't sure that it mattered much. He would hinder them rather than help.

Slowly the caravan started back up again. Darren didn't trust Avery with any of the goods, so the others horses were laden to the breaking point.

The light failed them as they grew closer to their destination. Stars pricked through the black blanket of night above them and the creatures of the night screamed, warbled, and clucked back and forth between themselves.

Men started yawning and stretching, Avery and Philip were too tired of sitting in their horses to care much about anything.

Suddenly, lookouts from ahead called out.

Darren halted the group, everyone wide-awake now.

"We've found them!" The lookouts from ahead bounded back to the main group. "We've gone so far to the south that we'll miss it entirely."

Darren nodded and turned his horse in the direction that the lookout had suggested. They pressed on. Avery and Philip felt the trip would never end. Would they always be riding through the forest in the dark of night? Would they always be to the right of their camp? Would they never get there? Could he ever get away from this waking dream?

It felt like forever before Philip and Avery saw the campfire looming in sight.

"Fire," Avery smiled, remembering the word that he had learned yesterday.

"Yes," Philip yawned, now half asleep. "Fire."

It wasn't long they were falling asleep to the crackling and sputtering of the fire as Darren's voice droned on with Lucas in the background. They had several things to talk about and several things that needed to be decided.

CHAPTER SIX

A very woke the next morning as the warm sun filtered through the boughs of the trees. He stretched and smiled as he basked in the warm glow.

"Warm," he thought to himself as he remembered how eager Philip had been to make sure that he understood the word. "Warm."

A shadow flitted over his face and blocked the rays of the sun.

"Cold," he mindlessly thought.

"Avery?" Lucas called to him as he opened his eyes. "I need to have a talk with you," he spoke in his language.

Avery sat up and focused his eyes on the tall man before him.

"Come on, we'll need to go a little way from the camp for this."

"But they can't understand what we're saying," Avery protested, "It doesn't matter if we stay."

"Come on. We'll be bringing the dwarf with us. He says his name is Grurhoum Greatbrow."

The name didn't ring any bells, but if the man wanted him to go, there wasn't much for him to do but go.

He stood up and followed Lucas as they mazed their way through the still sleeping forms around them. The dwarf was already waiting on the outskirts of the ring and he bowed as they neared.

"Sir," he nodded to Lucas.

Avery was as curious as Lucas about the dwarf, but he was sure he wouldn't get a word alone with him. Lucas knew that he needed them both to talk and he couldn't risk them conspiring against him and his group of outlaws.

"Alright," he said at last. "I want to hear your story Grurhoum,"

The dwarf bowed, "My history begins long before I was born," Lucas and Avery waited in silence waiting for him to continue. "My people are enslaved by humans, sir, and I have been a slave in the Bucan Dynasty."

"The kingdom to the east," Lucas nodded.

"I have been there since I was a child. There was a time when my people lived under the mountain to the north. We called it Gulrun but it is Vamkuldir now. So many sad things have happened there," he paused. "We were taken from the mountain and enslaved by Bucan but recently there has been an awakening. Enough of us have escaped to the mountain that they have begun to build our nation again to end this once and for all," he spoke with such passion before he paused, aware of his human audience. "Our beef is with Bucan and other nations that deal in slaves, not yours."

"Tell your story," Lucas reminded him.

"I lived in this mountain. I was born into freedom," he smiled. "I was torn from my family when I was ten though. My cousin, the heir to the throne under the mountain, will free us all someday."

"But why are you here?" Avery asked. "Our country has never held slaves, and we have never traded with Bucan."

"Grurhoum," Lucas asked hesitantly, beginning to draw conclusions. "Are you sure of this?"

"Yes? How could I not be?"

"We intercepted a regular tax caravan. Why is the kingdom of Davia taking taxes from Bucan?" Lucas's brow furrowed. "This is wrong, very wrong."

"I have never seen taxes collected in the way that I saw," Grurhoum spoke up. "This was violent, almost a raid."

Avery looked away, he knew what was going on. He had heard things in the castle that led him to conclusions of his own. Conclusions that would mean dire circumstances for regaining the throne.

"Avery?" Lucas asked as he turned to face him. "Do you know anything about this?"

"Yes," he said slowly. "I heard things in the castle."

"And?"

"The Phoenix Followers are attacking Bucan. I don't know why."

"Do you know anything else?" Lucas' lips pressed into a thin line. Things were worse than he had thought.

"Not much," Avery began, "I'm sure that the Phoenix Followers just want more power, and they are using Davia to do it. They will be getting more money, they will be getting slaves for the first time, they can even use Bucan as a jumping point to go further east. I'm sure that they will be requiring more slaves from the dwarfs. They will stop at nothing!"

Lucas had already figured those things out in his head, but he had to push them aside. He still didn't trust either one of them and to draw conclusions with them around could be dangerous. He changed the focus of the conversation. He still needed to know what had happened yesterday.

"Avery," he began, "Where were you during the attack yesterday?"

"I went with Philip," he replied. "Our men attacked and one of the enemy made it into the woods. He was heading straight at us and I threw my dagger at him. Another one was coming at me quickly, so I ran. I fled into the woods and he followed me until he tripped. I turned back and struck him while he was down. After that, I wasn't sure how to get back to the road. I thought that we had moved in a straight line from it, but I wasn't sure. Finally, Philip showed up and I walked back with him."

"Good," Lucas said—he still trusted the boy. "And what about you Grurhoum? I heard a little bit about you attacking the guards, same with you, Avery. What was that about?"

Avery looked to the dwarf.

"After our caravan started out was when you attacked. I did not know what was going on—changing hands to people I didn't understand."

"Did they mistreat your?" Lucas asked.

"The tax collectors did or whoever they were. Your men were considerably well behaved and I was confused and in a panic."

"Do I need to have a talk with my men?" Lucas asked.

"No, no! Your men were exceptionally well behaved! There is no reason for violence. They only held me back when I decided I wanted to leave. Up until that point I was treated well," Grurhoum assured him.

Lucas nodded and urged him to continue.

"Then the young man Philip came back to make sure everything was under control. When I addressed him everything got very confusing."

"I guess I just was a little excited," Avery added.

"Right. Then when you tried to come and talk with me, they held you back. Everything just happened so quickly."

"What then?" Lucas asked leaning forward.

"They held her back—" Grurhoum began, rubbing his nose thoughtfully trying to remember.

Lucas held up his hand to pause him, almost unsure if he had heard what he thought he had heard.

"Her?!" Lucas reached out to the dwarf and Avery, his face a study of fear, took three steps back and fingered the dagger that was still in his belt.

"You can't tell?" Grurhoum asked, taking a step back and looking at the lord in disbelief.

"Is this true?" he asked turning back to Avery, glaring as the small boy stumbled back against a tree.

"Sir—" he began, his eyes darting from tree to tree.

"Come on!" Lucas screamed at him.

"Alright! Yes!" tears streamed down her face and everything about her changed. "You know I'm of noble birth because of my language," she began quickly, trying desperately to explain. "I was living in Falkerstone when it fell into the hands of the Phoenix Followers. I had to escape or they would kill me," she unconsciously reaches up to rub her injured arm. "The only way to escape was disguised but even that didn't work. They followed me out and I would have died if it weren't for you. When I woke up I was surrounded by people I didn't know or understand. The disguise was for my protection. I didn't know who to trust and I still don't."

"How can I trust you if you don't trust us?" Lucas cried, looking disappointed. "I trusted you! I fought for you to stay here. I accepted the responsibility of taking you in. I took a risk. And now what am I to do with you?"

Avery was sobbing and the forest grew quiet as Lucas waited for a response.

"Sir," Grurhoum cleared his throat. "Perhaps you should ask what her real name is first and find out who she really is."

Lucas stood there unsure. He was angry, but being angry would not fix his problem. "Who are you?" he asked quietly. "What is your name?"

"Avery is my name," she replied, suddenly standing up as tall as she could and looking the lord straight in his eye. "I am the daughter of his highness, the Duke of Alnor citadel, may he rest in peace, youngest of three brothers, the crown prince and his royal majesty, King of Davia."

Lucas stepped back in astonishment, every trace of anger leaving him as everything fell into place.

"Thank you," Avery began, coldly stepping further away and taking her hand off her dagger.

"Your highness," Lucas dropped on his knee, his mind still racing.

"Thank you, but I am hardly even a lady and women cannot ascend to the throne." She smiled despite herself. It was past time for people to realize who she was and her importance.

Lucas cried out in surprise. "If we retake the kingdom, there is no reason why that rule cannot be changed."

"There is no reason for me to take the throne," Avery reminded him. "There are many people in line for it before me, law or no law."

"The Phoenix is out there to eradicate anyone of royal blood, what chance do you think any of them had?" Lucas began. "Lords from all over the kingdom are gathered here, each of them bringing some variation of the same story. They're dead. Do you understand what this means?"

Avery took a step back. "They're all dead?" she whispered unbelievingly.

"I'm sorry," Lucas answered.

"I'm the only one left?" her hands made their ways to her heart.

"I said I'm sorry, your majesty."

"Don't call me that!" she lashed out at him angrily. "And saying that you're sorry doesn't change anything!"

She turned her back to them and leaned against the tree. "What am I going to do?"

"Do you have any choice?" Lucas asked. "If you leave, someone will find out who you are and you'll be killed. Besides, you're needed here," Lucas paused for a moment. "It's not any less dangerous for you to stay here though. Everyone thinks that if they prove themselves they might become the next king since there is no hope of returning him or his bloodline to the throne. They might contest you—especially if we change the old traditions to do it—but we can keep you safe here for the moment."

Avery nodded. "Now stand up!" she cried. "There is no need to kneel."

Lucas rose.

"No one will know about what we have spoken about today," Lucas began, "Unfortunately I will have to tell Wellington, he is my second in command and there is no reason not to tell him. He will support me in whatever choices I make."

Grurhoum stepped forward and Lucas started, "I had forgotten that you were here," his job had just become a bit more complicated. "Can I trust you to keep this a secret?"

"Of course!" he bowed. "I only want to get out of this mess as soon as I can. It doesn't belong to me and I never wanted it." Grurhoum did not continue though he had many questions. The problem of language still plagued him. Why did she know his language? She wasn't from Bucan. She was Davia Royalty!

"Good," Lucas smiled again. He gestured the camp and they turned to go back.

"Here," Lucas handed Avery his handkerchief. "Your eyes are red."

She wiped her eyes and gave it back to him. It would never do to arrive in camp with red eyes that would show something was wrong.

Silently they entered the camp.

"Be careful," Lucas called to her as she turned to sit by the fire.

She watched as he pulled Wellington off to the side and took him into the woods a way off. When they came back out she could see several emotions on his face.

Avery turned back to the fire and traced her finger through the dirt.

"Hello," Philip called down.

"Hello," She smiled up, strangely aware of lying to him. He didn't know that she was a girl, and at this point he would never know until she ascended the throne. How funny that sentence felt to her ears. Never in her wildest dream had she ever imagined ascending the throne.

Philip sat down and began rattling out words that she didn't know. She turned her head back to the fire and tuned him out.

He turned to her with a concerned look. He knew that his friend wouldn't be able to understand him, but he decided to ask anyways.

"Are you alright?"

Avery didn't move. He tried again.

"Are you good?" he asked, knowing full well that Avery already knew the word good.

Avery struggled within herself. Did she want to tell the truth and have him bring his father back over so he could question her? Or did she want to brush this off as nothing even when she did want to talk about it to someone?

"Yes," she answered at last. She could think it through later, by herself.

Philip sat back knowing full well that something was wrong. He tried to think of something that he could do to make Avery feel better.

"I've got it!" he snapped his fingers together. "Come on." He pulled Avery up by her sleeve and dragged her to gather some things, namely his bow and arrows.

"I'll teach you," he pointed at Avery and then at a tree a good distance off.

Philip shot first, his arrow flying straight and true as it hit the target with a satisfying thud.

"Now you do it," he handed the instruments to his friend and stood back.

Avery had never touched a bow and arrow before, much less shot one, and she wasn't sure where to begin.

Philip stood there unsure of how to describe anything to her as she fumbled with the bow and arrow.

Suddenly an idea hit him. From where he stood he mimed the action of pulling the string of the bow back. Avery tried to do the same feebly. She pulled the string back as far as she could.

"Good," Philip nodded.

"Yes." Avery answered quietly.

"Try again." Philip handed her another arrow.

She fumbled with the arrow for a moment before she drew back with her right arm, her left holding the bow out in front of her. Her elbow shook and dipped as she tried to hold it steady. She drew the string as far back as her other elbow, and let loose. The arrow flopped to a rest at her feet.

Philip took the bow from her and demonstrated without an arrow.

"You have to pull it back as far as the corner of your mouth," Philip explained even though she wouldn't understand him. He then pulled the string back. "See?"

Avery took the bow and tried as hard as she could to get it back that far.

"Good," he handed her the arrow and watched as she pulled it back and aimed.

She held her breath, sure that she would miss again and that pulling it back this far would have no effect on the overall outcome of the shot. She let the arrow loose and watched as it flew right past the tree.

"*Mina ist*—" she began, "Good."

"Yes," Philip grinned. "That was good. Now go get it."

Avery frowned in puzzlement.

"Here," he walked down to the tree and she followed. "Look for it." He scanned his eyes along the ground and watched as Avery did that same.

He grinned to himself. He had done it!

Avery held the arrow as high as she could, quite proud of herself.

"Good," Philip was getting tired of that word, but he wasn't sure how else to get the message across to Avery.

They walked back to where they had left the bow and arrows and they shot a few more before lunch was called.

Avery took a bite off food. It was warm. Warm was one of the few words she knew.

Philip was getting really tired of those few words that Avery knew. His progress with her was slow and repetitive.

Philip saw his father walking toward him and he stiffened. Lucas had yet to speak with him about what had happened the day before and Philip could feel that the floodgate was about to open.

"I need to talk with you," Lucas stood, towering over Philip.

Philip stood, trying to gather himself up.

"Every person on this team has a job that only they can do," he began. "And everyone has to do their part or we fail."

"Is this about what happened yesterday?" Philip asked.

"After lunch we're sending out a party of men to find a new campsite," Lucas continued. "I trust you, which is why I need you to look after Avery. It's not that I want you out of the way, but we need to keep an eye on him and make sure he doesn't get into trouble. I want both of you to go with the group searching for the campsite."

Philip was angry. He still hadn't proven himself to his father and the others would never accept him until he did.

"Alright, I'll take Avery with me," he reluctantly agreed.

"Thank you," Lucas smiled, "I want to have a talk with you before you go, though. I need to tell you something when the others aren't around."

Philip nodded and turned back to his lunch of venison and water.

Avery sat there, her eyes flitting across the several faces around the campfire. Not for fellowship or personal gain had they gathered, but for nourishment and the promise of being part of something that was greater than themselves. Her heart reached out to these people. She knew what it was like, those days back in the castle, how could she forget them?

CHAPTER SEVEN

*M*y eyes teared up as the carriage pulled up the drive and came to a halt at the door of my father's manor house.

"You're going west Avery," he pulled my small childish frame into a hug. "You're going to learn so much while you're gone. I can hardly wait for you to come back when you're grown and polished off."

"But Daddy! I don't want to go! I want to stay with you and Mommy ..." I cried.

"You can't. I can't teach you the things that a young lady like you needs to know." He released me from his hug and pulled me gently toward the door, "You listen to your elders, alright?"

"Yes, Daddy."

"Good," He helped me up into my carriage, glancing back at the several boxes we had been planning for months. He knew the contents by heart, as did I. Each dress that my several aunts on my mother's side had planned for me in preparation for my trip, each dress cooed over with pride and told that it was "The height of fashion" and that, "Everyone will love you."

"You'll be fine."

But will I? I thought to myself as the carriage pulled away. I stretched my head as far out of the window as I could and I twisted so I could look behind. Father had already gone back into the house. He didn't even wait for me to pull out of sight.

I tried telling myself that he had gone back in to look after my mother, but at the time I couldn't think that. Even now I can't think that.

The miles stretched out behind me as I looked forward to the time when I would reach my destination. I couldn't go back. They didn't want me back, so why should I want it?

Days passed in a blur, traveling forward, always forward, stopping only to rest each night.

Finally, I reached my destination. Falkerstone Castle loomed in the horizon, my past life—my mother, father, and memories—no longer belonged to me. This castle—its language, culture, etiquette, and people—was my life now. I could no longer go back.

The carriage stopped in front and the door was opened by a servant. He helped me down, bowing and mumbling something polite under his breath. I hardly noticed him. My short legs hit the ground with a hard thud and my new full-length dress touched the ground of the courtyard. I had only just been considered old enough to have full-length skirts and they scared me. I would never have been in them this early in my life if I hadn't been invited to court. The skirts symbolized what had happened with my life. If my mother and father had loved me and wanted to keep me, I would never have been thrust into the adult world so soon. I wouldn't have the long skirts that every young girl wants, and I wouldn't have the life at court that everyone covets.

The servant led me to a room through corridors lit by torches, other servants following behind with my five bags. I would never have had any of the things in those bags if I hadn't come here. I would trade all of my things—the advantages of living at court, the education I would get, the polish that would one day get me a husband—all of it, to have stayed at home. But it was too late.

I was left in a very large room, my fifteen-year-old self in a room decorated for a forty-year-old woman. The bed was covered in a dark red blanket and all the furniture was dark and heavy.

The servants left the room and I dragged myself to the window that overlooked the garden below. Light poured out into the darkness. I could see nothing. I turned from the window, pulling the curtain to shut out the night and the thoughts that lurked within it, and I pulled open the heavy door to the wardrobe.

The servants had left the bags by the door to my room, and I opened them now. Each dress lay there with only terrible memories hiding between the folds in their cloth. What had happened to the three dresses my aunt had added a panel to at the bottom? The only three dresses that I had any fond memories of?

I dug down to the bottom of all five boxes and I found them. Tomorrow I would wear one, but for now, I needed sleep.

The next morning, I woke and put on one of my old dresses, the familiar folds hugging me and making a useless attempt to comfort me. Somehow the added length at the bottom kept it from being the dress I had remembered from my childhood, but I would wear it. I needed anything I could grasp my hands on.

I slipped out of the room on soft slippers. The morning sun streamed through the windows of the thick-carpeted hall as I tip-toed my way quietly down it. Stairs greeted me at the one end, and so I took them. What else was I to do? I followed them and found my way into another hall, then another, then another—could this place go on forever? Finally, I found a room that seemed to be set up for eating, servants flitted to and fro.

"Who are you? What are you doing here?" suddenly a harsh voice called from beside me.

I jumped and swiveled to meet that voice. "Avery," I gulped.

"Oh," the servant that accosted me suddenly had a knowing look. "You're the king's bratty niece."

I didn't answer.

"Well, you're in the wrong place," he began with mock politeness as he led me through several more halls. *"You don't eat with the servants, your place is with the nobles."*

We entered a great hall where several people were already eating. I turned to ask him a question, but he was gone.

I stood there, uncertain what I was to do. Did anyone expect me? Could I just sit down at any of the four tables here? Or was there a hierarchy?

I turned to go when the room quieted. Slowly I turned back, all eyes were on me.

"Avery?" a questioning voice came from somewhere in the room.

"Yes?"

"Come here," I scanned the tables, my eyes finally resting on a man, much like my father, wearing a crown seated next to a young woman, his wife.

I walked to the table and curtsied, unsure.

The woman looked over my dress with scorn, was this her niece? In a beggarly-patched dress with length added to the hem to make her more grown up?

I blushed.

"You may sit here," he gestured to a chair nearer the end of the table. *"It seems only yesterday I was writing to my brother about you. I didn't realize I had forgotten to have a servant call on you this morning."*

I nodded, and sat down, all eyes still on me. Food was already on my plate so I picked up my fork and dug in, hopeful that I wouldn't break any rules of etiquette.

CHAPTER EIGHT

A very gazed into the fire, remembering when her life turned upside down. It seemed that once again, she was being thrust into something she wasn't ready for yet, once again she was dressed unacceptably by societies standards, once again she wasn't wanted.

Philip finished his lunch and went to speak with his father.

"What was it what you wanted to tell me?" he asked.

"Lord Wellington wants to send a few men to inspect the border between Davia and Bucan. I want to know everything about the current relationship between the two. I want to send you and Avery along with Grurhoum the dwarf. There will be a few others, but you are my main choice. I need people who can speak the Bucan language, and I don't want you here when we ..." he cut himself off. "I think you would be better off on this mission."

Philip wanted to ask him what he was going to say, but he stopped himself. If his father were going to tell him, he wouldn't have stopped himself. He still felt angry and guilty about trying to prove himself.

"I'll think about it," he replied, knowing full well that this was a requirement, not a request.

He turned back to the fire before his father could say any more.

Wellington looked up from his food and surveyed his group. They were a fine lot of men. He couldn't have asked for better.

"Men," he called out when he finished his mouthful. "We need to find another campsite. I'm sending all of you that aren't on watch today to help with this effort. We need to relocate soon before the Phoenix Followers find us. As soon as they feel safe in Falkerstone Castle, they'll be out here for us, and we are going to need a better place to hide." He turned to Lord Lucas. "Should Philip and Avery come with us to look?" he asked with a knowing look.

"I don't see why not," he answered looking at the two.

They had turned to each other again, and Philip was pointing out things and Avery was trying her hardest to understand what he was saying.

"They'll be fine," he assured Wellington.

He turned back to his bedroll to get some more rest. He would have the watch in another five hours.

"Alright everybody! Let's move on out!" Wellington stood up and headed toward the horses.

The horses had almost doubled in number since the raid on the caravan. Even if they didn't need the money from it, they certainly used the resources.

Avery and Philip mounted their respective steeds and turned to follow the other men on their way.

They followed the stream uphill.

"Water," Philip absentmindedly pointed and told Avery.

She nodded. "Water is cold."

"Yes," he replied. "Shade," he pointed. "Is cold."

"Tree is good," she smiled, finally using the word good with another. "We look for shelter."

Philip smiled. "You listen to everything, don't you? I never said shelter, Wellington did."

"You ... " she floundered. "Are help?"

Philip smiled at the compliment so tentatively given, "Thanks."

"You're welcome," she replied, remembering what he had said earlier.

They followed the stream until it came out of the mountain. Hardly a hundred yards away from it there was a clearing and much to everyone's excitement, a cave.

Wellington lit a torch and picked out a crew of people to take in with him. Philip and Avery were chosen to go with him in case the going got tight.

"We'll explore as much as we can. I can't think that a wonderful cave like this doesn't have something foul living in it," He pulled up to the mouth of the cave and gave the remaining men instructions, "If we don't come back in an hour, go back to the camp and get Lord Lucas. If he thinks it wise, you may come in after us. But only if he says so." The men acknowledged him.

"In we go!"

He nearly dove into the cave, the men already lagging behind him as they cautiously tiptoed their way through the entrance.

In a moment, the cave grew and they could see that it was much larger than they had expected just by looking on the outside. It was the size a great hall and Avery gasped as she remembered her days back at the castle. It was the same size as the dining hall at Falkerstone Castle. How nature had made something so impressive stunned her.

Wellington made his way to the back of the cave where he saw an opening like a side hall. His men followed him, slower as they looked at their surroundings. Wellington walked through the corridor, his light outstretched before him, fighting with the darkness.

"It looks like it gets narrower," he called back.

They continued on until one man could no longer fit through the tight space.

"We should turn back!" he called up to the front. "We already know that the cave is good, we don't need to know where this goes.

"No! We have to know where this passage goes. The entire cave—every entrance and exit—must be explored. We can't have anyone coming upon us unawares," Wellington yelled back. "We've come too far to stop, but I will light another torch, I have an idea."

They backtracked a little till the men could change places in line and then they stopped.

"Let's light another torch and send the two boys ahead. They're smaller and when we can no longer fit, we will stop and wait for them to go ahead and tell us what they find. Philip has a sword he can use and I trust his head."

Philip looked up. He was surprised that Wellington trusted him and was sending him on a mission.

"Avery can be given a bow and arrow. He'll follow Philip and we can give them a torch."

No one disputed the idea because Wellington took action at once, lighting a torch, and explaining his plan with Avery in her language. Then the two squeezed past all the other men and make their way to the front.

They quickly set out again, this time with the young, small people in the front. It wasn't long till they reached the same spot as before and the other men could no longer squeeze through. Avery and Philip were on their own.

They silently made their way down the long corridor. Not much time passed before they found that it turned nearly around and was getting wider. They looked at each other without a word and hurried on. In another moment, the corridor had turned into a cave again. This cave was smaller and seemed to have a glow about it. They searched the walls without a word and came to another corridor that took them back to the forest. They blinked their eyes at the bright sunlight and took note of where they were. It must have only been around the corner of where they had gone into the other cave. They both looked at each other and smiled. The cave made a full circuit and they could use it to hold themselves and their things. Lord Lucas and Wellington would be proud.

They quickly retraced their steps back to Wellington, and Philip told him what they had seen, "The corridor makes a turn not far from here and then it turns into a cave that opens up to the forest probably not far from the opening of this cave."

Wellington motioned to his men to head back out. His job here was done. No one had seen evidence that either cave or passage was in use. This would be the perfect place for them to move their camp to.

Philip was proud of himself. Not only did Wellington trust him, but he had just completed a mission that everyone in the camp would thank him for.

He turned to Avery who was staying quiet and grinned.

"We just found the place where everyone is going to stay," he told her, aware that she wouldn't understand what he said. "They're going to be so proud."

Avery didn't say anything and Philip grew silent.

As they were leaving the cave Philip spoke two more words.

He blew out his torch. "Dark, cave."

Avery nodded, "It is good."

Philip smiled. Avery was learning words that could connect other words together to make sentences. He had worried about those because he couldn't just point to an "is" and say "is."

They exited the cave and mounted their horses. They followed the stream back to their current camp, glad that they had good news to bring back to Lord Lucas.

"We found a great place," Wellington began, and he told Lucas about the cave that they had found.

"It sounds great. Tomorrow we'll have to go and find the other end to the cave that Philip said he found. Then if we like it, we'll move in. Also," he continued, "We had a few more nobles and gentry come in today while you were gone. There is a knight and his son and the eldest son of a lord who was killed. I'm going to introduce the knight's son to Philip. They are around the same age and will be a part of the same group when we execute the plan," Wellington thanked Lucas and turned to leave. "Wait," he turned back, lowering his tone. "Are we still going to follow the plan?"

Wellington looked around and lowered him tone. "I see no reason not to. However, let's put it off a few more days. We'll want to get moved into our new camp."

"Thank you," said Lucas. "That was all."

Wellington bowed and went to take care of his horse. Avery and Philip disappeared into the forest, both carrying something under their cloaks.

"Philip!" Lucas called after them. "Come here!"

Philip turned, dropped what he was carrying, and retraced his steps back to his father.

"I would like to introduce you to Ian, the son of one of the king's knights," Lucas led his son toward the young man who he pointed to. "I hope that you'll allow him to join you and Avery in whatever you were planning on doing."

Philip looked at his father. So now he didn't even trust him to keep an eye on Avery by himself?

Philip sighed as he bowed to the knight's son. "Philip, pleased to meet you."

"Ian, at your service," the other man said coldly.

Ian's golden hair danced in the breeze that meandered its way through the forest and his green eyes reflected the essence of the wood back at anyone that dared look in them. "I am eager to make your acquaintance," Ian continued.

Philip tried push his thoughts to the side while his father looked at him expectantly.

There was nothing to it. Philip would have to invite the other boy to walk with them in the woods, and he was going to teach Avery how to sword fight too! Surely this other boy would scorn his efforts to teach the few moves that he knew to his friend.

Lucas cut into Philip's thoughts. "Philip was just about to take a walk in the woods with his friend, Avery. I'm sure that the two of them wouldn't mind if you came along."

"Thank you, I accept gladly," Ian gave a cold smile to Philip, surprised that the favor was half-heartedly returned.

Philip only nodded before he turned back to the woods, this time with Ian following him.

"I've heard about how the leaders of this group are trusting you with watching this strange boy," Ian prodded, trying to gauge his new acquaintance.

"Really?" Philip replied waking himself just a bit.

Ian knew he had already struck a note and his plan was already forming in his mind. "Yes, I know that it's nothing in comparison to the work that my father and I do—defending the kingdom from attackers—but he seemed really proud of the work you were putting into it."

Philip sniffed. So, this boy was going to try to outdo him?

"I've never had the opportunity of fighting for my kingdom," Philip began, "But perhaps if you had worked harder at it, we wouldn't be in this predicament right now."

Ian did a double take. "You're old enough to fight, why weren't you with us on the battlefield? We could have used a man like you—that is, if your sword fights as well as your tongue."

They had neared where Philip left Avery and she slipped out from behind a tree.

Her eyes furrowed and her face showed confusion. Who was this person and why was he fighting with her friend?

"Avery," Philip began. He knew full well that he was breaking manners by first introducing the older to the younger, but he was disgusted with the new comer. "This is Ian."

Avery's head whirled, she could see what was going on though she only understood a few words.

"Ian, this is Avery."

Ian knew that he was insulted. By being older than this other boy, he had the right to be introduced first. He of all people knew that—being the son of a knight sworn to the chivalric code and his time at court.

Ian could do nothing about it but bow stiffly. "Pleased to meet you," he said and proceeded to show little interest in the other boy.

Avery's mind raced, having only understood about half the words Philip had said.

"What?" she queried, a confused look on her face.

"He is Ian," Philip replied.

Ian recoiled, who were these unmannered people? Why did they think that they could just walk right over him the way that they did? Why didn't Avery reply with the usual formalities? How rude of him …

Ian. Avery's mind raced. She remembered the boy. He had been at Falkerstone Castle only a few years ago, though she had not met him.

"Pleased to meet you," she replied at last, repeating the words he had said to her, hoping that they would make sense like that.

Philip grinned. Those words—pleased to meet you—said in such a cold tone made him so happy. Avery was going to side with him against Ian. What could be better?

Ian could feel that he was losing, two against one. It wasn't fair! How many times his teachers would say: "You're a knight, nothing will ever be fair, you need to accept that and move on," but those words would never mean anything to him.

Avery's mind whirled. Ian knew her language. She knew that with his time at court and high birth that he would be able to speak it fluently, though she had never heard him speak it before.

She turned her eyes back to the trees as Philip led the way. She knew Philip had been planning on teaching her sword fighting, but now that Ian was with them, she felt that his presence had disturbed their plans.

Why did he have to come? Why couldn't he mind his own business? She thought to herself.

Philip couldn't take in his surroundings, and he didn't dare speak to Avery for fear that Ian would interrupt in the other language and leave him behind.

Ian could tell that he was interrupting something—a rhythm between the two—and he wasn't mad about it.

"*Aline sine est,*" Ian said to Avery at last. He had read Philip's face and he knew that he was afraid of having the one thing his father trusted him with taken away.

And he was right. Philip looked away with a fake air of indifference.

"No," Avery replied angrily to his statement.

Ian smiled, he didn't care about Avery's reply. Philip's face had been enough.

Birds flitted through the air and sunlight poured through the trees making beams and pools of light. Petals fell from the air almost like snow, but the effect was lost on the three.

"How about we go look at the river?" Ian said at last, bored with wandering and wanting to show that he could speak his mind.

"Sure," Philip replied. "We were there just this morning but we can go there so you can see it."

Avery followed the two boys, not really sure where she was going, or what the others had said, but she wouldn't stoop so low as to ask Ian.

The tension in the air did not dissipate after they reached the river. It wasn't long before Ian, Philip, and Avery found themselves back at camp and just barely in time for dinner.

Ian left them without a second thought or a look back, and Philip and Avery sat down on a log to wait for the meal.

They were silent and the other men who gathered around the fire were too. Something hung in the air with the smoke, and as Philip and Avery breathed it in with the men, they too grew quiet. Something pressed in from every side, but they couldn't bring up the courage to ask what it was. The men spoke in hushed whispers around them as Avery and Philip's thoughts raced through their minds. Somewhere in the background they could hear Ian talking with his father, his loud rasping tones falling on their ears like rocks. He seemed oblivious to the men around him, as was his father. The two conversed for several minutes together, men exchanging looks with each other as the two switched from topic to topic, but finally, they were brought to the fire and grew silent.

"Men," Wellington began. "Phoenix spies have been seen patrolling the forest today. Until we move our camp away from here we must be quiet. Is that understood?"

Lucas stood behind Wellington, but all eyes were on him, the true leader of the group. His head held high, overlooking Wellington with ease, he nodded seriously at the group. His graveness spreading even to Ian and his father.

Men around the fire nodded and then served the food. Ian made his way to the front of the line, while Philip and Avery silently took up the end. They hadn't been working as hard as the other men, and so they figured that they could wait till the hard workers were fed before they got their own food.

Ian took up residence on a log with a full plate. When Philip and Avery finished the line, there was nowhere else to sit but next to him.

"Avery," Ian began, speaking to the girl in her language. "I have been at Falkerstone Castle several times, but have not had the chance to live there."

Philip looked at the two. It angered him that Ian could monopolize his friend just because the two could speak the same language. It was infuriating knowing Ian now had a hold over his friend.

"The city is absolutely stunning, though the ones from Bucan are much better looking. I think Davia could benefit from some more Bucan architecture," Ian answered. "But I'm sure you already know that."

"Why should Davia change her identity?" Avery asked. Memories from her time at Falkerstone flooded her senses. She could remember the first time she had found out about the relationship between the two countries.

"Bucan has such a rich and refined culture!" Ian debated. "Davia has so much it can learn from other kingdoms!"

"I resent that!" Avery cried, standing up and glaring him in the eye, her food spilled to the ground in her excitement. Something had woken up inside her. Her passion for her country was rising within her again. "Take it back this instant!"

Men from around the campfire that were silent now turned and listened to the words that only a few of them could understand.

Ian's father, Henri the knight, was the first to react. He had heard the entire discussion. "Boy, I would pardon you this one time for your ignorance concerning the Bucan culture."

Avery had seen Ian's father at court and she recognized his way of speech immediately. She looked up at the tall man, not aware of what she had gotten herself into.

"Davia should not be envying other countries," she laughed. "It is disgusting how we take on their cultures like they're an extra garment of clothing."

"Silence!!" Ian's father stood before her, his eyes red and his hands quaking. "I will make you sorry!"

Fire coursed through Avery's vanes as she stared the grown man in the eye. Her pale face growing even paler as she spat out her words. "I am sorry," she began, "That men like you lead our kingdom astray!"

Ian's father grabbed her injured arm in a viselike grip.

Men who had been content to stand by and watch now sprang into action, some having understood the words that had passed between the two. Philip, who had been standing back dumbstruck now ran to Avery's side.

"Are you alright?" he asked, surveying her from head to toe.

Avery gasped, her wounds reopened.

"Good?" Philip asked, wondering if perhaps the language barrier was to blame.

"No," Avery absently rubbed her arm. "Not good."

Philip's eyes searched the crowd. Ian's father was fighting the men still, his face a study of rage. Ian himself was standing, watching, his face a study of stone. No one could read his thoughts. Lord Lucas rushed out of the woods, his face a study of alarm.

"Father!" Philip called out to him. "Come here!"

Lucas heard his son's voice and dashed to his side. He looked Avery over.

"What's wrong?" he asked her in the language.

50

"They were slighting Davi and saying we should follow Bucan," her mind had moved from her injuries to the insults. "I told them to take it back but they wouldn't."

"Never mind about that. What's wrong?" he asked again.

Avery took her hand away from her arm, revealing small spots of blood seeping through the bandage she already had there.

Lucas examined it. It seemed that the scabs that had formed over her arrow wound had broken and the bleeding would stop in a minute.

"You'll be alright," he told her at last. "Keep an eye on it for now. Let's settle this dispute."

The accusations he had heard made him angry. He was loyal to his country and they would pay.

Ian's father seemed to have reluctantly submitted to the other men, and Ian himself was nowhere to be seen.

Avery sat back down on the log, her face turned from Ian's father.

"Now, can someone explain what happened?" Lucas began, his stern face turning from man to man as they withered under his gaze. Philip took his place next to his father, his face angry.

"The boy has no respect for our kingdom or those who protect it," Henri the knight accused, straining at the many hands that tried to keep him back.

"And where is Ian?" Lucas asked. "He started the disagreement. Has he shied away from finishing it?"

"Ian is doing the best thing he can right now," his father began, "I told him to stay out of this. This is between me and the boy. The chivalric code does not stand for this disgrace to my and the kingdom's honor."

"I have reason to believe that your son started this," Lucas told him, ignoring his accusation. "Now, where is he?"

Ian's father had no time to reply before another man pushed his way through the crowd that had gathered, dragging the man in question along with him.

"Right, now we can begin," Lucas's face was still stern.

Avery watched in silence, the words that they said floating around and above her head. Sometimes a sentence would come through, its meaning known to her, but then meaning would leave her and the words went back to floating around just out of reach.

Lucas—his face a blank wall, his hands behind his back, his mind racing as he put two and two together—fought hard to make the two answer his questions. He asked everyone except Avery, knowing full well that it would be best to leave her alone.

Finally, he came to some version of the truth. He was disgusted as he reviewed the facts.

He was angry. Many people shared the opinions Hanri and Ian held. It would be impossible to do anything more than reprimand them for breaking the peace and give them a warning not to do it again.

This upset him beyond measure for he hated what they stood for and they were about to get away with it.

"Ian, you and your father Sir Henri should make a point of keeping the peace. There are people with differing opinions here but we are gathered to take the throne from the Phoenix Followers and restore the throne and it to a worthy successor," he switched over to the other language. "And Avery, in the future try to be less sensitive?"

Avery looked up, words with meaning awakening her from her reprieve.

Lucas would have said more but there were others around who could hear him so he gave her a meaningful look, reminding her she had to be careful.

"Alright, I'll try," she answered.

Lucas turned to the other men. "You are dismissed. If you're on duty for the new watch, go relieve the old one. If you have nothing to do, go find something to do. Remember to keep it quiet, the Phoenix Followers are out there."

Instantly everyone seemed to have something to do. Men went to change out the watch, others went back to their bedrolls and went to sleep, still more went to mend things.

Lucas turned to Philip and Avery, "I want you two to come if I call you. Understood?" he repeated it in both languages and the two nodded their heads.

"Now, Henri and Ian, I recommend you come with me," the authority made his voice sound hard. Henri and Ian reluctantly followed, fearful of disobeying a voice that displayed so much power.

The two watched the men walk to the edge of the woods and then disappeared. Philip sat down on the log next to Avery and waited.

"You were interrupted during dinner," he said pointing to where she had left her plate as he picked up his own.

"Thanks." She picked it up and began to eat.

"I thank you for your help," she told him when she was done.

Philip smiled, it had only been three days since this boy had heard the first words of this language and already he could make sentences that made sense.

"You're welcome," Philip replied. "Tomorrow I will show you how to sword fight."

Avery smiled blankly before continuing to eat.

I guess not everything gets through to him. Philip thought to himself. *Only a little bit.*

The two sat in the deepening dusk. Clouds covered the sky, blocking out the moon they had both been looking forward to. Stars peeped through the blanket of cloud every few minutes, but all was dark. Rustling could be heard in the forest all around them and the conversations being held all around camp in hushed tones. Everything around them was expecting. Whether it was rain or something more human, no one knew.

Lucas came back, the other two nowhere in sight.

"I talked with them Avery," Lucas told her quietly in her language. "They will no longer bother you."

"Thanks," she replied, in kind. She hesitated a moment before continuing. "I saw Ian once when I was at court."

"He knows you?" Lucas asked. "Will he figure anything out?"

"I don't know, but we have nothing to do but live with it," she replied, her eyes on her folded hands.

"I know," Lucas sighed, "And that's what makes this all so hard. All of the king's knights are like this. It seems as though there is something about being so close to the heart of our kingdom that makes them this way. I once had the opportunity to become a knight of the king, and I'm glad I chose against it. Philip too had the opportunity at a very young age, but his mother had just died. I didn't want him to go away."

Avery looked away, sure that this disclosure was not for her. "We'll find a way."

Lucas was silent for a moment before he stirred. "You should be fine," he stood up. "I'll see you in the morning."

Avery turned back to her plate as Lucas spoke a few words to Philip and left them alone. His feet breaking the anticipating silence by snapping branches and twigs, crunching leaves underfoot.

Philip had been sitting there while his father spoke with Avery. He watched as his father left and wished hard that Avery knew enough of his language to tell him what had passed between them, but not even a star was in the sky to help him.

CHAPTER NINE

T hey woke up rather early the next morning to rain. It dripped off of leaves and branches and soaked into the ground and the men's clothes.

Lucas and Wellington conversed over breakfast as to what the best course of action would be. They wanted to go look at the cave again and if possible move in before the end of the night. But morale was low and they weren't sure how people would feel about it. In the end, they decided to follow through with it, focusing on the fact that tonight they would have a roof over their heads and dry clothes to put on. The day after they could move on with more important missions. The two had been making plans since they had arrived, and it would be time to put them into action soon.

"Alright everyone! We move out in half an hour. Start packing your things. We'll take them with us. I don't expect to find anything wrong with the cave and I'm willing to take the gamble," Lucas called out to everyone at breakfast. "Those of you who are on watch this afternoon, I want you to take double duty. You'll start watching our new location for the Phoenix Followers. You'll have extra time off tomorrow, a roof over your head and dry place to sleep. What do you say to that men?"

His speech was greeted with rousing approval from all.

Instantly the entire camp was thrown into action. Men wolfed down their meals and turned to pack up the few belonging that they had. Some finished earlier than others and helped their neighbors. Philip and Avery had little to do but watch the other men after they had packed up their bedrolls and saddled their horses.

Philip was back to expanding Avery's vocabulary and he was pointing to things and miming out actions as he said the words that went with them. Ian looked at them several times, his nose upturned at their "quaint little ways" as he and his father spitefully called them.

They talked for a little bit in simple conversation before Lucas mounted his horse and motioned for the other men to follow.

He took up the head of the group with Wellington while Philip and Avery fell into step just a few paces behind them.

Grurhoum Greatbrow, the dwarf, had been given a horse and tagged along at the end. He didn't like the many stares many of the men gave him. It appears Bucan ideology ran deeper with more men than Lucas had suspected.

Philip knew he had only half of Avery's mind, but he continued with his words, hopeful of reeling her back in.

She sat there in the saddle for a moment before turning her eyes back to call to the dwarf.

It only took him a moment before he joined them Philip and Avery welcomed him with smiles and nods as they rode. Avery asked after his health and laughed with Philip as she tried to translate it for him.

"You've been treated alright?" she asked Grurhoum.

"Very fine," he replied, not mentioning the disgust some of the others treated him with. "I hope you have been treated well also?"

"You probably heard the fight that I got into yesterday, but I think we have ironed out those details for now. Do you know of any plans that Lord Lucas has for you?"

"Yes actually, and I'm surprised you haven't heard them," he replied, looking at her.

"Really?" she looked at him curiously, thoughts racing through her mind as she tried to put her finger on what this mission might be.

"Yes, Lucas wants to send a team into the Bucan Dynasty to do some surveillance. He's going to send you, me, and a few others who know the language to find out what the relationship between the two kingdoms really is," Grurhoum told her. "I will be there to make the mission look realistic and help translate some of the customs."

"But don't you have a life that you want to go to? Don't you want to make use of your freedom?" she asked him.

"Am I really free?" he asked her. "I owe this freedom to Lord Lucas and this company. My life is not my own. How can I use it for anything but helping them?"

Avery struggled within herself. Something told her that he was right, he wasn't truly free, but again something told her that he was wrong, that he should swallow his pride and take his freedom without paying for it. "It was a gift."

"Is there ever a gift that you don't end up paying for?"

"I understand," she said at last.

They rode on in silence.

"Look!" Avery pointed quickly, a flock of deer was to their left, the rain barely touching them as they flitted between trees.

Philip watched, hardly taking in the sight as he reveled in that simple word.

"They are good," she told him.

Philip reminded himself that he needed to come up with more words that meant good to teach to Avery. Something like pretty or nice would be fine with him—anything but good. It was an overused word he never wanted to hear again.

"Pretty," he said at last. "Very nice." He hoped that the words meaning would get across.

Avery did understand the words. Nice was not a new concept to her, however, pretty was.

"Pretty?" she asked.

"The flowers," he pointed. "Are pretty. The rain," he pointed again. "Is pretty. The water is pretty. The horse is pretty. Do you understand?"

Avery tried to think. Flowers were beautiful, was that what he meant? The rain was overpowering, but flowers weren't, neither was water or horses.

She shook her head, "No, I don't understand."

Philip sighed. He would take up the challenge another day. Right now, they had to unmount and lead Lord Lucas through the caves while the others unpacked.

"My Lord," Wellington called out to him, "Perhaps I will take Philip and go to find the other outlet of the cave."

"Good thinking. Philip?"

"Yes sir," he caught up to Wellington and led a small group in the direction he believed the outlet to be in. He was proving his trustworthiness again. He was proving himself.

Back at the cave Lucas grabbed a torch and in less than a minute everyone who was left was entering the mouth.

Lucas held the torch as high up as he could, searching the ceiling and walls for cracks. Nothing caught his eyes, and they stepped back out into the rain.

Lucas turned to his men. "Unless Wellington finds anything out of the ordinary on the other end of that tunnel, I think we have made our new headquarters. Everyone move your things into the cave and start lighting a fire. You might as well get that roof over your heads right now and start drying your clothes."

The men followed his instructions immediately, each man doing his share of the work and then moving on to help his neighbor.

Avery found herself in a corner, far removed from the others. She was fine with that. The extra privacy that she enjoyed would be nice, but she had less to move than everyone else. What could she do now?

Slowly and purposefully she made her way so as not to attract attention and left the cave. She reached the edge of the clearing and passed through the soaking trees that now offered her peace. Alone, something she had not been since before she had joined this group or even before she had gone to court. People always pushing her, prodding her, making her do things she didn't want to do. All the balls she had gone to, every moment of her day devoted to education, to the arts, manners, and social status. She was not alone for a moment. No one would have stood for it. Those days seemed so vivid and yet so far away from her right now.

She remembered every detail of her years there, but the days since she had lived it seemed like forever. And well they might have been. Years of learning can happen in days, and those days age us like the years that they should have been. The same thing happened to her when she had left her home for the first time.

CHAPTER TEN

*A*fter that fateful morning at breakfast and those moments I had alone before that, I was rushed about from place to place. Examinations trying my patience, people trying to figure out what I knew and what I didn't. People pretended they cared about me, but would turn around once I was gone and say something like: "That little Avery girl, was she taught nothing?!"

Those days following my arrival hurt my feelings like no other before. The three dresses that had had been lengthened by my mother's servant were no longer worn. My old life no longer fit my new one—my old dresses no longer befit my new life. There was no place for the familiar. There was only space for the new, what my aunt the queen thought I should learn before my coming of age in another year. Sixteen felt so far away, but time flies and how could it have been any closer?

I went from riding lessons, to dancing, to lunch, to manners, to socializing with dignitaries and visitors, to parlor tricks like playing the pianoforte, to sketching, and finally to writing. My aunt hardly oversaw anything that I did. She oversaw the people that taught me, but she never saw me herself. I was a girl brought up by my teachers and hardly ever had an ear to vent my feelings to. Perhaps that is what makes me so pale and pent up now. Perhaps I would have turned out as more of a credit to my aunt if I had the chance to vent my pent-up feelings more often.

After having been at court for nearly a year, my sixteenth birthday arrived. My uncle and aunt threw a ball for me. I was to be presented to everyone at court. According to the customs, I would probably be engaged to one of them by the end of the evening.

The idea repulsed me. I had known many girls who had thrown away wonderful and promising lives to "wonderful and promising" men. They realized their mistakes too late and wept for themselves.

It was a week before the ball and my birthday. I had attended several fittings for the dress that I was to wear, and was about to add another study to the long list. This was to be the only study that my aunt gave.

I walked into my aunt's quarters not sure what to expect.

"Darling!" she called to me. "I feel like you've only just come to live with us and now I'm to give your ball. Isn't this all just so ... sudden?"

"I suppose," I answered her, not sure what she expected. "Thank you ever so much for hosting me here." I changed the subject but not to be impolite.

"You're such a darling!" she exclaimed. "How about we sit down?"

I followed her lead and sat down on a small chair that she offered me.

"Now, I've heard from your teachers. They say you are moving along very well, especially in sketching, and that you have become a fabulous dancer. Is that true?"

"I wouldn't know," I answered truthfully. "I've never had anything to compare my work with."

"Ah well, your teachers do," she smiled. "Imagine, I'm sending out my youngest niece in less than a week and she's so accomplished that I'm quite proud of her. Avery, you don't know how happy I am that I successfully raised an eligible young lady."

"Thank you Aunt, but hadn't we better get on with my lesson?" I asked, wincing at the praise.

"Ah yes, for what are talents and manners and eligibility without a young man to share them with?" she asked laughing at herself. "For you know, I do expect a beautiful girl like you will be engaged by the end of the ball. Why, I wouldn't expect less!"

So, my aunt wants me to become one of those girls. *I thought. And just moments before I had vowed not to be like them! I won't, it's not worth sacrificing my personal happiness for my aunt's. How could she be so silly?*

My aunt carried on. "I've come up with a list of all the eligible young men who will be at the ball in a week and I've had sketchers draw their pictures so you can recognize them by sight on the night of the ball."

"But," I protested in disgust.

"It will be easy, you'll be fine," she assured me.

"It's not that, but what if I want to stay single?" I hesitantly told her.

"Don't you think that's rude?" she stared at me, her eyes searching my face, wondering how someone could think so differently from herself.

"How would it be rude?" I asked.

"I've prepared you with everything you'll need in life and now it's time for you to take advantage of it," she explained.

"But what if I'm not ready?" I asked.

"You'll be fine. I was," she tried to sound understanding.

"But," my tone escalated in panic. "What if I marry him and find out later there is another man that I love more?"

"I'm sorry, love, but when your father entrusted you in my care I promised him I would secure you a future," she said at last, putting her hand on my arm. "Can we sit down and be friends again?"

I sat down again but in shock this time. My father had betrayed me.

Aunt pulled out a few sketches from where they had been leaning against the wall. I had noticed them when I came in.

She grazed through the first couple, naming several names I both did and didn't know. There were even a few faces I recognized from events I had been to since coming to Falkerstone.

She came to the end and put the pieces of paper away.

"There are several young men who are worthy of your station, but for one reason or another are not eligible," she continued.

I could not hold my curiosity in check. "And why not?"

"Well," my aunt looked at me out of the corner of her eye with a small, knowing smile. "There are many who do not know the language of the court or our ways, even if they are high up in the nobility. It's a pity too, though many years ago a man came to court, found a wonderful lady, and learned our language so he could court her. The lady died when their son was young. He refused to teach him the language that had been love to him for so many years."

I didn't care about the story but something she had said prompted me to ask a question that I had always been wondering.

"Why do we speak a different language from the others? Wouldn't it be best for our country to unite under one language?"

"Well," she pulled her chair in closer in an attempt to make me feel more at ease, but I tightened up. "The Bucan Dynasty has always been looked up to by our kingdom and our fashions have always been an echo of their culture. One day it was the highest fashion to speak in their language. Everyone was doing it. I'm sure it had been started by the king in an attempt to make the other kingdom look down their noses at us and give us a benevolent smile, but the truth is that they looked on us with disgust at our attempts to be like them and perhaps one day join underneath one flag and one ruler," she sighed, obviously thinking that the other kingdom might have been nicer. "Our goal as a kingdom always seems to be making other kingdoms like us and perhaps one day join under the same flag."

My mind tried to wrap around what I had just heard. Davia, the kingdom I loved since birth, was just mirroring other countries to make them like her. I looked at my aunt in disgust. It was almost like the kingdom I loved was willing to hire itself out to anyone that would take it.

"That's disgusting." I turned my face from her, shameful of the language that I had thought of as beautiful up until this day.

"There are many people who would disagree." Then my aunt pulled out one more portrait. It was almost as though she had left it for last but forgotten about it until now. His long, prideful hair was pulled back and the high cheekbones that protruded from his face gave him a stern look. "I have saved the best for last, this is Lord Alonzo. His father died a few years ago, and though the boy was only fourteen he took charge of his father's estate. He has never been introduced at court and so he has some strange ideas as to the proper state of the kingdom. Because of the amount of power he holds he is the second most powerful person, right after the king. Unfortunately, if he decides to use this power to break away from the kingdom, there is a high chance he'll be able to make it. And that's where you would come in," she looked at me. "If it sounded like he was going to make moves to break away, you would send us a messenger so we could be ready in time for him."

I cringed. "So I would be a spy? And marry him with that purpose in mind? I could never do that!"

My aunt looked at me pityingly. "It would be best for your country, but perhaps you don't care about your country."

I stood up. "Thank you for your time."

"I expect to see you again tomorrow so we can review."

"I don't believe that will be necessary."

I left the room, conflicting thoughts filling my head. Marriage was not to be tossed around the way my aunt wanted it. Kingdoms were not to be tossing themselves at the feet of other kingdoms in the hopes of being conquered. If Davia wanted to add to its own every culture that came its way, what was I to care? And if it became part of my power to further it, I would flatly refuse even to dance with the person. I had become the daughter my aunt wanted, but if that meant being her political pawn, I would break her heart.

CHAPTER ELEVEN

A very's eyes smarted with rain, or perhaps they were tears—who cared? The trees around her offered her quiet solace after the morning activities, and her soaked clothes clung to her making her shiver. Her short black hair was plastered to her pale face and felt itchy as it dried.

She relived her past over and over again, realizing how much more she knew than Lucas and Wellington. She had information they could use, and now that she recalled it to her memory, she realized the importance it had. She rebuked herself. She should have brought it up earlier.

She remembered the ball vividly, but she would have to think about that later. Footsteps closed in on her. She stood up, turning to face whoever it was.

"Avery?" Philip's voice came through the rain as he pushed back hanging vines and branches out of his way to reach her.

"Yes?" she called back.

"I've found you!" he sighed, his pent-up anxiety leaving him as he sat down on the log and motioned for her to sit beside him.

Avery thought for a moment about the story she hadn't paid attention to the first time. About the man who had fallen in love with the lady and learned the language of the nobles only to lose her. But who was the son she had spoken of? She said he had not been taught the language of the nobles.

"I came looking for you," he broke into her thoughts before she could finish them. He went on even though she would only catch every few words. "When I came back from showing Wellington the other cave. Everyone is pleased with it. When I saw that you were gone, I came looking for you. It must be hard living with people you don't understand. I know I would be furious. And can you think? My father isn't even around when important things are being said so he isn't always there to translate for you. You are getting along in learning the language. I'm really proud of your work. You're doing such a good job and you're learning faster than I thought that you would," he sighed, "You don't understand everything though." He sounded discouraged and tired.

He turned back his memory to what was really bothering him and the real reason he had left the group to seek some quiet.

His role in finding the other entrance to the cave had been smaller than he had thought. But when Lucas and Wellington decided to put a watch on it he had been the first to volunteer and the first to be rejected. His father had reminded him he had other responsibilities.

He put his head in his hands and Avery watched as the raindrops fell on his neck and dribbled down his shirt, sending chills down his spine.

She wanted to reach out to him but she didn't know what was wrong or what to say.

"You are good?" she asked at last.

"No. It's 'Are you alright?' Not, 'You are good?'" Philip absentmindedly corrected her.

Avery stood up, her feelings hurt. He had never corrected her before.

"Come," she angrily pulled at his sleeve. "Come!"

Philip stood up, but mostly in surprise. He had never heard her sound so determined.

"I'm coming," he followed her as she led him down to the river.

"Look," she pointed and smiled, wiping her face as drops of rain fell in her eyes.

Philip looked at it puzzled.

Raindrops were splatting on the water of the river and it looked very tranquil, but he had no idea why she had brought him here. Suddenly his eye caught something: fish were coming up to the top because of the rain.

Philip's mind raced trying to come up with the words to say what she wanted, but in the end, he resorted to miming it out.

"You want to catch them?" Philip asked. Fish would be a great addition to dinner.

"Yes, catch," she mimed grasping them out of the water just in case catch didn't mean what she thought it meant.

Philip took off his cloak, put it gently on the bank and waded into the river, his boots already soaked through. His slow movements captivated Avery as she watched him reach down and feel with his hands.

"Come." Philip whispered so the fish wouldn't get scared away. "Catch."

Avery wadded a little bit further upstream and knelt in the freezing water, feeling for fish but not entirely sure of what she was doing. Suddenly her hand felt something smooth and scaly. She grasped at it as fast as she could while trying to stand up at the same time. It worked. In her hands, she held proudly a glistening fish.

Her eyes were wide in surprise.

"Look!" she called to Philip. He waded over to her and took it from her. She knelt back in the water to find another one while he went back to the shore to flip the fish's head against a rock and then place it on the shore.

In another minute, he was back in the water feeling for another. Avery's luck seemed to leave after her first one, and she watched as Philip pulled out another three before she had even the faintest touch of a fish. She grasped at it quickly, its scaly skin resisting her attempts to pin it down. She reached forward as it started to slip out of her hands. Her balance became precarious, her feet slipped out from underneath her, her arms flailed for a moment before she plunged under the water, its cold waves closing in over her head.

It took her a moment to put her feet back underneath her, but when she stood up, the water had done its damage. She had been soaked to the skin by the rain before, but now she was freezing. It would be insane for her to stay out any longer. She crossed her arms and stamped her feet, trying to stay warm.

"I guess it's time to go back." The four fish they had caught sitting there on the bank where they had left them. It suddenly dawned on him that they had no way to carry them back.

"Here," he slogged his way back to a bank, Avery in tow, and tossed her the cloak from where he had left it on the bank. "Take this." Avery turned from him and pulled the warm cloak around her shoulders. Philip took some vines that he found and threaded them through the fish's gills before throwing them over his shoulder.

The cloak was soaked through with rain and didn't do much to warm her but she pulled it closer around herself in the hopes of getting any warmth out of it.

"Come."

He led the way back to camp, slow enough to not miss the beauty of rain, but still quickly because Avery was growing colder by the minute.

It hardly took them a minute to get back to where Philip had found Avery, but it took them another minute after that to get back to the cave. It felt like they had been gone hours but in reality, it had just been the quiet waiting for the fish that made it feel like that.

Steam rose out of the cave, they both guess that I was from the gear drying off. It only took them a second to enter the cave. The wall of heat the greeted them both was welcome as they were soaked, and the light that dazzled their eyes was beautiful in contrast to the deepening dusk around them.

"Avery! Philip!" Lucas called out to them from across the cavern.

He stood up immediately and made a straight line toward them.

"What happened?" he asked Philip.

"I went out looking for him and then we went fishing because the fish in the river were so plentiful," at this point he handed the four fish he had caught to his father. "Unfortunately Avery lost his footing and fell in. We came back as soon as we could."

Avery's wet clothes had bled through to the cloak and it was already soaked through. Lucas inspected both of them.

"Both of you get to the fire and I'll bring you a change of clothes," he switched to the other language and addressed Avery in a hushed tone, "I have your clothes that we found you in, you go sit next to the fire and I'll bring them to you. You can go to the corridor in the back to change, its protected by a curtain that we hung up while you were gone."

"Thank you," she said, trying to keep her teeth from chattering as she turned to go to the fire.

Philip had already made it there and he gestured for her to come over.

As she made her way over she noticed that Ian and Henri both left the fire to go to their bedrolls. She shrugged it off as a good thing and sat down next to Philip.

The men around the fire chatted with each other as they passed around bits of bread. Avery and Philip nibbled on their bread, silent as they waited for dry clothes.

Avery's came first. Lucas handed them to her and she slipped away to the corridor at the back of the cave to change. She was done in a moment and came back to the fire with her soaked clothes so Philip could have his turn to change.

Lucas had put the fish over the fire right after he had passed out the clothes, and she waited only a few minutes before they were cooked and ready to eat.

He served her first and she sat down to fill her empty stomach with warm food.

She watched the men around her. They all had perked up after moving into the cave and she was glad of it. These men didn't deserve what fate had served them. They had homes they should be at right now, families to be with, servants to be cooking their food, children to spend their time with. How was any of this what they deserved?

She finished her food—tired as she was—and fell asleep before she could move back to her bedroll.

Lucas watched as the stars came out and the rain stopped. His son had given him a start when he came in soaking like that and with Avery wrapped up in his cloak. He would have done anything to keep the both of them out of trouble, to keep them safe. He smiled looking at them now. Philip had gone to bed and was passed out while Avery was asleep by the fire, she hadn't moved since she had finished her dinner. She looked so serene. She was well fed, dry, and warm. She looked tired and happy, but with a strangely sad and hungry look.

He turned his head back to Philip. He too looked tired and happy, but the hungry and sad look that Avery had was missing on him.

"Friendship can only go so far for her," he sighed, turning from the stars and making his way to her.

He stooped down and picked her up, her light frame giving the strong man no trouble.

At closer range the sad look was even more evident than the hungry one. She wanted to reach out somewhere and find her place, but she knew she didn't belong in that place, and the place she really wanted was gone and could never be reached again.

He walked over to her bedroll, and placed her gently there.

"Sweet dreams," he whispered to her. He had never had a daughter, and she was the closest thing he had.

He looked back at her, the hunger and sadness gone from her face.

"I can't replace that life," Lucas whispered, "But I can give you a new one."

CHAPTER TWELVE

P hilip woke up the next morning and stretched. He felt so rested and peaceful, but it was soon to change. His father was already up, thoughts troubling him and keeping him from sleep.

"Son," he softly called to him over the sleeping forms of the other men.

Philip silently went toward him, careful not to wake anyone. "Yes?"

"I want to talk with you." Lucas made his way toward the opening of the cave.

They both stepped out, the cool air greeting them and waking Philip more than he had been before.

He had still not been reprimanded for anything about the raid on the caravan, and he prepared himself for the flood. Darren must not have said anything to him about it until now.

"Son," Lucas began, "I have a mission for you."

Philip looked at him in surprise. He had been expecting to be reprimanded, but here he was getting a mission.

"I'm listening," Philip told him.

"In a few days Wellington and I are going to make a sneak attack on the castle ..."

"And you want me to come!" Philip grasped at his father's arm, his smile filling his face. He was finally going to be accepted for the man he was. Somehow, he had proven himself.

"No," Lucas frowned. "I don't want you anywhere near the battle."

Philip's face fell. His father didn't trust him. "Ian will go, won't he?" he accused. Disappointment and anger filled his voice.

"No," Lucas told him, "Even if Ian has been in battle before I refuse to allow him to go."

"Why?"

"You're both needed on another mission," Lucas assured him. "I don't need to remind you that everyone on this team needs to play his part or everything will fall apart. I'm not saying I don't trust you. I do! That's why I need you."

"So you've just come to tell me that I can't join you in battle?" Philip turned from him to go back into the cave.

"No," Philip stopped and turned back to his father. "I'm planning on sending a secret band of spies into the Bucan Dynasty, I need you to go with them. I can't trust anyone else to go with them."

"But I don't know the language." Philip looked at his father, confused.

"No you don't, but you will be going with Grurhoum Greatbrow who will be there to bring credibility to your group and make sure that their customs are observed. I'm also sending Avery who will pose as a son of one of two other lords and Ian will pose as the son of the other."

"So you trust me with the same things you trust Ian with?" Philip scoffed. "It doesn't sound like I'm really needed in this group."

"I need you to go because I don't trust him," Lucas explained. "You're the only one who has bonded with Avery and he'll need someone on a mission like this."

"I still don't see why me. You have Grurhoum and two other lords. You don't need me," Philip told him.

"You will be posing as one of the guards on a convoy. I have to yet chose who you will be escorting, but it will be a fictional little-known low noble of some sort." Lucas paused for a moment, debating on whether or not he should continue. "Avery was never taught how to defend himself and I need fighters on this team because it needs to succeed. I know your skill and that's why I chose you."

Philip thought about it. He was being chosen for a special mission, one where he hardly played a large part, but was yet vital to the survival of the team. He could think of himself as a bodyguard.

"I'll think about it," he said at last.

"Philip, you can't think about it, I have already decided. You are going on this mission. You are the only friend Avery has here, and they need your skill. This mission must succeed. If it fails, we all fail. I need my best man on the job."

Philip struggled. The responsibility that his father was giving him made him proud, but being told he had to do it without having the choice made him want to rebel. But he forced himself to yield. His part was one that no one else could play, and even if it meant that he would be working with Ian for a few days, he would give it his best shot.

"I'll go," he said at last.

"Thank you," Lucas took him by the shoulder. "I knew I could trust you. You're going to have so much fun on this mission, and you'll get to experience another culture, something that you haven't really had the chance to yet outside of Falkerstone," they headed back into the cave. "I'll find someone who can translate between you and Grurhoum. I'm sure there are some things that he'll want you to know. I've put him in charge of the trip, I don't see any reason not to."

Philip didn't answer. Other men were already stirring and someone had started breakfast.

He glanced around the room, looking for Avery. But he was talking with Wellington already and he didn't want to interrupt.

They were talking intently, and after a moment, they summoned Lucas and stepped out of the cave to be alone.

"Lucas, Wellington," she began. "As you know, I have lived at the castle for several years." Lucas and Wellington nodded. "I have a few things that you should know," she stopped, looked at them, and continued. "Back during my time at Falkerstone I was at the center of the entire kingdom and learned many things."

Lucas and Wellington waited.

"I heard a lot of gossip about many of the lords including Alonzo," she looked at the two. "I was told he was the most powerful lord. Where is he? Why hasn't he joined us here? Did he know?"

"Rumors have spread that he is dead," Lucas told her, turning to go back into the cave. "We have nothing to fear from him."

"Lord Alonzo is possibly behind the Phoenix Followers," Avery stated.

"Lord Alonzo?" Wellington asked, his attention grabbed.

"Yes," she confirmed. "He had never been introduced at court until a year ago, and I was informed that he has some strange ideas about the kingdom. And spreading the rumor of his death sounds like just the trick the Phoenix would pull to get suspicion off himself."

"What kind of ideas did he have?" Lucas pressed her.

"He was considered a threat by my aunt. He is the second most powerful person, right after the king. Unfortunately, if he decided to use this power to break away from the kingdom, it's possible he could have formed the Phoenix Followers in secret and is using the poem to hide behind his true intentions of taking over," Avery cried, looking away angrily.

Wellington looked at Lucas. "Alonzo knows about the rendezvous plans here in the forest, it would explain the guards that we found the other day. He knows we're here. He just has to root us out."

Lucas reluctantly nodded. "For the moment we'll assume the Phoenix knows we're out here and Alonzo might not be dead.

Wellington ran his fingers through his hair, and Lucas leaned against a tree.

"And what are we supposed to do against such a powerful man like that?" Wellington cried.

"I don't know," Lucas answered. "We don't even know if Lord Alonzo is the Phoenix. However, if he isn't and he is still alive, it might be best if we could make a friend of him."

"Either way we need to look into his whereabouts," Wellington began. "Perhaps we can spare a few of the older men to go scout out the east in search of a few clues as to his standing on the matter."

Lucas sighed and stood up. "Sure, I think we can spare Garret, Sterling, and Darren. That will leave us with ..." he paused, thinking through each man individually. "We have seven people now on separate missions and that leaves us with twenty fighting men excluding ourselves which brings us up to twenty-two men to sneak into the castle, find out everything that we can, and do as much damage as possible."

Avery spoke up, "I didn't know that this was happening. When is it?"

"In the next few days. We've been preparing for since we got here," Wellington began. "And Lucas, do you want to tell her what her part is in all of this?"

Avery's eyes switched from one to the other, her heart racing. She was to have a part in this plan?

"Well," Lucas began. "I'm planning on sending you, Ian, Philip, Grurhoum, and two of the lords, Sir Vincent and Lord Edward, on a mission to the Bucan Dynasty for surveillance. You'll all be posing as an escort for a little-known noble, which will explain why you have a dwarf servant and will give Philip a reason not to say anything since guards are supposed to hold a respectful silence. Grurhoum will be the leader of the mission since he knows the customs and what to look for. Philip will be an asset because of his skill in fighting. Since you've never been taught how to fight, it will be important to send strong fighters with you."

Avery tried to take everything in, her pale face scrunched up trying to smooth out all the details.

"I have only one question," she said at last. "Can we trust Ian to behave? He's obviously mad at me after our scuffle the other day."

Lucas sighed and leaned against the tree again as Wellington continued to run his hands through his hair.

Avery bit her lip and looked at the mouth of the cave. Maybe it was time to tell everyone who she was.

Avery's heart went to her mouth. Something about that prospect did not make her happy. She couldn't imagine telling these people that she had been lying to them about something so big for so long. What if Philip was mad at her?

"Sir," Avery began. "Would it be a good idea to let everyone on my team know who I really am?"

The two looked at her blankly.

"I think it might be a good idea, Avery," Lucas said at last. "It would solve the problem of who the little-known noble is."

"But I lied to them!" she blurted out at last. "What if they hate me?" she tried grasping at other excuses but her hands came up empty. She didn't want to break their trust after she had been trying to build it up for so long. She didn't want to expose herself.

"So?" Lucas smiled. "You might as well tell them now instead of later when it will be harder or could destroy the entire mission. It is the best thing for your team and your country. They need someone to escort, and you're the perfect fit. They would never expect a girl to be on a secret mission."

"The fewer secrets you take into Bucan, the fewer chances there are that your mission will be exposed. It is best for everyone and will put your team at less risk. The closer to the truth we stay, the better," Wellington argued, trying to persuade her to his side. "It's the best for you, your team, and your country."

"And what do I care about this country?!" Avery began, her rage becoming delirious. "All it wants to do is become conquered by another one. I hate this language! I hate what it stands for! I hate that it means everyone who speaks it wishes for Davia to be conquered by Bucan! I hate it all!" she dropped her hands in desperation, her face red and hot with the anger that burned within her. "This country does not deserve our efforts because it doesn't want them."

"If that's how you feel," Lucas sighed, turning his back to her and walking back toward the cave. "Then we might as well turn ourselves in right now."

Avery looked up, the expression on her face frozen in her surprise. She hadn't expected him to let it go that easily.

"But then we die," she said simply. Lucas had forced her point of view around on her, showing her the consequences of her beliefs.

"If our country dies, then so do we," he confirmed, turning back to face her. "And if we die, so does our country."

"When we take back the kingdom, I can change it," Avery hesitantly began. "I can make it proud of itself, worth fighting for." She waited to hear what he would say.

"You won't be the only one," Lucas reminded her. "There are many people out there who believe in our kingdom and will join you. You don't have to do it by yourself."

Wellington and Lucas turned to go back into the cave.

"Alright then."

They stopped.

"Let's do this. It's going to happen sooner or later."

Avery turned her face back to the wall of stone as the two men went back into the cave, their mission complete. She only had a few moments, but she cleared off her face as well as she could and attempted to make it like the wall of stone in front of her—hard, unmoving, and emotionless.

She gave a grim smile as she thought about the entire conversation they had just had. She had been the one to suggest this course of action in the beginning, and she had also been the one to object to it the most. It was the right thing to do though and she knew it. This would take a load off of her during the mission.

Steps sounded behind her before she was ready, and when she turned around she found them all there, waiting for her.

"Ian, Philip, Grurhoum," she began. "Sir Vincent, and Lord Edward, I have something to tell you," she searched with her eyes, sensing their confusion until they met with the Lords Lucas and Wellington in the back.

She shuddered but continued speaking in her language. Someone would translate for Philip and she was glad if it. It meant that she wasn't telling him directly and something in that gave her comfort.

She took courage and began speaking again. "As you already know, we have been assigned with a mission to the Bucan Dynasty. However, Lucas, Wellington, and I have conferred and there is some information that we believe you should know before we go in," she took a deep breath. She knew in her heart that this was the right thing to do and it should have been done long ago. "As you might have noticed by the fact that I only speak the Bucan language, I am a noble of close relation to the king. One thing you do not know is that I am the only daughter of the king's youngest brother, and due to the conflict, I am now heir to the throne. I am the crown princess to the Davia Kingdom."

She breathed out, the only sound that could be heard above the confused looks that Ian, Philip, Grurhoum, Sir Vincent and Lord Edward were giving each other. In the back, she could watch Wellington and Lucas translating for Philip. His face had not changed yet, and she knew that the news had not yet been broken. "You are not to share this information with *anyone*. This information is privy only to the people in the group going on the mission to Bucan. You are not to share this information outside of this group and the Lords Lucas and Wellington. The only reason you are being told is because the fewer secrets we take into Bucan, the higher our chances of coming back out. You are not to tell anyone else because many of the lords believe there are no heirs to the throne left, and that they have a chance at it. If they knew who I was, my life could be in jeopardy."

No one spoke. Avery's eyes searched theirs.

Grurhoum was the only one besides Lucas and Wellington who already knew and did not look surprised. He was to be the leader of the group and he was glad that she had told them. It would make his job as team leader easier if they didn't have to come up with lies to protect her on their mission.

He was still puzzled as to why they would expose her like this. If the information someone left this group, her head would be marked.

But slowly he put the pieces together. She would be the one they were escorting. She was the perfect fit because she was already a noble and both looked and acted the part. It wouldn't make sense to have a small boy with no fighting skills on someone else' guard.

Next Avery's eyes found Sir Vincent. Avery hadn't spent any time with the younger brother of Lord Edward and had only seen him in passing, but she could see his surprise, realization, and how he began putting two and two together.

Then her eyes met with Lord Edward. Sir Vincent's older brother was having the same kind of thoughts. Things were beginning to make sense to him, and her pale features and dark hair made sense now that they were on the face of a girl.

Finally, she locked eyes with Philip, watching as his father translated for him. He looked confused, almost as though he didn't believe anything.

Lucas left Wellington to fill in the details as he addressed the group.

"Are there any questions?" Lucas asked quickly and in a voice that said that they had better not. A moment passed as they looked at each other. "Good. Right now, we're planning on making our move in the next few days. We're gathering supplies. We will have to be careful because the Phoenix Followers are still roaming the forest and we don't want them finding our hiding place," he looked around at the faces. "Grurhoum will be in charge of the group. He knows the culture and customs better than any of you and will help you blend in better. Edward is second in command and the rest of you are to follow their orders and as you might have guess, Avery is the one who you will be escorting. We'll have meetings each day until you leave and we'll give you the rest of the details then. Are there any questions?" Lucas looked around at the group. He had spoken in the language of the nobles because he had already spoken with Philip about this.

No one spoke up to ask anything. They were still absorbing everything.

"Alright, go get breakfast. Remember, you are not to tell anyone," he didn't look at anyone specifically as he said the words. He waited a moment for his words to sink in. "Now go, eat!"

Still taking in all the information, they slowly went back into the cave leaving only Lucas, Wellington, and Avery.

Philip followed the rest of the group almost mechanically as though his mind were somewhere else.

The three stood in silence for a moment before Avery broke it.

"We have to retake the kingdom," she spoke with passion. "We can't let it die."

Lucas nodded. "The Phoenix is tearing it apart, nothing seems right. Davia is collecting taxes from Bucan and taking on slaves. We have to help."

They stood in silence. "Not just for ourselves," Wellington broke the silence. "Or even for the kingdom itself, but also for the people who live in it."

"It'll be alright," Lucas told him, turning back towards the cave. "Both of our missions will succeed. They have to or we have no chance of restoring the kingdom."

Wellington and Lucas went back into the cave and all was silent.

She felt surprisingly calm about how it had gone over with them, but something nagged at her and she couldn't quite place her finger on it. She brushed it off. It probably didn't matter anyway. But her mind kept going back to it. Why did she feel this way right now?

She slowly and purposefully moved her mind away from it and thought about going in to eat breakfast. She reminded herself that nothing had really changed for her. She still had to act her part, but something about the thought of seeing all those eyes looking at her stayed her in her place. The last time she had felt like this was during the ball as she stood before the door, knowing she had to go in but didn't want to.

CHAPTER THIRTEEN

I *do indeed remember it clearly, not just the ball itself, but the entire day of the ball. And how could anyone forget such a day as that?*

It started early the morning of the ball. My aunt woke me up herself, coming into my room before it was even light out.

"Wake up," she called softly. "It's time to get up and seize the day. We have so much to get done today."

I groaned. I needed my sleep, but more importantly I wanted to put off the day for as long as possible.

"It's not day yet, the sun has yet to come up from its resting place, and if the sun hasn't gotten up yet, then no one should."

"But today is a busy day for you," she argued, pulling at the blankets. "It only comes once in a lifetime."

I muttered as I pulled myself out of bed. I slipped a dress over my nightgown to bar the cold that crept in from the outside. I could see the moon—lady of the night—reflecting off of the soft, fluffy flakes that fell relentlessly from the sky. My clothes wouldn't matter. I would end up having to change them before the festivities anyways.

"I'm ready," I mumbled, shivering.

"Then come with me!" she slipped out the door of my room and quietly turned down the hall

She had a grace about her that allowed her to move quickly without running and I hurried to keep up with her.

"We have a quick refresher on the nobles we will be expecting and the procedure of the ball, then breakfast, then we'll go to another dress fitting to make sure everything is ready, then we have to buy slippers for you because you wore your others to rags, then we'll be back for lunch, and then we'll have the afternoon to get your hair done before our guest start arriving at four," she told me breathlessly. "You'll be required to hide out of sight. Our guests are not to see you until you are presented. Unfortunately, that means you will have to be ready by four because I will be down stairs welcoming them and will not have time to

prepare you after they arrive. The ball itself starts at seven, there will be fifteen minutes while the nobles greet each other before your uncle and I are presented, and then you will come out a few minutes afterwards," she took a deep breath and continued down the hall.

We turned a few corners before she took up the conversation again.

"After you have been introduced, you will be called upon to take this first dance. As you know, there are three ways this could happen," she explained. "The first is with your father."

"He'll be there?" I turned to her, my voice surprised. I hadn't heard anything about any of my family being there.

"He was invited," my aunt explained. "But he had to decline. In this case, the king would act in his stead. Seeing as he hasn't said anything about it, it is unlikely that he will take the first dance with you. He has been very busy recently. There are many things going on in the kingdom."

We walked down another hall in silence. I shouldn't have expected my father to come.

"Besides," she continued as she slowed her pace. "The whole point of this ball is for you to meet eligible young men and that will not be accomplished if you dance with the king, although you will be obligated to do it at least once during the evening."

She had slowed her pace but she still hurried on, regardless of my feeble protests.

"The second way to take the first dance is if you ask for a specific young man himself. But I know you," she looked at me. "You won't do that, will you?"

I didn't say anything.

"No matter what you decide, I know you are adequately prepared for this. You have excelled at just about everything we have given to you to learn and you're a great dancer."

We had reached my aunt's room where she stepped in for a moment to grab a thin shawl to go over her dress and keep her warm, and we hurried on. "The final way to decide the first dance is if one of the young gentlemen comes up to you himself and asks for it. Of course, if this happens, you are obligated by the rules of etiquette to accept unless you have already promised the dance to someone else, or have someone specific in mind."

I was so out of breath with running about through the halls, that I could only manage a nod and a lick at my parched lips. I wondered if there would be water in the hall.

"Good," she turned from me, satisfaction gleaming in her eyes. "Then we agree."

I wondered if my aunt could hear herself. Anger rolled itself into my hands that now lay clenched at my side.

"Ah, at last!" she pushed open the door to the ballroom, nodding to the two guards on either side. "This is the place where your destiny could be written," she sighed, looking at me with sparkling eyes.

She quickly turned, her skirts rustling across the floor as she glided up to the dais where her throne stood sparkling in the soft lamplight. The effect was quite beautiful. The soft light glinted off of the gold and darkly illuminated the tapestries and paintings that lined the whole hall. Everything stood at attention, ready for the gaiety of the night, ready for lights to stream in through the windows, ready for the rest of the lights to be lit, ready for the music to start, ready for my doom to be sealed. It looked so innocent that I could hardly blame it for being the device of my doom.

"Darling?" she called out softly.

I turned to look at her, her face grown soft in the soft lights, but perhaps it was only an illusion.

"I'm so happy for you," she pulled me into a tearful embrace, "I had this chance myself when I was your age, but since I have no daughter of my own to lead out into the world, you are the next best thing. I'm so proud of my adopted daughter, you're going to be the talk of the entire country, and maybe even Bucan Dynasty and the Wrorid Empire," she smiled down at me to see how I took that information.

I looked away.

"Darling?" she tucked her hand under my chin and lifted my head to look into her eyes. She paused there for a moment, searching my eyes. I expected her to say more but she didn't.

She sighed and turned me away. "Perhaps you are right. It is too early. Shall we find breakfast?"

Without waiting for a response, she slipped out of the ballroom and I followed behind her. We dashed down many more familiar halls before we found ourselves in the dining room. The royal family—my uncle and a few of his advisors—had already gathered and were waiting for us.

My aunt left me to join the king where he sat, but in a moment, he called me up to him, my heart in my mouth.

"Niece," he began. He had hardly spoken to me since I had arrived almost a year ago. "Good morning."

"Thank you," I whispered, in awe of his smiling face. His arm was wrapped around his wife. I had realized long ago that he truly loved her, but in return all she cared about was his station. Tears almost always came to my eyes when I thought of it. My uncle was a very noble man, kind, generous, wise, and always chivalric. His deep sense of honor had gotten him into trouble many times because he couldn't take the faintest insult without having to defend his honor in a gentlemanly way.

"You will save the first dance tonight for me?" he asked teasingly. "If you do not, I would feel like you do not care for your old uncle who is useless to the world."

He smiled as he said it and without thinking I blurted out my answer. "Your majesty! Of course I will save the first dance for you."

"Good," he held out his hand to me and I curtsied the way my teachers had taught me. "Without my brother here to introduce you to the world, it is my own duty to do so and if my wife ..." he kissed her on the cheek bashfully. "Had decided on anything other than doing this small thing for my brother, I would never be able to face him again. It is a matter of honor to me. If my brother cannot pass you off to the world, then I will do it in his stead."

I glanced up to my aunt with joyous eyes, but she pretended to have not heard him. Her eyes did not betray any emotion.

"Thank you," I curtsied over his hand again and went to take my seat further down the table.

"Wait!" he called back. "You are about to be introduced to the world," he began. "You may take a seat at my right hand after the queen."

I glanced to the seat next to my aunt that he motioned to and stood behind it, waiting for him to sit down. In another moment he did.

Everyone could sit now, and after the king had taken his first bite, everyone plunged into their breakfasts with an energy that denoted something big was going to happen that day.

I could see my aunt to my left eating her meal as quickly as she could without being rude, and stealing glances at my plate to gage my progress. She finished quickly and quietly waited until I had enough food. Though she was quiet, she was still impatient for me to finish.

At last, the inevitable could be put off no longer. I finished and she whisked me away from the table as fast as she could, trying to make up for lost time.

She pulled me up to my room where she basically threw a cloak and winter boots at me and dragged me out the door again.

I hopped along beside her, stuffing my unwilling feet into the boots and trying not to drop the cape. I felt irritated. I knew we had plenty of time.

But in another moment, we were outside in the thick fluffy snow that came up almost to our knees. If today had been my birthday back at home, I would have gone out and played in it. I would have gone sledding with the others in my town and then gone to ice skate on the nearby pond.

My aunt would never hear of it. Such pastimes were for peasants, not the daughters of noblemen.

The carriage pulled up to where we stood and I was hustled inside. In another moment, we were off, down to the town where the kingdom's dressmaker lived and where we would find a pair of slippers for me to wear with the gown.

I watched out the window, reveling in the beauty around me. But it only took a moment before my aunt asked me to close the window. She was clutching her shawl tightly and I reluctantly closed it.

I sighed, but I could follow her rules for one day. It couldn't be that bad.

We were let out in front of the dressmaker's residence and were hurried inside.

The old wizened lady who greeted us with a smile asked the queen to sit down while she took me away to try on the dress.

She took me into a bare room with only a small chair in the corner with a box on it. She left, closing the door behind herself, and I turned to the box.

I opened the lid resentfully, pulled away the brown paper that covered and protected it from getting splinters, and saw the dress.

It was dark gray blue with trim around the neck. Other than that, nothing could be inspected from the way it was folded. I pulled it out of the box with a sigh, the long skirt dragging against the dirty floor as it went.

I had almost didn't put it on but then I remembered my aunt would be waiting to see it.

I slowly put the dress on and in a moment, I had the lacing at the back tightened and I pushed open the door.

"It's very well done." My aunt smiled at the old lady and pulled out her purse to pay

her. *"You have outdone yourself."*

I glanced down: the dress was a gray blue with light blue trim around the sweetheart neckline and draping sleeves. A single band of the same light blue was around the arm of the sleeve, and the few slashes in the skirt also sported that color. Silver ran around as a trim, but seemed hardly to make such an effect as the light blue. I gave it a twirl, hardly even trying to resist the temptation that the full skirt posed.

"I do think I have," the wizened old lady said at last, her fingers catching a fold of fabric between her bony fingers and giving it a rub. "I refrained from using silk because you wanted an even look that only wool can give you," she explained. "I made sure that you had the finest quality, only lambswool. And when you pair it with the belt that my assistant made," she pulled out another wooden box. "I'm sure you will both be satisfied."

She handed the box to my aunt. She pulled the lid off and lifted out the small garment.

The delicate band of silver sank through her fingers like liquid moonlight. She admired it and passed it to me, I placed it around my waist twice before tying it in the middle and letting slide down to my toes.

My aunt muttered to herself as she gazed at me, pleased with my appearance. Then she spoke aloud to me, "Change back so we can get the shoes."

Though it twirled nicely, I still couldn't wait to take it off.

As I slipped back into the bare room, I overheard my aunt speaking to the dressmaker, "It really makes her complexion look less queer. Her hair is so dark and her face is so pale that it's quite a pain to dress her."

"I agree. I wasn't too sure about the fabric choice myself. She looks so strange," the dressmaker answered back as I closed the door behind me, my heart back in my boots.

I changed back as fast as I could and then carefully wrapped the dress in the brown paper before I placed it in the wooden box.

I crept out the door and my aunt thanked the dressmaker before she hurried me on.

"We still have to find shoes," she reminded me. "Lunch is in two hours and we need to be back at the castle before that. Hurry!"

She dragged me back into the carriage, leaving both boxes with the manservant who came for that very purpose. She gave directions to the driver, James, and sat back, satisfied with the transaction.

I groaned, forbidden from looking out the window, but not having anything to look at in the carriage.

In less than a few minutes we reached the shoemaker and I was once again hurried into another workshop.

The shoemaker greeted us. "I have been expecting that you would come by," he began, smiling at my aunt. "You hadn't made any orders for your niece's ball so I took the liberty of designing a few." He turned to pull some shoes out from behind the counter. "I still had both of your measurements from last time you came in here, so I came up with a few designs for both of you." He looked at my aunt with a sly grin. He knew she cared about showing her wealth and status and wouldn't pass up any of the delicate footwear he had made.

My aunt called to the servant in attendance, ordering him to bring forth the box to carry things in so that a choice could be made.

I looked at them, my eye passing over the ones made for aunt. She had an assortment of shoes—some in gold, some in silver, some in purple and other colors of royalty. Embroidery graced several of them, but on others semiprecious stones seemed to be the decoration of choice.

My aunt glanced them all over and paid the man. The servant placed the box with the dress on the table and went to packing the five or so pairs that my aunt had already paid for.

In front of me, she looked over the four pairs that had been made for me.

The first could have been made for the queen and not me. Embellishments covered the whole of them until you could not decipher what color they really were. My aunt paid for them without a second thought.

The second pair seemed simple enough. The man explained that they were all in fashion before she paid for them and moved on to the next.

The third pair seemed to be a walking shoe in green suede. Once again my aunt motioned for them to be put with the others in the carriage.

The fourth pair seemed to be boots made for a man. They were ridiculously tall, but the man explained that they were lady's riding boots and that the top was to be cut down to the lady's height. My aunt reluctantly paid for them, but only because they were "in fashion."

She turned from the counter with a sigh. "None of these will do for a ball," she cried.

"Don't worry, madam," said the shoemaker. "I have saved the best for last."

He pulled out another pair of shoes from behind the counter and watched my aunt's surprised face.

I did have to admit that they were beautiful.

"I copied them from the ballet dancers from Bucan," he informed us. "They are very supple and will stay on your feet without trouble."

The shoes he had set down were a beautiful shade of silver, like the dress. They did not have the awkward look and shape that our shoes had, but instead a pretty rounded toe, a top that would expose my foot, and ties in the back to make sure they would not slip off as I danced.

"I'll take them," my aunt told him, pulling out even more money than she had for any of the others. "I want you to make me a pair like that before the end of next week."

The man smiled. "I already have," and he pulled out another pair just like it, but a little bit big, and began to wrap them.

"I am very satisfied with your work," my aunt told him as we left. "I'll be back in a few months for spring shoes."

"I'll be ready, your majesty," he called after us, congratulating himself on selling so many shoes.

I could see how he had played us but decided not to tell my aunt. It would be a secret between the two of us, the shoemaker and me.

We were pushed back into the carriage and whooshed away on the long ride back to the castle. My mind, heart, and eyes were bound to the confines of the carriage.

After a few moments, I notice the early morning had caught up with my aunt.

I grinned and without hesitation stuck my head out the window to watch the people and the sights.

I waved at several people, the harsh winter wind blowing the color red to my cheeks.

The streets seemed more crowded than normal. Perhaps it was because of the big event happening at the castle that night, but I couldn't tell. I didn't recognize any of the faces outside the window, though many of them probably recognized mine.

As we continued through the streets of the town I did noticed the large number of people who recognized the royal carriage and bowed to us as it went by.

Two men on horses caught my attention specifically. The elder seemed haggard, but with noble blood. The younger was obviously his son as they had the same golden hair and the same eyes.

The father looked up at the castle with eyes like none I had ever seen before. They signaled hurt and hardship, but also seemed sad with remembering. But overall he looked expectant.

The center of the town was congested with horses and carriages so we were not moving.

The son seemed careful of his father. He was always watching the things around him, sometimes pointing things out because they were interesting, and to him almost everything seemed interesting. It was almost as if the young man had never been to a big town.

His father did not reprimand him for being rude, but rather seemed to pour information from his mind to the inquisitive boy.

I liked the way they looked together. The father protective of his son, and the son protective of his father. I almost wished that their worn wool, graying tunics and faded boots were replaced with the extravagance of the nobles. How I wished that the father at least had an insignia denoting him of noble birth, but I could find no such mark. I could tell their horses were as pure as could be, and that they should be dressed better to go with them.

Our carriage moved forward at last, the father and son dropping from their horses to kneel on the ground as we passed, their cloaks covering their shoulders and draping into the cold slush that covered the ground.

CHAPTER FOURTEEN

P hilip sat in the cave, his mind taking in the words Avery had said. He watched as his father made the circulations among the men, gathering people for a meeting to set up the day watch.

Philip watched and listened. So much had already happened today and he wasn't sure how to take it. Something inside him urged him to slip outside and find Avery, if only to sit with her silently. But then another thought urged him to stay. Avery didn't need company, but she did need a friend, and not just any time, but right now.

She must think that everyone hates her for being alive to take the throne from them, Philip thought as he made up his mind, gathered some more food on another plate, and slipped out of the mouth of the cave. Lucas's eyes followed his son, thankful that his boy had made the right choice not to shun Avery.

Outside the cave Philip scanned the area until his eyes rested on the unmoving shape of Avery.

She was sitting on a log right outside the clearing, her head was in her hands staring at the ground and for a moment Philip almost went back inside, but his heart reached out to this girl. What else could he do?

He silently walked out to the edge of the clearing and sat down, keeping his eyes away from her and her inner struggles.

Avery looked up in surprise, revealing her grave face.

"This is for you." Philip passed the plate of food to her and was silent.

She took it without question, almost in shock, and ate the contents slowly but without really tasting them. When she was done, she placed the plate on the ground beside them.

So, he wasn't mad at her.

"Thank you," Avery broke the silence at last.

"You're welcome," he answered simply.

They listened to the silent woods, washed clean by the storms of yesterday.

I would never have forgiven myself if we had passed her up when we found her. Philip told himself.

"Thank you for everything," Avery brokenly said at last. "You are good."

"Thank you," Philip answered from the bottom of his heart. "You have been good to me, too."

Those words now meant something to Avery—she actually knew what each of them meant—but the tone he said them in meant everything to her.

They sat there, watching the cleanly washed woods around them spring to life.

Days later, they set out for the Bucan Dynasty. Lucas watched as his son left, trusting in him to bring everyone back safely.

Avery's wounds had healed nicely and Lucas had allowed her to take the bandages off that morning. They had peeled them away, revealing the gnarled scabs that would soon turn into scars. Her head wound had turned out to be only superficial, just a simple graze that had bled a lot. But it still pained her to move her arm in such a state it was.

Grurhoum clinked the coins in his pocket. He felt confidence in his position of leadership. He knew the most about the county they were visiting, and there wasn't a doubt within any of them going on the trip as to who was in charge.

Lord Edward could feel the same responsibility that Grurhoum felt, but in a different way. He was to be the leader if Grurhoum came upon something that he was not capable of undertaking himself, and he was to be head spokesperson when they got there because Grurhoum would be seen as a slave and it would not be appropriate for him to speak in their company.

Philip looked back at his father, still not sure if was trusted. He reminded himself of their last conversation when Lucas had told him that he was going on this mission. He was here because his father trusted him and knew his skill with the sword.

Avery felt lost and unsure. Lucas had given her a bow and arrows to go with the dagger Philip had already given her, but she hardly knew how to use them. Sure, there was the one time with the caravan and the one time Philip helped her shoot, but if push came to shove, would she be able to protect herself? She would be up against men and wouldn't have the help of the forest or Philip—could she do this on her own?

They pushed through the forest, away from the cave where Lucas and Wellington waved goodbye, away from the warm fire that had soothed them during the night, away from its safe stronghold.

They pushed onto the path, sure of their way. Lord Edward was the only person who knew these woods and could navigate them to the safe path from there to beyond the forest and into the great countryside that would await them. From there, Grurhoum would navigate their wandering pilgrimage to the Bucan Dynasty.

Philip settled down into his saddle. With Ian up at the head of the caravan, he felt he could speak with Avery without being looked at in contempt from the other boy.

"I haven't talked with you these past few days," he said.

Avery looked up at him, catching only half his words.

"We don't talk much," he simplified.

"I'm sorry about it," she answered. "It's hard to talk. To think up words, to speak with people. I have ... " she broke off, unsure of how to continue.

Ian called back as he slowed his horse to pull up with them and then switched to the other language.

Philip looked away in disgust.

"Many people envy your position," he began. "I'm sure you've heard that many of them are interested in proving themselves worthy of the throne since they know of no living heirs."

"I didn't ask you for your opinion," Avery answered him coolly.

Ian didn't answer her.

"Philip," she smiled at him, his head turning at the sound of his name. "Is on this mission because he is a good fighter."

"I thank you for your high opinion," he answered, looking at her in surprise.

"Your father said so," she answered him, turning her attention back to the road and rocky terrain.

Ian spurred his horse on. Avery's laugh followed him and spurred him faster toward the front of the line.

Light bounced off the bubbling brook they followed and cast shifting patterns of light across their faces and horses. How could anyone not laugh? The small buds that had begun to bloom a few days ago were now falling from their twigs, creating the effect of snow falling. Flowers that had been only green plants the day before now bloomed for all to enjoy. The sun that had its way of hiding behind clouds decided to make itself known today, and nothing could stop it.

They walked on through the forest before turning onto the beaten path that they had been on only a few days before when they had attacked the caravan to keep supplies out of enemy hands.

Philip pointed to a few things and said their words for Avery before he fell silent like the rest of the troop.

Lord Edward focused on making sure they followed the path that they should.

Sir Vincent leisurely read a book, trusting in his horse to keep on the path.

Sir Ian seethed in his own rage at the front of the line.

Grurhoum sat in silent contemplation of what he was about to do. Going back to the country that had enslaved him and his people was probably the most dangerous decision he could make. If he were caught, these people who had rescued him would be killed for stealing him from his old master, and he himself would be killed to set an example for his people.

Philip watched the world go by, realizing that his childhood was closed, his time to enter the adult world had come, and he felt strangely prepared for it. His sword was ready and sharp, his heart was not divided in anything, his place in this world was clear. He was to take his father's place as head of his household, and currently that meant protecting Avery so she could ascend the throne and restore the kingdom.

Avery's mind was full of many scenarios. Her heart was divided. Her place was not known yet. This country didn't seem to want her, and she certainly didn't want it. What reasons did this country give her to fight for it? What did this country mean to her? Was it worth replacing her own life and dreams to serve another's?

CHAPTER FIFTEEN

Days passed in this manner as they headed east. Sleeping in the few tents they had brought with them at night and avoiding the gaze of the common people during the day, until finally Grurhoum got off his horse to take the position of a foot slave. The others laden his horse with their things and he led it, always aware of the looks other travelers gave them.

He led them to the border of the country and Lord Edward became the spokesperson as Grurhoum became silent.

"We'll rest outside this city tonight," Lord Edward began, looking at Grurhoum to make sure that he approved. "And tomorrow I'll take Grurhoum, and Ian into the town to scout things out. If anyone asks we'll be waiting for the rest of our group. Sir Philip and Lady Avery, will stay with my younger brother Vincent until we have scouted everything out and are ready to rent a few rooms at the inn."

No one objected, so Philip and Vincent slipped off their horses and settled down to wait for the others to come back.

The surrounding trees sheltered them from being seen by people on the path from a half mile away. Everything had warmed up as time passed, and the group shed their cloaks.

Philip continued to point things out now that Ian was gone.

"Grass," he stroked the soft green blades. "It is the color green."

"Color?" she spoke with curiosity. "What is color?"

Philip sighed, tired of having to explain things. "The sky is blue, the clouds are white, my shirt is white."

"The trees are like the grass, green?" she questioned.

"Yes, the trunks are also brown," he pointed to their tired, grazing horses. "The horses are brown too."

"And white," she smiled. "My shoes are brown."

The conversation about color only lasted a few more moments before both of them grew tired of it and became silent.

Sir Vincent paid no attention to the two, preferring to read his book over speaking with them.

Suddenly, Philip stood up and grabbed his weapons.

"Come with me," he told Avery, taking her by the hand. "I'll show you how to use a sword and you can have some practice."

Avery jumped up in excitement. This time there would be no Ian to interrupt their practice.

She grabbed the bow and arrow and dagger and followed him a little way into the woods where Sir Vincent could still see them if he chose to look up from his book.

Philip had grabbed Sir Vincent's sword for Avery to use since she had no weapon herself, and in a moment, he fell to teaching her some basic moves.

"Attack me," he began, sure that he could keep up with anything that this girl could give him.

"But ..." she began. She was not sure of the words she needed to tell him she was afraid of hurting him and she ended up staring at him like he was out of his mind.

"No fear, I can defend myself," he guessed her reservations.

Suddenly she attacked. Her sword moving like a snake had attached itself to her hand and she controlled it. However, the attack had no method to it and Philip defended himself with considerable ease.

"You're not good enough to hurt me," Philip assured her with a smile. "You need to think out your attacks more."

Avery attacked again, this time making sure to watch his moves and not just her own.

"How did you learn these moves?" he asked at last.

"I see people," she answered, paying close attention to his moves. "They fight like so."

Philip moved in for his own attack, upsetting the rhythm that Avery had fallen into. His sword broke through her defense and stopped inches from her injured arm.

"You are not good, but can be better."

Avery took meaning from context and answered. "Make me better."

"Then attack!"

Avery's sword flew again, this time making sure to be wary of her opponent's moves also, and when he switched from defending to attacking, she was ready.

"Good!" he called out to her above the noise of their swords. "Much better!"

It would never do if she came up against a person who was actually trying to kill her and not just teach her.

"Keep it up!" They moved quickly, Avery picking up moves and nimbleness as she went, watching and waiting for the right moment to make her move.

"You are good," she called out to him, hoping to take him off balance.

"I am only an amateur," he replied, smiling and letting his mind wander from the battle at hand.

Avery moved in quickly, sure to take her chance.

Her sword slipped and slithered through his guard and came to a halt right in front of his heaving chest.

"Good," Philip called out as he swung his sword to the side to pull it away from himself. He attacked again, a little annoyed that she had managed to catch him off guard so easily. What had he been thinking to let her get into his head like that? It would never do if that had happened in a real battle.

Their swords clashed in midair and Avery's feet staggered back as the sword came clashing down in front of her, missing her knees and feet by inches.

Without waiting for him to ask after her, she swung again only to be deflected with an easy flip of the wrist.

Philip's sword slipped, crashing down close to her face as she dropped her sword in terror, the sudden movement surprising her and catching her off guard

"Are you alright?!" Philip cried, turning and dropping his sword to run and inspect her.

"I'm alright," she replied, taking the hand that he offered her. "Thank you."

Philip led her to a log to sit down and rest. Perhaps they should stay away from swords for a little bit. Besides, teaching Avery how to use a bow and arrow would be more worth her while because they didn't have a spare sword for her to use.

Philip walked back to where Sir Vincent sat reading his book. He seemed unaffected by the clashing of swords and other ruckus that they had been making.

Philip ignored the man and brought his watcher jug back to Avery. After their little fight, they both needed something to drink.

"Here," he handed her the water and sat down.

"Thank you," she took it from him and uncorked it. "Teach bow and arrow now?" her broken words came again.

"Rest a little, then I'll teach you."

Avery drank the water, its coolness refreshing her weary arms and parched mouth.

"Teach me now, please," she ordered, handing the jug back to him.

"Alright, alright!" he smiled, taking the water jug from her and replacing the cork.

She walked over to the bows and arrows, carefully picking hers out from among his.

"We'll have the target be that tree," he pointed while standing up and walking towards it. "Aim for it and we'll see who is better."

Avery placed her arrow to the string and raised it up to her eye, drawing back on the string as far as she could.

He watched her aim and then release. The arrow flew inches past the tree.

"You're getting so much better," he praised her as he prepared his own arrow and bow.

Philip pulled back, aimed, and released. His arrow hit the center of the trunk.

"You're good also," Avery replied, admiring his shot.

They shot a few more arrows, Avery hitting the mark once, much to Philip's admiration. They had to go back and pick up the arrows, and when they had finished that, no one really felt like shooting any more. So they went back to Sir Vincent waited.

Slowly Avery dozed off, the long days in the saddle and her training making her tired.

Philip grew tired with waiting and paced the grove of trees, unable to sit still. He didn't want to be there doing nothing while the others got to get started on the mission without him. He itched to be down there in the town with them.

They waited in the quiet grove for three long hours as the sun sank below the edge of the forest.

Just before the sun plunged below the horizon and brought darkness, Lord Edward, Grurhoum Greatbrow, and Sir Ian pulled into the grove.

Philip woke the still-sleeping Avery, "Come on, wake up! They're back."

She stirred and groaned, woken from a dreamless sleep.

"I'm awake," she muttered in her language, her eyes still closed as she pulled her hands across her face. "Stop bothering me."

She settled back into a comfortable position.

"Now, Avery!"

"Alright!" she snapped back, her eyes flashing open in rage. "I'm awake!"

The returning party dismounted, Lord Edward carrying a small bundle wrapped in brown paper.

"We've scouted out the area and planned our next course of action." Edward handed the package to Avery.

She caught a glance of some fabric between a tear in the paper that wrapped around it.

"We said we were going to move in tomorrow, but I think our presence would be missed. We're going to have to go in tonight," Grurhoum spoke quietly out of habit. His back bent over again like it had when they had first met him and his voice was more subdued.

Avery noticed the change in him as she left the group, tearing the paper away from the package.

Edward and the rest of the returning group stretched and yawned, it had been a long day and it still wasn't over.

Vincent looked up from his book, noticing the returned group for the first time.

"How did it go?" he asked.

Edward gave him a brief play by play of what they had spotted, including the inn where they would be staying that night.

They sat in silence for a moment, the dusk deepening around them.

"Well?" Vincent stood up. "Shouldn't we be getting on?"

Edward nodded, gathering up his things from where he had left them.

Avery had returned and now stood on the outskirts of the group.

It took them a moment for their eyes to see her. The dark green dress that she now wore blended into the night and forest around her.

It had been so long since she had been dressed like this. She had forgotten how restrictive it was and how hard to maneuver around things and impossible to go over things.

"Alright crew," Lord Edward called out. "It's time to hit the road. Remember what our mission is, and from here on out, unless you are Philip or speaking to him, you are to speak in the high language of the nobles."

Everyone nodded and began mounting.

Philip turned back to give Avery a hand up her horse.

"Remember," Edward spoke out again in the language that even Philip could understand. "We're escorting Lady Avery. Philip, Vincent, and Ian are guards, Grurhoum is her footman, and I am the head guard."

Everyone nodded and they moved out into the silent darkness that had gathered around them while they waited.

Their slow caravan was cloaked in the shadows as it made its way down the hillside. Edward found the path and followed it into the town below them. They passed the dark fronts of stores, their horses clip clopping through the cobblestone street.

"It's around the corner, my lady," Edward spoke in the other language, breaking the silence.

Philip sat back having not understood a word. Now the tables were reversed. Instead of Avery not knowing what was being said, it was him. He shrugged it off, sure nothing of importance had been said.

Lord Edward slowed to a halt in front of one of the inns and dismounted. Sir Vincent and Ian followed.

Grurhoum, playing the role of footman, offered his hand to help Avery down from her horse.

Edward walked purposefully toward the inn, the others following him. He spoke a few words to Grurhoum before leaving him outside to take care of the horses.

Grurhoum had informed Edward that it was customary for servants to sleep in the stable, so he and Lord Edward exchanged a look before he led the horses back, disappearing into the darkness behind the inn. They would reconvene in the morning.

Vincent, Philip, and Ian followed Avery into the inn.

Lord Edward strode up to the innkeeper and spoke to him in hushed tones, bargaining for a room.

Several other noble people seemed to be staying the night. A few rough men and a couple of peasants conversed together in the warmly-lit dining room. Men hugged their beers close and respectable gentlemen refrained from touching anything for fear that the establishment might turn foul on them and be a non-respectable place.

Avery rather liked the look and feel of the place, but Ian turned up his nose despite it being the best in the town.

Edward paid the innkeeper and he turned back to the others.

"You have three rooms for the night, my lady," the innkeeper addressed Avery as he picked up a lit candle from the table and turned to the staircase at the back of the room. "We don't get many travelers through here now," he commented as he held his candle high and mounted the stairs. "Ever since Davia came on a raid here a few weeks ago, everyone has been on edge."

Lord Edward pricked his ears. "I know. I heard of it. It was terrible, wasn't it?" he pried for information while trying to sound like a worried guard. It was his job to worry about their safety.

"It was, though, I'm not at all sure why they did it. What is surprising is that the king hasn't taken up action against Davia. I wonder at it," he turned at the top of the stairs. "I have lost so much business because people have heard about it and no longer want to come to our town."

"I'm sorry to hear that," Edward replied.

"We're not in any danger, are we?" Avery looked up at her head guard, pretending to be the young noble who cared about her safety. "I do not fancy being around if they chose to attack again."

"I assure you, my lady" Edward began. "You are perfectly safe."

"Yes, you are," the innkeeper continued. "I regret even bringing up the subject. The raid was so long ago and was so small that it's not likely to happen again," they had reached the top of the stairs and gone down the hall a bit before he pointed out three rooms. "These are the rooms you paid for. They are each double bedded as you requested."

Edward thanked him and the innkeeper went back downstairs.

"I could only secure three rooms," he told them, "With Grurhoum in the stables we'll have Sir Ian in one room with me, Sir Vincent in a room with Philip, and Lady Avery has the room in the middle to herself."

He paused, watching everyone's faces. "I'll see you all in the morning. Goodnight."

Ian turned in to the first room and Vincent, whispering a few words in the other language to Philip, took Philip and a candle into the other room.

Edward looked at Avery, the only one left in the hall.

"If you see or hear anything, don't be afraid to say something," he reminded her. "If I had known about the raid beforehand I don't think we would be here. It sounds too suspicious to me. Davia has no reason to attack Bucan while it's still at war with itself."

Avery nodded and taking the last candle, entered her room. The hall fell silent and dark.

CHAPTER SIXTEEN

Morning found the group eating breakfast in the dining room of the inn. The other people around them seemed to accept their story.

At last, Avery asked the question they were all thinking. "What is our plan for today?"

Lord Edward pushed his chair away from the table and leaned back. "We are ahead of schedule by a day so you can stay here and rest for the day if you would like, or you can do some sightseeing around town," Edward worded it as a choice, but Avery knew Edward wanted to look around the town, hunting for information.

"I'm fine and wouldn't mind seeing the town a bit," she answered him and Edward nodded.

"I'll make sure the footman knows to have the horses ready."

He called the innkeeper over, telling him to have Grurhoum get the horses ready for them.

He did what they asked and in a moment Avery was being helped up her horse by the dwarf.

Edward and Grurhoum led the way into town, sharing the information that he had gained from the innkeeper in low, authoritative tones.

Everywhere Avery looked, things were so much different from Davia, and yet there seemed to be the same underlying tones. The kingdom she had once thought as almost the same as her own now blossomed into an ugly and very different flower than the kingdom she now admitted she loved.

It felt so strange to be in a place that was like her kingdom, and yet so different with its own customs and traditions at the same time. The architecture that she could not study last night now glared big and vulgar in her eyes. She couldn't think for the life of her why Ian and Henri thought it was beautiful. It was repulsing. How could she allow her country to give in to such an evil and oppressive power as this?

Philip listened to the noises around him, unfamiliarity assaulting his ears. He too saw the vulgarity around him and was repulsed, glad the he didn't have the words to communicate with the people around him.

As Edward watched the ever-moving crowd, a strange feeling cast over him. He glanced behind him and caught a man's eyes on him. This had not been the first time he had been looking at them.

Avery had started out with her horse in the middle of her escort, but she pulled her horse a little off to the side so she could see the shop windows and the items that the street vendors were selling. Cheap and brightly colored things caught her eyes, wooden shoes with intricate carvings, purses with golden thread sewn all around them, and belts dyed in every color imaginable. She slowed without notice, her eyes glued to the things around her.

Edward looked back through the crowd, noting that Avery had fallen behind and the man following them had closed in.

Suddenly, above the hustle and bustle he heard a shout from in front of him.

"Stop in the name of the king!"

Edward's head snapped around, hardly noticing that Grurhoum had fallen back, using his horse as a shield.

"What do you want?" he called up, mastering his voice to keep it steady.

"You have stolen that dwarf." A muscular man emerged from the hushed crowd. "He is my slave, and you have no right to steal him from me."

The company looked at Grurhoum, his face betrayed recognition of the man.

"You have no proof," Edward began, "This dwarf is mine, I bought him but a day ago."

He claimed Grurhoum quickly so Avery wouldn't bring herself into the scuffle. He didn't dare look back at her and didn't notice she had fallen so far behind she didn't see what was happening.

"Untrue!" the evil looking man spat out. "You cannot take my dwarf from me."

"And as this is not your dwarf, then I am taking nothing from you and we can part ways as though this had never happened." Edward moved his horse forward, the others following his lead.

"I have the law on my side!" the man threatened as Edward's head twitched. Suddenly, he knew this wasn't just a joke. This man meant business.

"I believe that the law will side in my favor, so I would recommend you save yourself the embarrassment." Edward turned back to the man.

"Maybe I have spoken wrong," the man began as the group sighed, calling Edward's bluff. "I am the law!"

Suddenly, from all sides, men with weapons appeared.

"You are to come with me, stealing a slave is punishable by death," he grinned, watching their faces contort in anger, but there was nothing for them to do but follow him.

They were pulled from their horses with none too-gentle hands, and one of their men lead the horses away.

Edward scanned his group, counting everyone, trying to make sure they were all there and still together.

Suddenly it dawned on him. "Avery!" he whispered. Where was she?

She stood in place, riveted by the violence she saw, but not a part of it because she had fallen back to look at the things more closely. Edward watched as she slipped off her horse, blending into the crowd around her. He caught a glimpse of her following them on foot, her horse forgotten where she had left it.

He wanted to call out to her, to make her go back, but if he did that, she would be found out and there would be no one to go back to Davia to tell Lord Lucas and Wellington they had failed and been found out. So he kept silent, hoping she would make the right choice before it was too late.

Edward turned his eyes back to the situation in front of him.

Philip, Ian, Vincent, Grurhoum, and Edward each had more than one person hustling them on.

Edward called out to the leader, demanding to know where he was being taken, but no one answered him. Their arms were pinned behind their backs, and when Philip tripped on the uneven ground, he was roughly pulled back up again, his knee dripping in blood as he controlled his face to keep from wincing in pain.

The men pushed them into a side street, hopeful that they would shake any followers and keep public eyes off them.

Avery followed them through the dark side street, dashing in and out of the doorways that offered her little protection.

Suddenly the men pulled them into a small house where they were bound with tight ropes and blindfolded. They were then pushed through the back door and into an awaiting carriage. It pulled out, Avery following it on a horse she had taken from outside of a neighboring house. She prayed no one would notice her as she followed the carriage.

Edward was almost thankful they had gone through the house and were now in a carriage. It meant that it was impossible for Avery to follow them and get into trouble, although the girl was very resourceful. He relaxed, almost resigned to his fate, knowing that Avery would still be alive to go back and tell the others that their position was compromised.

She followed them anyway, somehow managing to not be seen. Something felt wrong about this, it was all too planned for this to have been a chance encounter with someone who recognized Grurhoum as a stolen slave. Someone knew too much about them and had planned this down to the last detail.

But Avery didn't have time to think about that. The carriage pulled up in front of a large castle and her friends were hustled inside, beyond her grasp.

She slowed her stolen horse to a halt, taking down every detail of what she saw.

The castle grew up and not out. Its tall spires seemed to want to reach up to the sky, to be the best at its own thing, to put everyone down and shame them. Avery shrank under its gaze, unable to keep her eyes in one place for too long.

She released her horse, giving it a small swat to send it back to its owner. He had served his purpose and Avery wasn't going to leave until she had found a way to release her friends from the dark, tall, foreboding castle before her.

She slipped into the woods nearby to wait and watch, sure that some small detail would come to light and would allow her to slip in.

She waited all day, oblivious to her growling stomach and only drawing her cloak further around herself.

Inside the castle, they were pushed and shoved through many corridors, always going down. Their feet faltered on the slippery stairs, but their captors pulled them up to continue their descent into the abyss that awaited them.

Darkness from their blindfolds seemed to oppress them on every side, and Edward questioned the real reason they were there. This could not be a city prison for slave thieves. This was—from what he could guess—at the least a large manor with a dungeon. Their journey had taken so long that he knew they could no longer be in the city. Some other force was behind their capture, and they probably knew every person in their group and could tell that Avery was gone. He now almost cursed her absence, sure that it would bring their captors to find her and perhaps take desperate measures with them to find her location. There was no way she could escape with trained hunters on her tail.

Without their knowledge they were split up, each person taken to a cell removed from all the others.

Finally, their bonds were taken away and their blindfolds torn off. They watched as their prison doors closed in behind them with the final clang.

Edward and the others listened as they heard their captors' steps echo away. Finally, he spoke up.

"Philip? Grurhoum? Ian? Vincent? Are you all here?"

Answers came back to him, each affirmative.

"Alright then," Edward strode to the front of his cell. "I don't think we're here because he thinks we stole Grurhoum," he began. "This was a very well-planned operation and they probably already know who we really are, and what our purpose is. There is no need to keep up the facade."

Things around him were silent except for the sounds of soft breathing.

"Come on gentlemen," he started. "We can't let them get the best of us. Besides, Lucas and Wellington will hear of our fate and that will tell him more about the relationships between the countries than any surveillance that we could gather would."

No one seemed much comforted by that information, but they were relieved when they heard Avery had escaped.

They waited there in the silent darkness, time meaning nothing. At one point, food was distributed to the cells and it was taken away again untouched. Some of them dozed off at one point, but Edward sat in the corner of his cell, his cloak wrapped around himself, listening for any sign that their enemies would come back down for them. He thought about who their captors could be, what they would want with them, and what they would do to them.

Philip couldn't sleep. His thoughts traveling to wherever Avery was, sure she was already on her way back to Davia to inform Lucas and Wellington of their fate. She would have no reason to think this was anything more than them being taken away as common criminals. Their trip would have come to naught.

Edward was infuriated. How could they have come so far and yet fallen so short? Nothing would come of their trouble. The group back at home would continue without knowing their predicament, and would perhaps fall prey to something he could have warned them of.

The hours blended together. Philip bound up his knee where it had cut open. Grurhoum chided himself a few cells away, sure that this fate had come upon his friends because he had been there. If only he had stayed home or stayed a slave in the first place!

Vincent pondered if they had gone wrong somewhere. Had they been seen in the clearing yesterday? Had they given away too much at the inn last night or this morning?

Ian seemed strangely agitated and aware of what was happening. He would pace about his chamber and in a sudden fit of emotion pound on the bars in front of him.

Food came again, and they did not eat.

From outside the castle Avery watched, waiting till her time would come. Night fell, but her eyes didn't perceive it. She focused in on the castle with unblinking attention. The moon came up and she continued to look, her eyes and ears open to anything that would give her safe passage between those walls.

A horse and buggy pulled up the dark path and Avery slipped out of the woods. She took the chance, and she would follow through with it.

CHAPTER SEVENTEEN

L ord Edward had dozed off, his eyes closing their unfaltering vigil and his chin falling to his chest as his breath slowed to deep sighs.

Off to his right something stirred. A door was opened, a breath was uttered, and something woke him. He heard steps on the stairs but they were soft and not strong and resounding the way their captors' footsteps echoed over the blank walls that held them in.

His head pulled up out of his light slumber. There was something very wrong in the way that those steps sounded.

"Who goes there?" he called out, his voice penetrating the darkness around him, seemingly swallowed up in the abyss.

The steps quickened. A swish followed the figure as its halting steps descended the stairs.

Edward noticed they seemed hesitant, unsure of the way. The swish must be from a hand feeling the wall for support.

He called out again, making sure to use the Bucan language. "Make yourself known!"

A voice came in answer to him at last. "Who is that?" it whispered.

Edward waited, "You tell me."

The figure almost shouted with recognition. "Edward?!" it called out, forgetting to whisper.

"Avery!" Edward dashed to the front of his cell his surprise turning to panic. His arms reached through the bars. "Get away from here! You'll be found out!"

Avery ignored him, the others now stirring and calling out to her.

She grazed her hands against the walls, feeling, searching for something.

"Avery!" Philip called out, "Leave before it's too late! Tell Lucas and Wellington what happened. Tell them that someone knows too much about our group, tell them ..."

"Shhh!" Avery whispered loudly back at him. "Listen?" loud echoing steps could be heard above them as her hand found what she had been looking for, keys.

"Leave now!" Edward almost yelled. "They're going to find you. Get out now! Leave us, that's an order!"

Avery ignored her order, the key already grating in the lock to his cell.

He pushed the door the moment he could, forgetting his order from before, searching for the others to unlock them.

"This way," he whispered, pulling her further down the dark hall as the steps grew louder.

They came upon another door, and Avery turned to unlock it. Edward was already moving on to find the next door for her.

The last door was too dark for them to see. Ian pressed his face as close to the bars as he could.

Edward already started moving back to the door to confront the steps.

"Come on everyone. Stay close," Edward whispered as he slipped behind the door. "We'll go out together."

Ian pushed open the door the moment it could be moved, snagging Avery's dress in the dark. Neither one noticed.

They all looked up at the as the door opened. Torchlight flooded the hall, blinding their eyes that had grown to be accustomed to the dark.

Edward stepped out from behind the door, grabbed the torch, and plunged them back into darkness.

Everyone pushed toward the door. "Is everyone here?" Edward called out into the darkness.

Replies flooded him. Unsure if everyone had answered, he took his chance and pushed through the door. The jailer knew full well he was outnumbered. There was nothing for him to do but stay out of their way and sound the alarm when he had the chance.

"I'm coming!" Avery called out from the last cell, unable to see anything. She took a step, her skirt ripping as she fell to the floor. Her head hit something hard and her vision blacked out. The keys slipped from her grasp and slid across the floor.

Edward, unaware, counted each person as they passed him, but in the dark he wasn't sure he hadn't missed one. He called back, "Everyone up?"

No one replied so he slammed the door behind himself and everyone pushed forward, finding an arm to touch to make sure that no one was lost. Edward wanted to do a head count, but they had already made too much noise for his comfort, so he prayed they were all there and pushed his men on.

Edward followed a labyrinth of passages, always heading up. It never occurred to him that Avery should be leading this since she knew her way out. He did have a funny feeling about something, but he pushed it off to the side in hopes that it meant nothing and plowed forward.

Suddenly they came to a great door and Edward pushed through it to see the brilliant light of day. He almost cried out in joy—their imprisonment being so brief. But he had no time to glance around himself or to gather his wits because he moved on even faster toward a door that looked as though it might lead them to the outside world. It opened with ease and they pushed through, ignoring the fact that there were no guards around such a castle as this, for now they could see that it was indeed a castle.

Edward saw the forest and made a beeline for it, sure that they must have been spotted at this point. But strangely enough, no one accosted them. Perhaps they were all inside looking for them, hoping that they had yet to make it out of the dungeon.

They reached the forest and Edward paused to look back.

Guards streamed out of the castle gate, scouring the countryside for them. There would be no going back.

He looked around at his group, each person leaning or sitting down to catch their breath and rest. He counted them off in his mind, *Philip, Ian, Vincent, Grurhoum, me, and Avery*. His eyes glanced around for the girl, but to no avail. "Avery?" he called out, sure that she must be behind one of the trees where he could not see her.

The others looked up, now aware that they hadn't seen her since the light had gone out in the dungeon.

Edward cried. "Where is she? Did anyone see anything?"

His query was greeted with stunned silence. No one said anything as they looked around at each other, still not quite believing that she wasn't there.

Edward stormed back to the edge of the wood as hands reached out to grasp him.

"Brother!" Vincent called back at him. "We can't go back! They will kill you."

"I know," he kept moving. "But how can we leave her behind?"

Grurhoum cleared his throat. "I was put in charge of this trip," he began, "We already know that we were not captured because of slave stealing, but rather because they knew who we were. They will not kill her because they have a plan for her. Trust me. We should go back to Davia, tell our news to Lucas and Wellington, and get reinforcements before we take this castle by storm. Look," he pointed at the castle now swarming with soldiers. "We've got to get moving or we will be taken by force and we might die."

Edward stopped. "We can't just leave he! Our mission is failing!" he cried. "Lucas and Wellington will never entrust us now that we've ruined everything."

"You have done admirably," Grurhoum told him. "No one can blame you. You have done what you set out to do. Others cannot boast as much." He turned to go deeper into the woods. "We have a choice now—stay and do nothing to get her back or leave in the hopes that we'll be able to bring back more people. I have chosen."

Edward, Ian, and Vincent followed him as Philip took one last look at the castle. It hurt all of them to leave, and he wished she hadn't come back for them.

Suddenly the picture of the soldiers pouring out of the castle registered in his mind.

"Run! They're coming!" he whispered, turning back to his friends.

The others looked back, transfixed by what they saw. But in a moment the spell was broken and they dashed through the forest.

It seemed to be just morning. Edward took gauge by the sun and tried to maneuver them back from where they had come. Philip brought up the rear. The wound on his knee hindered him.

We were only in the dungeon for the night, he thought to himself, though what puzzled him was how Avery, a girl, had managed to follow them.

Suddenly he stumbled upon a large, docile creature.

"A horse!" he cried, halting.

The others doubled back to him, staring in wonder at the creature before them.

The black horse, only the day before having been stolen from his master to take a long trip with a girl, had decided to stay around. It was nice here and there was plenty for a small horse like him to eat.

"What is it doing here?" Philip thought out loud.

"I don't know," Vincent replied. "Too bad it's not five horses."

"We'll take what we can get," Edward called back at him. "Somebody give Philip a hand up. He needs to give his leg a rest."

"I can't take that!" Philip cried out. "What about Grurhoum? He can hardly keep up because his legs are shorter than ours." As he said this, Grurhoum caught up, heaving deep breaths of air.

"But you're hurt," Edward countered. "You won't be able to keep up for long."

"I'll keep up as long as I can," he stifled the pain that coursed through his knee. "Come here Grurhoum. I'll help you up."

He took action to his words, even though the pain in his knee made him almost want to curl up on the ground.

How could something hurt so much? he thought to himself. But in truth, something hurt even more than that. The pain in his knee kept his mind of the pain of failing and leaving Avery behind with their enemies.

Grurhoum reached the back of the horse with much difficulty on Philip's part, but in another minute they were on their way west. Away from the sunrise and toward the sunset they went, each one wishing in his heart of hearts they could stay.

Deep in the darkness that they left behind, Avery lifted her head, her eyes open and unseeing in the unfathomable depths around her. Her breath quickened as she reached her hand up to her forehead and touched the large bump that had grown there.

From out of the darkness came a voice. It didn't surprise her. Something inside her knew it was coming.

"I know you're there," it said. "Your friends left you."

Something struck light in the darkness, and Avery pushed herself into a sitting position.

If only the darkness could stay! If only the darkness, her friend, would hide her!

The light caught, and she closed her eyes, blinded by it.

"They'll get away, but that's alright."

CHAPTER EIGHTEEN

They plowed through the woods, limping, riding, or just plain all out running.

For what seemed like hours they dodged low hanging branches and walked around fallen trees, always making their way west.

The sun hit its peak, they hadn't eaten in a day, and yet they still pushed on, sure of making it to the town with the inn by dusk.

At one point, they slowed so much that Grurhoum got off the horse because he could keep up and Philip was put in his place.

Philip could no longer feel his knee, and he took advantage of it, but always with a nagging fear that this could not be a good sign. Yet he preferred the painless walk to the gut-wrenching limp.

They put their discomfort far from their minds and plowed forward.

The trees in front of them thinned after a while, and they slowed down even more, trying not to come upon a path unexpectedly, and yet it happened anyways.

They followed the path from the security of the forest, sure it would lead them to some sort of civilization, even if it was just a small village.

Their hearts and hopes rose when they saw below them what looked to be the same town they had come from, the sun setting behind it. Every penny from their persons having been stripped, they had no idea what they would do there, or how they would get food or transportation, but any goal that brought them closer to Davia was worth reaching.

They descended upon the town, hardly bothering to keep out of public eye. Their faltering feet slipping out from beneath them at times.

They left the horse outside the city, strangely aware that they had stolen it from someone, but they didn't know who it belonged to.

They cut through the town, night falling upon them. The street sellers had already packed up their stores, some leaving their spoiled wares on the street for the dogs.

Vincent took advantage of a few things that he could find, but hardly any of it was edible. They nibbled on the things they could salvage and moved on, tired and weary, looking for any corner to spend the night.

From outside the town walls they could hear horses' hooves pounding. Their hearts quickened, the words of the innkeeper echoing in their ears.

Edward finally came to a decision, the noise growing louder by the minute.

"Take cover," Edward whispered. "The innkeeper said there was a raid the other day. I think we are going to be caught up in a second one."

Everyone stopped.

"The innkeeper said there wouldn't be any more," Ian whispered back, urging them to move on and ignore the noises around them.

"How is he to know anything about that?" Philip asked, his voice a mask of pain. "Nothing is guaranteed in this time, nor in this place." He gestured to the dark houses around them.

"I agree with Philip," Vincent began. "If nothing else we owe it to Avery to be as careful as possible, if we fail ..."

Edward nodded, his eyes searching the empty street for cover. "Spread out." he told his men. "We'll find something, anything."

Vincent helped Philip walk now that they could move slowly. Vincent's own legs cried out in pain and agony, begging him to lie down and rest, but he ignored them. If his tired legs felt that way, just think about how Philip's injured knee felt.

They leaned against a doorframe for a breath and moved on, Ian sullenly following behind. He kicked at rocks, using the energy he should have been devoting to helping the group as a whole to instead entertain himself.

Horses hooves clopped on the road around them and they pulled up their cloaks in a vain attempt to hide themselves from the prying eyes around them.

From around the corner, the first one could be spotted. A black figure on horseback riding toward them, almost as if he knew they were there.

"Show yourselves!" he called out in the language of Bucan, reigning to a halt in front of them. His black horse glistened with sweat.

The other riders pulled up around them, facing the small group with sneers and unblinking eyes.

"Who are you?" Vincent called out in the same language.

"You are in no position to ask the questions, cur!" the man shouted, bringing his cuffed gauntlet down on him.

Vincent melted under the blow, sinking to the ground.

"Who are you?" the leader called out again.

Ian slunk back leaving Philip to answer the man's question. Philip stood, transfixed—unsure of what to do, unsure of what was being said, unsure of everything.

The man smiled an evil, knowing smile and spoke out again, this time in a language Philip did understand.

"Who are you?" he switched languages, smiling in a knowing way.

Philip felt trapped, sure that if he responded he would be found out, but if he didn't he would be killed.

The horses began to surround their prey, sure they had found what they were looking for.

"Tell me who you are or your companion dies." The man continued to speak in the Davia common language while he gestured to one of his men who drew an arrow, nocked it, then aimed menacingly at Ian.

"Alright!" Philip called out, hating himself for what he was about to do. "We are visiting from Davia," he rushed. "We are no threat to you, we will answer any questions you have, just please leave us alone!"

The man on the black horse laughed, his mission complete. "I don't need to know anything more." His tone changed to dripping with condescension. "Don't you have questions for me?"

Philip shrunk back, unsure of the trap that lay in front of him. But perhaps he had already stepped into it? Whichever it was, it was too late for it to matter.

"Who are you?" he asked, his voice as calm as the night air around them.

"I am The Thief, sent by the Phoenix to collect you, Philip, Ian, Edward, and Vincent." He did not mention Avery, almost as though he already she was captured.

Philip knew then that something more was afoot than anyone first expected. Men dismounted all around him, moving in closer in a strategic ring of attack.

Philip knew arguing would be pointless, and he resolved that since the group had come to capture him, he wouldn't go down without a fight, knowing full well that they couldn't kill him if they wanted him alive.

"Well then," he replied calmly, the thoughts still bouncing around in his head. "I'm afraid I don't want to go with you."

He unsheathed his sword, its silver blade glistening in the pale moonlight all around them.

The Thief smiled, accepting the slim honor that Philip tried to pull around himself.

"As you wish." He signaled to his men who also drew their swords. Ian slunk into the background, already giving in to the many hands that reached out to him. "Take him down, give him the dignity he asks for." He spoke in a patronizing tone, smiling behind the black cloak he pulled around himself as he turned his horse away, leaving his men to do the dirty work for him.

As he dashed down the alleyway his hood fell from his face revealing a hat with a red feather in it.

Philip turned to the men around him, watching as they closed in around him.

One of them lashed out at him. Philip's quick reflexes deflected the blow almost before it was made. It almost seemed like the cue. All around him the men formed a rotating circle, stomping their feet and crying out in victory every time the man in black made a good move and every time Philip's feet and knees faltered from beneath him.

He knew it was over the moment it started. In his state, he could not have wished to hold out for more than a minute. But if he failed here, where it mattered the most, how could he ever face the others again? He was trading in the freedom that Avery could have paid her life for. He knew it, and it made him furious.

Slowly, the man he fought against disarmed him. His sword clattered to the ground with its final clang, and he dropped to his knees, forgetting his pain in defeat.

The men around him drew arrows, wary of any move he made, wary he might strike out again.

He noticed them and gave a weak smile. "I know you won't kill me," he told them, closing his eyes and taking a deep breath. "I'm not afraid of you, what you can do to me, or what you're going to do to me."

CHAPTER NINETEEN

*A*fter *my aunt had gotten me ready, I remember waiting the day away by myself. When the time came, I was presented to the room. It had changed so much from that very morning. The lights were all lit and the hall was filled. My aunt could not have asked for more for me.*

I was led up to the front where I was permitted to sit in the seat of honor, next to my cousin Prince Rupert and his sister Hazel, one of the many princesses in attendance.

Princess Eveline, the daughter of the brother closest to my father's age, sat next to me, her eyes encapsulating every moment of the night.

The first dance was called and my uncle stood before me, bent on keeping the promise he had made only just at breakfast.

"Niece?" he called to me, loud enough that the whole hall could hear him and stopping any approaching suitors in their tracks. "I call upon you to keep the promise you made to me but this morning."

"Yes, your majesty" I replied, taking the hand he offered, standing, and then curtsying over it.

He led me to the dance floor. All eyes were upon us, many in admiration. I didn't have a chance to see my aunt before we reached the flood.

He glanced over at the orchestra and they began one of his favorites.

I ignored the many eyes on us as I traversed the dance floor in the arms of my strong and tall uncle the regal king.

I whispered up at him, smiling. "Thank you for saving me from having to accept some stranger I don't know for my first dance."

"I wouldn't have had it any other way." He smiled down at me. I could see he was resisting the urge to kiss the top of my head, if only because it would have damaged his honor. "You'll have to dance with them at some point," he replied, "But I understand."

I thanked him with my eyes and turned back to the dance floor, focusing on keeping in step with the waltz.

If I ever have a daughter, *I thought.* I will never force her to marry as a political pawn, and I will never force her to have a ball unless she actually wants it.

I swirled over the dance floor with my uncle who was the envy of every young man in the room. I caught glimpses of faces as I went around, but none of them stood out to me.

"Forget about suitors." My uncle laughed, guessing what his wife had told me. "I will deal with your aunt when you aren't engaged by the end of the ball."

"Thank you," I answered him, truly thankful I would not have to worry about her insufferable rage. "But I wish she wouldn't be disappointed in me or angry," I continued.

"I know what you mean," we continued to dance as he smiled.

"I have never truly had the chance to thank you for having me here," I spoke up again. Even if I hated most of what went on here, I still could not deny the skills and lesson that I had been taught.

"You're welcome," he grinned back. "My brother and I would not have had it any other way."

The dance closed and we tore apart, curtsying and bowing to each other. I thanked him with my eyes as he brought me back to my seat.

He nodded in reply and went to fetch his wife for the next dance.

Prince Rupert offered me the next dance before any of the other men could, and I accepted. Now that the expectation my aunt had placed on me was lifted I was able to enjoy myself a bit more.

We took a few turns around the floor before someone he knew caught his eye, and he asked to be excused.

The dance ended and I was thankful to head back to my seat again, laughing inwardly, when I was interrupted by someone clearing his throat.

I turned, knowing full well it was another young man to ask for a dance. I was prepared, a smooth decline already formed upon my lips.

"Lady?" he began, his eyes looking up at me from the bow he had thrown himself into the moment I turned around.

"Sir?" I asked, unsure of how to continue.

"I am Lord Alonzo," he began. "May I have this next dance?"

The refusal vanished from my lips, curiosity banning me from declining his offer.

"Yes, you may."

He took my arm and skillfully maneuvered me to the dance floor, the next dance only having just begun.

I studied his face, anger permanently etched there.

"Lady Avery," he began. "I have heard much about you."

"Oh?" I asked absently.

"Your aunt recommended our acquaintance several times in her invitation to this event."

My attention was officially grabbed. "We'll I'm glad to finally be able to put a face with a name. And what do you think of the event?" I asked.

He looked at me as though seeing right through me. "I am eager to be introduced to Princess Hazel," I could see the greed in his eyes. It was easy for me to judge him and say he only wanted to meet her because one day she could be ruler of all of the Davia Kingdom, but I held my tongue.

"I only met her just tonight," I told him. "She is very pretty isn't she?" I asked.

Alonzo nodded, his head turned to her pretty face high above the rest of the crowd where she sat on her seat not joining in on the frivolities.

I turned back to the dance and shivered.

"Cold?" he asked, his head turning back around.

"Yes," I lied.

He led me to the side of the dance floor.

"I'm sorry we could not complete this dance," he told me as I left him to stand by the fire that had been built into one end of the hall.

"It is a pity. Perhaps another time," I called back to him, not meaning a single word that I said. I could tell he knew it.

A few other men asked me to dance as I walked to the fire, but I declined them.

The night passed slowly as I mostly watched the people around me.

My aunt's face grew darker the less I danced, and I watched as Alonzo dance with the unsuspecting Princess Hazel, her innocent blue eyes looking up at him in blind admiration.

In the morning after, I knew nothing I could do would spare me from my aunt's wrath, but in the moment I couldn't even think of it.

CHAPTER TWENTY

A very waited, locked up in the darkest cell they could find. Her breath was the only sound that could be heard in the senseless deep around her. Her mind turned from her present situation to that of her friends.

It was always a trap, she thought, digging her fingers into her knees where she had drawn them up to her chest. *There was no way we could have even won this.*

Tears sprang to her eyes. *We played right into it. I played right into it! They might not have even succeeded if I hadn't come back to rescue them.*

Her face contorted in anger. Everything had played out according to their enemy's plans.

Her heart reached out to the rest of her group, sure that something wrong had happened. What had become of the small company? Had they escaped? Had they already gone back to Davia?

Unspoken fears tugged at her heart as she tried putting the pieces to the puzzle together.

She was frustrated. How could they have missed seeing this?

Someone obviously knew who they were and what their mission was, but how? Someone in their group back at home must have been a double agent, or perhaps their attack on the castle had turned afoul and they were being tortured to death.

But none of that made sense. There hadn't been enough time since they had left for the others to attack the castle and for the Phoenix to send someone after them. The only option that made sense was a double agent.

Everything looked bleak. There was no way for them to fight a power that was among them that they could not see.

Hours passed but she was not aware of them. Deep in the bowels of the earth, how could she? Time meant nothing to her, meant nothing to anything down there, meant nothing to anyone.

Back in the city, Edward watched Philip and Ian from a doorframe the men had overlooked. He wanted to reach out to them, but he was no match for the group. He justified his actions, vowing he would stay to tell Lucas and Wellington as soon as he could.

He watched as Philip fell to his knees, the men around him drawing their bows. From behind Philip one of the men struck him on the head. The blow did not look as forceful as the one that had been dealt to Vincent, but Edward watched Philip slump down to the ground, unconscious.

The men tied him up, hands and feet, and draped him over one of their horses. Ian had already been taken care of to their standards, and been placed on another horse. They raced after their leader, leaving Edward alone in the street.

He raced over to Vincent as soon as he could, shaking him.

"Come on, Vincent," he whispered. "We've got to go after them."

Vincent didn't move as Edward picked up his head, turning it to inspect the wound.

It looked as though the bandit who had struck him had done it with his metal cuff. More than a bruise had already formed.

"Vincent!" Edward whispered to his brother as loud as he dared, becoming aware of the screams and shouts all around him.

The raid seemed in full force. Fires sprang up around the city, and he could hear panic and death all around him.

"Vincent!" he called out again, shouting to be heard above the noise around him. "Vincent!"

The wound on Vincent's head left Edward without a doubt as to what happened. Yet he still found himself reaching out to feel for a pulse, knowing full well he would not find one.

Tears sprang to his eyes as he lay Vincent's head gently back on the ground, grasping for his brother's hands.

"No," he whispered, his voice swallowed by the ruckus around him.

Grurhoum silently came up behind him. He took everything in at a glance, not wanting to break the moment.

Edward cried out again, dropping the dead hands and rising to his feet. Tears sprang to his eyes, unwanted and yet welcome.

Grurhoum watched as the man scooped up the body, tenderness still in his touch. He stormed down the street, his boots echoing above the sound of chaos around them.

Grurhoum followed as close as he dared.

Edward stormed through the hectic streets, oblivious to the terrible destruction and despair around him. His heart was numb—he could see and feel nothing. As things around him burned, so did his life. The only brother he had, the only tie he had to the life he knew before, was now gone.

Grurhoum watched the crumbling destruction around him, aware they were the only men left of their company. Avery, Philip, Ian, and Vincent were gone. It was up to him to take Edward back to Davia, but his strength and courage within him failed. How could he lead anyone beyond such despair?

He followed Edward outside the city, almost wondering if Edward planned to carry his brother all the way back to Davia.

Just beyond the city walls they stopped. Edward placed his brother on the ground, his heart gone. His throat choked up. Words ran through his head, but the courage to say them was gone.

Grurhoum watched respectfully, knowing that interruption in this process would sever Edward from the final good bye he was trying to bring himself to.

His voice came out scraggly, almost as though he were dead and not the man in front of him.

"Brother," his voice choked. "We have been through so much," he paused, swallowing and trying to keep his composure. "I love you. I will avenge your death. These men," he paused. "These men, who, have no regard for life, will understand what it means to have no regard for life. You will be avenged."

Grurhoum turned, unable to stay for this heart touching show.

"They have no regard for life," Edward whispered, kneeling by the still body in front of him. "I will not allow them to have Philip's, Ian's, or Avery's," he almost shouted. "They will not have another life! I will not give it to them." Tears came down in full force now. Grurhoum left him, heading anywhere but there.

Grurhoum waited on the path, unable to leave, but not wanting to wait another minute. They still had a mission to complete. No amount of morning would change that.

Finally, as the sun rose upon the sad unfortunate scene, Edward fell upon Grurhoum. They silently followed the path back to Davia, their meager meal from the night forgotten in the overwhelming tiredness that now assaulted them. They had not slept or properly rested in what felt like days.

At the top of the hill Edward turned back, kneeling toward the burning and broken city below them. Grurhoum's eyes turned to the grove where he had left the two, a plume of smoke rising lazily above the tops of the trees.

A cart maneuvered the trail up from the city and they watched as it passed them, its strangely guarded self rolling its way sluggishly and yet with haste.

Edward pulled his broken and ragged body from the ground. He turned his back to the city, never to look back again, following in the ruts of the guarded cart that had passed before them.

They walked on all day, silently pushing their way as close to Davia as they could.

They didn't sleep or eat until they reached the border of Davia. Edward collapsed on the road in front of Grurhoum, his energy sapped out of him since his brother had died.

Grurhoum left him to find food, his stomach unfeeling it was so empty.

He found sustenance and came back to share with Edward. Silently he thanked the dwarf and they ate the food.

Their hunger slightly abated, they slowly nodded off, unaware of their tiredness.

They woke an unknown number of hours later, and they pushed on. They walked on, stopping only a few times to gather food, eat, and sleep. They didn't exchange a single word till they finally collapsed on the front step of the cave days later.

They stumbled inside, unaware there was no one to greet them. They fell to the floor, exhausted, feeling nothing within them.

CHAPTER TWENTY-ONE

S lowly, Edward and Grurhoum woke up again, their aching bones rebelling against them, their painful heads throbbing with sleep deprivation, their stomachs growling, unwilling to continue without food to nourish them.

Edward looked around, finally something dawning on them. His blank eyes scanned the empty cave. The empty cave echoed with their small movements.

Grurhoum swallowed, sure that his suspicions had turned true.

"Something must have happened," he said. The first thing either one of them had spoken since Vincent had died.

Edward nodded, unsure of how to continue.

"We need food and sleep," Grurhoum reminded him.

Edward nodded again, his mind mechanically going through the motions.

"You start the fire, and I'll find some fish," Grurhoum told him, standing up and taking action to fit his words.

Edward still didn't move as Grurhoum left the cave. He needed to be alone, they both did, and they both knew it.

Grurhoum stumbled his way to the creek he had seen only for the first time a week ago. Had it only been so long? It felt like years ...

He dipped his fingers in the river, feeling for the plenty of fish he knew to live there.

He looked behind him, thoughts running through his mind, feelings running through his heart. Was that a rustle in the leaves? Was it an animal or another person? Did he just feel as though someone was watching him, or was he really being watched?

He turned to catch a glimpse of something human moving behind him.

"Who goes there?" he called out, straightening up and searching the woods, suddenly aware of his vulnerable position in the creek. A second later it dawned on him—he was back in Davia. If there was another person out there, they wouldn't understand him or would think him crazy.

"Grurhoum!" someone called out, breaking through the trees around him. "It is you!"

Darren exploded out of the woods, a giant smile on his face.

Grurhoum relaxed, smiling for the first time in days. "You finally came back, we were worried when we didn't find anyone in the cave when we got there," he explained.

Darren's face changed. "No one is there?" he asked.

"You didn't know?" Grurhoum asked, suddenly realizing his fear, his smile now gone.

"I haven't been there yet. We got sidetracked when we saw you fishing." Garret and Sterling slipped out of the woods, following their leader's example now that they knew it was safe for them.

"We just got back from Bucan," Grurhoum explained. "It's been such a long trip and we have a lot of information and pressing need. We also need food."

"I have some," Darren gestured to a bag slung at his side. "Come back to the cave with us, then we can talk."

Grurhoum thanked him, glad he didn't have to find fish anymore, and glad they weren't the only ones there. It would be much easier to find out what happened now that they had people who were more up to date on what was happening in Davia.

So much had happened since they had left.

"Where is Philip?" Darren asked. "And Ian and Avery? What about Vincent? Are they back at the cave with Edward? Why didn't you have them come out here to help you forage?"

Grurhoum sighed. "It's such a long story that I don't even know where to start it. I'll tell you about it when we get back, just don't mention Vincent to Edward. Vincent was killed when we got caught up in a raid but a few days ago."

Darren stopped in his tracks, bowing his head and lifting up a prayer for the soul of Vincent.

"I see you have a lot to tell me," Darren began at last. "And I have a lot to tell you. We know who is behind the Phoenix," he teased Grurhoum with the information before he chided himself. Vincent was gone. None of them should be in a joking mood.

Grurhoum glanced at Darren. "Really? That information is very important."

"I know," he smiled. "I'm very glad we got it."

Darren tried to keep from asking questions as they reached the cave and Edward and Grurhoum ate for the first time in forever, but he disciplined his mind, sure they would have time to talk later.

Without prompting, Edward told their story, his empty eyes scanning the walls of the cave, never for a moment making contact with another pair.

Darren, Garret, and Sterling listened, aware that the telling brought pain to him.

Edward finished his account when Vincent died, as though he had died in his stead and could not remember anything that happened after that.

Grurhoum quietly summed up the last part of their trip, skipping over everything with as little detail as he could.

"Our hearts reach out to you in this time," Darren whispered when he was done. Edward did not acknowledge him, so he moved on into his own narrative of the past week.

"Lucas and Wellington had us start out the day after you," he began. "We were to go south past Falkerstone Castle and then east. We were sent out to search the area around Lord Alonzo's establishment to see if we could find any clues that would lead us to think he was a part of the Phoenix. It took us little time to get there, perhaps a day and a half, and we secured a place to stay the night at the village near him. In the morning we asked around a little bit. It seems like Alonzo had become hermit-like the past few months and completely disappeared in the last few weeks. Apparently, he gets many visitors in the night, some speaking the language of the nobles in a strange accent. I think we can conclude he has some involvement in the Phoenix, even if he is not the head of them."

"So then they have a lot of money and friends in high places," Grurhoum sighed. "If only he were on our side. If only he didn't have the money he does."

"The world was not built on 'if onlys'," Darren replied. "The first thing we need to do is find out what happened to Lord Lucas, Wellington, and the others."

Grurhoum nodded.

"I agree." Sterling said. "Perhaps we should wait here for one day just in case they had to put off the attack and are doing it right now, and then we'll do some reconnaissance by the castle."

Everyone around him nodded except Edward, who was still gazing off into the distance.

Sterling was a young man, just barely old enough to join them. He had been close with one of the nobles and though he was not of royal birth, his motives were never in question. When he had heard the news of the Phoenix, he was the first to take it to his friend, knowing full well it would mean the death of both of them if they were found out. He had left his beautiful fiancée with his mother when he pledged his service to Lucas and Wellington. He was quiet and thoughtful, her image never quite leaving his mind. He knew in his heart of hearts that he would never truly come back to the woman he once knew, but that did not keep him from pushing on. In fact, it pushed him even more. He knew he would not come back from this the same, why should he expect her to come out of this the same? His heart tugged at his mind, reminding him that she was but an hour away by horse, and if they had all day to do nothing, why could he not take that opportunity?

"We don't have anything planned for today, do we?" he asked at last, taking courage. "We're just waiting to see if the others come back."

"Yes, we're just waiting. Why?" Darren looked at him, knowing the young man's wish before it was spoken.

"My lady is but an hour away in the castle city. I could visit her without becoming known," Sterling could already tell what Darren was going to say before he said it.

"Why can't you go tomorrow when we're all going to be there?" Darren asked, willing to grant the request but not at the risk of going into the city twice.

"I can't see her tomorrow because if we are found, she will be killed along with us, if only because I went to see her." Sterling turned with a sigh, sure that his request would be denied. "I don't want her associated with our mission."

"Go," came a whisper. Darren turned to look at Edward who had become strangely attentive in the last few moments. "Don't endanger her," Edward said. "But yet do not ignore her," he sighed. "I have lost the only person left in my life and there isn't anything I wouldn't do to change it. Please, learn from me. Seize your opportunity today and don't wait until it may be too late. You never know what tomorrow will bring with it, but it always brings sadness. Go."

Darren nodded, transfixed by the tone Edward used. His emotionless voice echoed with the pain and the truth he could not hide from himself.

"You may take a horse and go to her," Darren echoed, digging into his pockets and handing him a few coins. "Get something for dinner if you think you can do it without drawing attention to yourself."

Sterling took the offered coins, fear suddenly covering his heart with its blackness. But after the trouble he had caused, he could not give up now. He exited the cave, mounting his horse with a great leap. He turned his horse's head toward the city and let loose.

The miles passed beneath his horse's hooves like grains of sand between slender fingers, each turning into a forgotten memory before the other had time to pass by.

He reached the city, daylight still gleaming golden on the roofs of the houses. He left his horse outside the city. It was a purebred horse and he knew it would make him look out of place. He couldn't risk any suspicion.

He gave one last look at his horse before he ran through the streets he knew by heart.

At last he reached the one he wanted. It was still on the outskirts of the city, far away from the bustling heart. If it had been any closer to the center he would not have approached it, but he entered without hesitation, calling out to the two women he knew to be there.

"Mother! Lilliana!" he called out. "I'm back!"

Feet clattered down stairs in unladylike fashion, but no one dared chide them.

"I thought you were gone, Sterling!" an old woman embraced him.

"Oh Mother, you knew I would come back for you." He whispered into her graying hair.

The woman was not his real mother, but when her husband had died leaving the family business to her, she had hired Sterling as an apprentice. He had become like a son to her.

"I promised I would not put myself into any danger." His face turned red because he had faced danger, and had faced it willingly, but she did not notice him. A young slip of a girl had reached the doorway, her pale face flushed with excitement.

Sterling reached out to her, his eyes filling with tears.

"Lilliana," he whispered.

"Oh Sterling!" she took the offered embrace, tears pouring out of her eyes. "I thought you were dead!"

"Lilliana," Sterling began, love overshadowing his confusion.

"How could you?" she reprimanded him, pulling away from his to look into his eyes.

"What?" he asked, searching her eyes.

"The attack on the castle?" she began, probing his memory. "You joined that group of outlaws and they had you attack the castle but five days ago!"

"I ..." he was cut off.

"They were snapped up like flies!" she cried. "You probably escaped with only your life. Oh Sterling!"

Sterling held her in a passionate embrace, hoping to calm her.

"I didn't tell mother about it," she sobbed. "I didn't want to worry her with the news."

Sterling's mind raced. So they had attacked the castle! They had probably fallen into a trap; they were all captured!

"Lilliana," he called softly. "I was not in that group; I was off searching for a man we believe might be behind the Phoenix."

She quieted down, his mother watching the softly from a distance.

"Lilliana," he whispered. "I knew nothing about this."

She wiped her tears away.

"I must go now," he finally told her, cutting his visit short. "I was not to stay long. Only to see that you were still here."

"Sterling, we will always be here," his mother answered, her arm around Lilliana as she tried to hold her tears back that he was leaving so soon. "Don't put yourself in any danger."

"I can't help it, Mother," he replied, making toward the door. "If you want to have me back, I will have to risk everything. We cannot be together, my love, unless I risk something. And ..." he turned back. "It will be worth the risk. Love is worth any risk."

He kissed her and left, his mind full of more than just love. Traitors must have given away their attack. Why had it fallen through?

Grurhoum had hinted that there might be a traitor in their midst, someone who had told the Phoenix they had a contingent of men in Bucan. Someone who had told them that they would be attacking the castle. But who was he?

Sterling knew he had information that needed to get back to the others as soon as possible so even though the coins felt heavy in his pocket, he ran back to his horse, mounted, and kicked it into a gallop to get back to the forest as soon as he could.

Fear followed his back. Did the traitor know that he had gone? Did the traitor allow him to go so that he could be caught off guard and then killed? Or did the traitor go on the trip to attack the castle so he could be reunited with the men he worked with?

The night fell before he reached the cave. The forest around him seemed strewn with ill will, things that wished to exterminate him.

He reached the cave without much difficulty, although it felt like he had been riding in terror for hours. Grurhoum was still awake, and Sterling decided to confide in him, sure that the dwarf could not be a traitor seeing as he had the most reason to hate the Phoenix.

Grurhoum nodded, convinced that the evidence did look bad.

"I think we can tell the others," he told Sterling. "Edward can obviously be trusted, his anger and wish for revenge can only be genuine, and as it cannot be the three of us, as long as we stay in a group we should be safe. However, I'll take the first watch tonight."

"Don't," Sterling stopped him. "You need rest, and I need to think. I'll take it, thank me later."

Sterling ducked out of the cave, the other men already asleep. Grurhoum was out in a minute, but Sterling watched the sky, its beauty reminding him of the beauty he had left behind today. That beautiful girl who he could only see when he closed his eyes to dream.

CHAPTER TWENTY-TWO

Philip woke from his dream, his heart full, his mind rushing. He sat in the dark, his breath slow and easy.

Avery had been rescued! Or was that just his dream? She had told him that she loved him! Or was that just his dream? He had come back for her! Or was that just his dream ...

He opened his eyes, his ears suddenly aware of noises of a cart all around him. He peeked through the cracks in the boards. He could just barely see two men, faint outlines against the bright sun. They looked down on the city moldering in its own destruction.

In a flash they were gone.

Philip labored at his bonds, careful so as not to make any noise, but the ropes that held his hands held him fast. He tried stretching his legs to remove them from their strained position, but his feet were also tied together. He tried to move his cracked and parched lips, but the foul gag that wrapped around his head stopped him.

Elsewhere in the cart, he could he someone else move, perhaps Ian, but Philip knew better than to even think about him. He was angry at him for giving in to their captors so easily, and Philip knew he would probably become too furious at him if he allowed his mind to dwell on it too long.

He waited, unable to resign himself to his fate, but unable to do anything else.

The cart rumbled on. Philip couldn't tell which direction they were going, but he could guess. They were going back to Davia. From that one glimpse of the red feather in the Thief's hat he could only guess they had been captured by the Phoenix. Something much bigger than any of them had thought must be going on. The Phoenix had been hiding something besides just who they were. Their motives were no longer as straightforward as they had had been told. Now that he thought about it, what had they told anyone?

And why should they trust them to tell the truth?

Philip waited for what seemed like forever. He dozed off now and then, but they never seemed to stop.

The cart just kept on going. It also kept going faster, or was that just his pounding head? Was that just his parched mouth? Had they been going on forever? Would they ever stop?

Suddenly they did.

Philip waited in silent anticipation, steps sounding near the cart.

The door opened, and he closed his eyes, unable to see in the only light he had seen for days. He would have called out, but his gag and parched lips stopped him.

Someone untied his feet and dragged him out, forcing him to open his eyes so he could walk. What he saw before him made him gasp. He was back at Falkerstone Castle. He was looking at the same stones he had seen for the first time that one day in the winter with his father and for a second time but a few weeks ago.

But he was hurried on as quickly as he could with his limp. The doors of the castle opened and closed behind him, sounding what seemed like a final doom.

In the darkened halls of the castle, he could see Ian. He looked to be in better condition.

They were hurried on as quickly as their captors dared, slowed down only by Philip's limping.

Doors opened before them and closed behind them as they were pushed deeper into the castle, each door slamming with a finality that made them both quake with fear.

Suddenly they were stopped in front of a great set of doors. Soldiers stood on either side of them, guarding the contents. The man in black bowed to them, seeking an audience. The soldiers pushed open the doors, allowing the men to enter. Philip's eyes searched the room, not resting on anything for more than a second. To either side of them there were pillars, white and creamy, reaching up as high as the ceiling. Tapestries depicting scenes from Davia's history covered the walls, their faded threads bearing witness to their years of service. A long, blue carpet reached forth to the dark wood and gilded throne where a man sat, his disinterested and proud gaze leering off into nothing. His head rested on one hand and no crown could be seen on his person. His golden green jacket was slashed at the sleeves and given a collar of dark fur.

Only one other man of importance seemed to be in the room and he stood next to the man on the throne. More aware of his surroundings, he had perked up at their entering the room. His chin was held at an angle that only meant he thought himself better than anyone else. His hands, folded in front of him, were adorned with many gold rings, and his feet, stuffed into elaborate boots, stood at shoulder width. His clothes were slightly less elaborate than the ones on the throne, but he still took pride in the things he wore.

"Your Majesty," the man with the high chin brought to attention the new comers to the man on the throne.

He looked up, his disinterested eyes scanning them. "Yes Lord Arlington?"

"These were the men you ordered to have captured from the Bucan dynasty."

The man on the throne stood up, his proud features still scanning the faces in front of him.

"Thank you Thief," he addressed the man in black. "You have made yourself known. You will be rewarded."

The man in black bowed, his powerful features in submission to the proud man in front of him. "Send Ian to his father, it is time for him to take his place among us."

Philip watched in confusion as Ian's bonds were taken from him and his arms were released from the vice like-grip that the guard had him in.

"Sir Henri has bartered for both of your lives," the man on the throne informed him. "I have also arranged a few things to make your conversion worth your while."

The men had been speaking in the language of the nobles and Philip's heart raced, confusion showing in his features. "What is going on?" he called out to the man from the throne. "Who are you?" he strained at his guards. "I demand to know what's going on!"

"You are in no place to talk like that!" the one called Arlington called out to him in his language, gesturing for the guards to put him back in his place.

"Enough, Arlington," the man from the throne smiled condescendingly and he switched to the common tongue. "If the common man who thinks he's worthy of being a noble wishes to know what's going on, then who are we to stop him? He might as well hear it from us—the geniuses who came up with the plan to begin with."

Arlington looked on in disapproval as the man from the throne took a step forward, studying the face in front of him.

"Philip," he began. "Your group of illegal outlaws from Farvel Forest, so close to the castle," he paused to laugh, "I knew you were there because all the lords were told what to do in case of something like this, but I would never have found you if you had not given yourselves away!" Philip shivered. He continued. "Your friends attacked the castle a few days ago, but one of them had already informed us that you were coming," Philip's face gave him away. "I see you already knew that information," the man from the throne noted. "What you don't know is that all of your company is now in my dungeon except for Sir Henri. I know," he smiled again. "You realize now that you should never have trusted him."

Philip looked away in disgust. Now that he saw the plan laid out before him, it was all so clear. They had walked right into it and it would cost every life within the kingdom if the man on the throne had anything to say about it.

"I know," he man walked toward him, stopping a few feet from his face. "You will never trust anyone ever again."

Philip swallowed, gnashing his teeth together, his jawbone flexing.

"Your friend Henri has given me a lot of information," the man from the throne continued. "He told me about the group that was being sent to Bucan before it had even gone out. He told me about the girl, Avery. We met before, though now that the throne is mine, she is only in the way. In exchange for the information he gave me about my rival, I gave him an offer: he would give me the information—tear your group apart from the inside—and he and his son would be given their lives and a high position in my court."

"You can't do that!" Philip cried out. "We will retaliate! You will not follow through with it!"

"I already have!" the man cried out. "You can't stop me because I'm already done! I sent men down to attack that small Bucan city because I had already attacked it in the past and it would be almost expected. Bucan has been paying me to help take over this country. I would get their support, and in exchange I would turn the country over to them and they would give me a princeship over it."

Philip's head felt weak. Was there more to this than just the Phoenix?

"Bucan wanted to be sure no one would expect it," the man continued. "They gave me some easy prey from the country so it wouldn't look like I was receiving the money directly from them. It was all so well thought out!" the man congratulated himself again. "No one would have even found it out, and no one has!" He smiled at Philip, enjoying the emotions that crossed his face. "I captured you all, and then Avery broke you out again, but she was left behind in the dungeon so it was not a waste of time. I only really needed her, but I also needed to return Ian to his father since he was the one to give us the information to begin with. The only reason you're here is because I figured you would make a great addition. It's really your own fault you're suffering right now."

"Where is my father?" Philip asked, giving up. There was no way to take back the country. "Where is he?"

"He is in the dungeon. He thought about giving in to me to save you, but I guess he didn't know the full danger you were in. Either way, they're all going to the executioner tomorrow. It will be a wonderful spectacle, and I'll make sure that you're there to witness it."

Philip struggled as the men pulled him away. "You can't do this! Someone will stop you! It might not be today, or tomorrow, or even this century! But tyranny will never prevail! You will be brought down!"

"I have a prophesy about me!" he called out. "No one can challenge me! Me! Lord Alonzo! The most powerful man in this kingdom!"

Philip closed his eyes, giving into the pressure around him, allowing the men to drag him away to the dungeon. What did he have left? Someone, someday, would resist the power around them, but he had given in. That fight was no longer his. He was going to die. It would be easier if he knew that it would spark revolution and bring down the Phoenix. Was that the only thing he had left? Potent last words? A legacy? Chaos? Death?

He collapsed on the floor of his cell as the door clanged behind him. So many things had closed behind him today—his life, his purpose, his emotions. He could only move forward, and it was his job to move forward in a way that would start people thinking. That was all that was left to him.

His eyes closed and his breath slowed, passing into deep sleep out of exhaustion, not even reaching for the food and water there beside him. What did he need it for?

CHAPTER TWENTY-THREE

A very glanced to the door of her cell, examining the faces that had come to get her.

"Princess," they began, showing full well that they knew who she was.

"'Lady' will do," she answered mechanically, sure that her doom had come upon her. "I'm ready."

They opened the door to her cell and escorted her out, ascending many stairs to reach the outside world. The sun hurt her eyes. One of the men handed her a cloak, threatening her to keep the hood on. She took it without question, pulling it around her, almost glad that it hid her from view.

She was helped onto a horse and then the others mounted. They guided her down the long path she had followed them up only a few days ago. They took her into the village and Avery prepared herself for what she knew to be coming next, but they passed through the village without stopping. No hanger's noose obstructed their view. No executioner's block came upon their path.

So, they are taking me into the woods to be rid of me, she thought. *Cowards. They won't even kill me in front of people!*

But the more they walked through the woods, the longer they went, the more perfect opportunities for a drowning passed without anything taking place, she began to wonder if they were taking her back to Davia to face her fate. Somehow these people must be connected to the Phoenix—that much she did know—but they had known that before, hadn't they? Something bigger than any of them had imagined must be taking place, she was sure. Someone had ratted on them and they would now pay for telling that person in the first place.

The woods passed around them. They didn't stop to eat their meals, but bread and water was passed to each rider as they continued their journey.

When they stopped at night, Avery was tied up to keep her from running away and a guard was set up to make sure they were not come upon unawares at night.

Avery slept fitfully, unable to get comfortable with her hands tied behind her back and her feet tied together. She nothing warm to cover herself with. In the morning, she was back in the saddle, another day of riding ahead.

They rode on for days in this manner, pushing themselves on but still taking time at night to rest. The men seemed to sense urgency from their orders, but they didn't want to push the lady to go too quickly too fast, and for this she was glad. Anything to push off what felt like impending doom.

They finally reached the castle city of Davia. Falkerstone Castle could be seen leering ahead of them. The last time she had been there she had been shot in the arm. She touched the wound as she thought about it, flinching because it still pained her. She turned her eyes away from the castle, unwilling to look at it until she had to.

The village around her boiled with villagers and townsfolk. Some uniformed men with the feathers of the Phoenix stood at street corners, and she began to be glad of the hood they forced her to wear. It concealed her face from curious passersby.

She scanned the crowd, searching for any familiar face. Voices called out in both languages and she prided herself in knowing most of what the commoners were saying as they called out to each other. Half-recognized voices tugged at her memory—Grurhoum calling things out, Edward countering him, Darren trying to keep them from fighting because it would give away their position.

But were these things really in her mind? What of the short man only a few paces away? What of the recognizable gait of Lord Edward?

She thought quickly. It had to be them! How could she get their attention?

She had stopped steering her horse as she tried to think of a way to make herself known. Someone bumped into her bewildered horse, startling him and balking from under her. Instantly her mind changed from getting attention to trying to stay on her horse.

He reared back till it almost felt like he would fall back on top of her. Her hood fell back, revealing her dark hair and pale face. Everyone around her watched as she slowly slipped off the horse before it galloped down the street without her.

Gurhoumr watched, his eyes transfixed as the men on the other horses gathered around her, his argument with Edward forgotten.

"Is that?" he whispered the questions his mind had already answered, the others already transfixed to the spot.

They watched as she stood up, shaken but unharmed. One of the men led her up to his own horse, her hood still down for all to see. They mounted and turned back to the castle. She turned to look for Grurhoum, but she had lost him in the moment.

She was inwardly crying, had they seen her? Did they know she was there? Did they know she was still alive? Had they left right before she had shown herself?

The men reminded her to pull up her hood and she did so reluctantly, savoring every moment she had to show who she truly was.

The people around her moved on, the spectacle over for them. They had their own lives to worry about.

They continued, but Avery could only think of Edward, Grurhoum, and Darren. Thoughts plagued her mind, taking it off of its impending doom.

They reached the middle of the city, that very same square that her carriage had stopped in on the day of her ball, but it looked very different now. This time the crowd was larger, but it gave way to them, allowing them to move forward.

Avery watched as they pulled away from in front of her, noticing through the crowd that they seemed to be gathered around something. Suddenly her heart fell. She had caught a glimpse of an executioner's noose standing at the ready.

She didn't notice as they dismounted and led her into the crowd, pulling past everyone to reach the place where the nobles sat. But they didn't stop there. They pushed on even more until they stood in front of where her uncle the king should have sat, but in his place was someone she recognized.

"Alonzo!" she cried out, anger and confusion rising within her. "What is the meaning of all this?"

"Ah!" he called out to her in delight. "My Lady, Avery! Come, sit by me and I'll explain everything all over again."

She sat down in the open chair, and her guard sat in the other open chairs around her. She glared at them. It would have been easy for her to run and disappear into the crowd, but that was no longer an option.

"I expected you yesterday when your friends arrived," he began. "But I heard you decided to be heroic and were captured by my men at another time. But none of that mattered since you all ended up here in time."

Avery glared at him, not sure where this conversation was going. "I am not interested in anything you have to offer," she informed him.

"You thought I didn't know that?" he told her. "And that's what makes this so very nice." His eyes turned back to the place that would soon be carnage. "Let me tell you about what is going to happen today and for what reasons," he began.

"I know enough about it," she told him, looking away. "You just conquered a kingdom and you're intoxicated with power. You have people to execute and a point to prove. Is that not enough? Is it not enough to see people suffer and then die in agony?"

"You are insolent," he glared at the square in front of him. "I am the

Phoenix as you might have guessed, and I just happen to have a bunch of people you know to execute today."

Avery waited in silence for a few moments, only now remembering that he was about to execute her friends.

"Who do you have?" she turned back to him, her eyes wide, not caring that he could see her fear. She needed to know.

"Well as you might have guessed, one of the outlaws within your circle is a traitor. He told me about the attack that was being staged against the castle. He told me about how you and a few others were being sent into Bucan to find things out. He knew who you really were so I knew to send for you because you're a rival and must be eliminated. By the way," he smiled. "I already have your friends Philip and Ian. I was ready for your little group of outlaws when they attacked, and now they are all my prisoners and about to be executed."

"Who?" she asked again.

"Oh, Lord Lucas, Lord Wellington, and a few others. Henri has saved himself and bargained for his son Ian." Alonzo pointed to the two men a little way away. They had already noticed her, but this was the first that she had noticed them. "They gave me information, and I gave them what they wanted."

"And what was that?" she asked.

"A pardon and power. There isn't much else they can ask for. The information they gave me was important but it wasn't necessary, I would still have won in the end."

The sun shone through the rooftops around them. The bright, late spring day felt cheery and fake considering innocent people were about to die.

Her eyes scanned the crowd around her, searching for the short dwarf, the tall lord, and the noble man, but they were met with simple faces here to watch the execution.

The prisoners were brought out. She recognized them. Their faces were proud and unbending to the last.

Alonzo gave the signal to the executioner to begin, and the first person was brought up.

Deep within the crowd Edward, Grurhoum, Darren, Garret, and Sterling watched as the first was brought up to the noose. They clutched their weapons, determined that their friends wouldn't go down without a fight, even if they had to go down with them.

The executioner put the noose around their friend's neck and Edward placed an arrow on his string, vowing to not let another man die because he had not been there at the right time.

He called out to the crowd, breaking the anticipating silence around him. "Shall we stand back while the men that fought for our freedom die?"

People around him grew louder, whispers circulating, but no one dared look him in the eye.

"Shall we stand here watching this man kill more because he wants to?"

The crowd stopped whispering, listening to him.

"This man has killed our families! Our husbands, our sons, our brothers!" he choked back at those words. "This man claims to be the Phoenix!"

"'From the ashes of the old shall he rise!'" someone called out to him. "Our kingdom has been reduced to ashes by this false Phoenix! Let the true one come forth 'like the Phoenix of old,' let him stir from the ashes of this broken kingdom!"

The man was hushed with a swift arrow from a guard and people broke out into a panic, suddenly realizing how they had been duped.

"'The time for new has come!'" another called out. "Down with tyrants! 'From the old ashes of the kingdom shall a ruler rise!'"

Edward pulled his arrow back, aiming at the heart of the executioner.

"'He shall be known as the weak!'" an old man called out. "When has Alonzo the tyrant ever been weak? When has he ever not had all the power he could want? He tyrannizes the weak, but isn't one himself!"

Darren could see Alonzo up with the other nobles, his proud face contorted with rage.

"But the poem says he shall be made strong!" a young woman cried over the din. "We must help the true Phoenix come to power. We must help him become strong! Let us truly fulfill the prophesy!"

Other people around Edward whispered the rest of the verses.

> He shall be known as someone
> But in truth is another
> He shall be hunted by hypocrites
> The ones he came to save.

Finally, as he loosed his arrow, someone called out: "'With the lawless he will dwell and one of them he shall be!' This Phoenix could be one of the men we were about to execute! Alonzo has declared them outlaws, who else could it be?!"

The arrow could not have struck its mark, but something in the wind changed, bringing his arrow to its target, striking with a thud that set off the crowds around them.

"'The time has come for change!'" they screamed out. "'Change in the bloodline of rulers!' Change! Change! Change! Change!"

Edward watched as the executioner fell down the very trap door he would have sent several others down that day.

"Come on!" he called to his friends. "We must fight the guards around our friends before they are taken back to the castle, hidden by the chaos around us!"

The outlaws followed him, their weapons drawn.

Faint whispers could be heard over the raging of the crowd, spoken in a tongue that none of them knew.

People around them organized themselves into attacking parties, defending the women and children from the many guards who poured into the small square.

Grurhoum and the others reached their friends and fought the many guards around them. The whispers continued over the noise, their swords swinging faster than they had ever imagined, their success becoming more than they had ever imagined.

Wellington grabbed the closest guard and tackled him, Lucas doing the same to the one next to him.

They all fought any way that they could. This was their last chance to break free.

And just as quickly as they had begun, it all stopped. More guards than they could fight entered the square. Grurhoum called the retreat, his men following him.

The prisoners slipped out without being noticed, heading toward Farvel Forest.

They ran along, hiding in the woods and not taking the path for fear of being seen. They were halfway to Farvel when they collapsed. Wellington called a halt, his fist shoved into his tunic, blood pouring out of the gaping wound that he vainly tried to cover with his hand.

Everyone began to go about caring for their injuries while Wellington, Lucas, Edward, and Darren came together for a meeting.

Lucas explained what had happened, how they had been captured and how he was told that Henri had given away all of their secrets. Then Edward explained how Philip, Ian, and Avery had been captured and how they had seen Avery in the city just moments before they had come upon the execution.

"We didn't expect to see you having an execution, we also didn't expect to see Avery either," Edward explained. "Philip, Henri, Ian, and Avery must still be in the castle," he thought out loud. "We just got the common people riled up. I think we can expect things will never be the same, and that Alonzo will not feel safe at night."

"We'll have to use that to our advantage," Lucas tried to think. "But I'm not sure how. One thing is clear though—we can't go back to Farvel Forest. Alonzo knows that is where we like to hide out."

"I agree. Let's take ourselves a way from the path and we'll stay here for the night," Wellington leaned against a tree for support.

"Yes," Grurhoum agreed. "Now let's tend to that wound, how did it happen?"

"It's nothing really," Wellington answered, removing his hand from blocking the flow.

They tended to it, Wellington flinching with pain as they bound cloth around it.

"I'll be fine," he finally pushed them away. "Let's worry about the rest of our men."

They pushed them on, moving further away from the path. They finally collapsed, Grurhoum setting out to be the first guard, Edward promising to take the second watch, and Darren the third.

They lay down, Grurhoum sitting down on a log, resolving to keep watch all night and not wake the others up. He would sacrifice for their rest.

He waited in the dark, watching the stars and the animals that passed before him, listening to the sounds around their camp.

Footsteps came upon him as the moon began to rise. He drew his bow, aiming into the dark where he knew them to be.

"Show yourself!" he called out in the few words of the comment language that he knew.

A small group of men walked into his circle of vision. Their torn clothes bore witness to the fact that they had traveled far.

"We have come to join your group," the leader cried out. "We are fed up with the false Phoenix."

Grurhoum lowered his bow.

"We accept you," he invited them to the camp, showing their weary feet a place to rest.

He turned back to guarding.

Another group came. Grurhoum invited them in. More and more people kept pouring into their camp, each group bigger than the last. He was surprised the Phoenix had not shown up yet, but it started to make sense. The outlaws were a snake and that afternoon they had bitten the Phoenix's hand. It would come back for them, but it would be more careful this time. It knew the bite it could receive.

Finally, right before dawn, a single person came in.

"I have come to help you fight the Phoenix," he told Grurhoum in the language of the high nobles and Bucan.

"Who are you and why are you here?" Grurhoum asked, cautious of the only man to come in by himself all night, but yet drawn to him at the same time. Something like fate stopped him from drawing his arrow. Something like destiny stayed his hand and made him step forward. Who was this man? Why was he here?

Grurhoum could almost tell what the answers would be before it was even said.

"My name is Crovprix, and I have already helped you fight the Phoenix. I am a wizard."

CHAPTER TWENTY-FOUR

Morning light had come. Grurhoum was reprimanded for staying up all night, but it was only halfhearted. Edward and Darren were glad of the extra sleep, although it did go against principle.

Grurhoum was sent to rest after breakfast, but his mind could not stay away from the wizard. Who was he?

He sat in the corner of camp, watching, but not partaking. Approachable but standoffish. His black cloak touched the ground beside him, and his long gray beard reached his waist, which was cinched in with a belt. Unlike everyone else, he did not seem to be armed. His belt held nothing to defend himself with, but anyone who looked at his shriveled face knew he had something up his sleeve and was not to be reckoned with.

Edward, Lucas, Wellington, and Darren conversed together, unsure of how to proceed. The wizard was not looking at them, but they had the distinct feeling he was listening.

"There haven't been wizards in our country for hundreds of years and when they were here, they weren't always one side or the other. Can we trust a wizard?" Wellington began, looking at Lucas.

"I don't see why not. He says he has already helped us, although I don't know how," Lucas replied.

"Perhaps we should question him," Darren suggested. "I'm sure his true intentions will show through."

They all nodded in agreement and made their way to the wizard who sat in silent anticipation.

"Ah, my lords," the wizard stood and bowed. Everything about him seemed rusty, as though he hadn't used them in years. "I'm sure you have many questions. Allow me to answer them as your humble servant."

The men nodded at him and he began.

"I am Crovprix Nightcrest the wizard," he told them, pronouncing the x in his name with extra emphasis. "The second wizard to ever be born of magic. You have heard stories of us passed down from your ancestors, and you do not trust me. What I can tell you is this: my past and its stories do not belong here, but when I have fulfilled my duty here I must continue my journey east. I am here for such a time as this and I am here to offer my help."

"You said you have already helped us. How?" Lucas enquired.

"Yesterday at the square. You did not notice?" he asked, looking at them in amazement.

Wellington cleared his throat. "I regret that I have not come in contact with enough magic to tell when it is being used."

"Ah well," the wizard sat down again. "I hope you don't mind." He glanced at them while they also sat down. "I guided your arrow," he glanced at Edward. "You might have noticed it should not have hit its target the way that it did and the effect would have been lost. I guided your arrow so the revolution could start."

Edward silently thanked him, but something was lost now that he knew he hadn't really killed the man, and that he still had to go on to avenge his brother's death.

"I know about your brother, Edward," the wizard looked directly at him. "I know that his death will not go unavenged, but ..." he trailed off as though there was information he could have given away, but chose not to.

"Do you read minds?" Darren asked. As the youngest there, his curiosity ran deeper than the others.

"No," Crovprix answered. "Thoughts are private, but the past is not."

Edward looked away, a sore spot touched.

"I was telling you about my involvement in the battle yesterday," he continued. "You might have also noted that the crowd shouted out parts of the old prophecies. I helped that—whispering thoughts in the minds of men."

"Is the old prophecy true?" Lucas asked, leaning forward to catch his answer.

"Yes, it is," Crovprix told him. "However it will not come true the way Lord Alonzo thinks it should, nor even the first way the people think it should."

The others sighed. "Then we have destiny on our side. There is no way for us to lose."

Crovprix looked away, "I cannot tell you that," he whispered. "Destiny must play out in its own way."

The men around him looked frightened, suddenly aware that they might still die to place the real Phoenix on the throne.

"Let us not think of that anymore," the wizard told them. "The future will take care of itself in due time," he continued. "And those whispers that you heard over the ruckus? Those were spells to hasten your swords and spells to slow your enemies. That is why it took them forever to reach the square."

They all sat there, soaking in the meaning behind those words. They had already decided to trust him, if only because he had helped them before they had asked for it.

"So what's next?" Darren asked.

"We need to attack the castle again," Lucas sighed.

"I have spells that can make us get there unseen," Crovprix offered. "I haven't used them in years, but they shouldn't take too much time to iron out and dust off."

"Thank you," Lucas told him. "We'll need it after our last attempt."

Crovprix nodded. "What about the men you have inside? And what about the girl? It is important that she is brought back as soon as possible seeing as she is the heir to the throne. I can read the past, and the past writes the future. I have reasons to believe that the past will write a terrible end for her if we don't intervene soon."

"Is she going to die?" Lucas asked, his heart going out to the girl he had basically adopted.

"I don't know for sure, not by my reckoning anyways," Crovprix answered. "But that doesn't mean she isn't going to wish that she were."

Avery looked out from the room where she was held. She had been led there after the riot in the square. It was nothing like the one that she had been in before. The cell paled in comparison to the room above ground that she now held. The window overlooked the dark and wet garden, reaching out till Farvel Forest could be seen on the hazy and rainy horizon. Her heart was there, unable to be captive by the heights, doors, and locks that held her in the place where it was now. But still its oppressive lighting and drip dropping rain made her feel like there was nothing left for her, that she could do nothing to stop her fate.

Henri was a traitor who had told Alonzo who she really was, but she had never told Henri who she was in the first place. That meant Ian must have been in on this too, and now they were all in the castle. Henri and Ian would be given their lives, a pardon, power, renown around the world once their treachery was exposed.

Philip was probably in a dungeon waiting for death.

And what about Lucas and Wellington? She had seen their escape, reveled in it outwardly. Their escape had made her realize that this terror could not last for forever. The people of her country would not stand for it. Especially as she realized that when it was revealed that Alonzo was taking over the country only to hand it over to the Bucan dynasty, they would never stand for it. She would never stand for it.

The door to the room opened and Alonzo entered, his two bodyguards taking either side of the door as it closed behind him.

"Ah," he glanced out of the window she had been looking out of.

She slipped off the window seat to stand a way off. "Leave me here in my pain, but do not come to make it worse. My country will not stand for you and your antics. You have seen how they respond to your displays of power. You have seen what they think of you. It will not be long before my friends gain enough power to attack again."

"Enough," he sighed. "You, don't, know, anything!" he glanced at her angrily before sitting down on the now vacant window seat.

She turned her back to him, arms crossed over her chest.

"You know that not everyone escaped yesterday," he looked at her. "I just figured you would like to know what is going to happen to your friends."

Her face changed, but she was glad he could not see it and could only see her indifferent back.

"Philip is such a proud boy, and I know that you would love to have revenge on Ian and Henri because they hurt you so much."

"I can forgive," she lied. "That is something that you might not be able to comprehend."

"But perhaps if you save Philip from death, pain, and hurt, then you can get that revenge on Ian and Henri, and perhaps save yourself some pain at the same time. I'm only saying that it makes sense and you win all around."

"Me? Win? No, I cannot win," she admitted to him. "You will make sure of that."

"What?"

"If I take advantage of your offer, if I so-called win, I can guarantee you will win even more. I cannot allow you to do that. I would rather take you down with me than give you a boost at my own expense."

"If that's how you want it, if you don't even want to hear my offer, then I might as well start planning your and Philip's execution."

Avery didn't say anything. She was angry at him but not sure she was angry enough to die for it. Her words had shown force, but they lacked the resolve behind them.

"Are you sure Philip would be willing to die because you're stubborn?" he turned to look back at her.

She felt like she was slipping. She knew there was one thing that she could do to save Philip and herself, but her pride would not allow her to stoop so low as to ask, even if it meant that Philip died.

Alonzo sensed that and smiled. "If you chose to, I can promise you Henri and Ian will meet with death at my hand and that Philip will be spared. I will leave you with that."

He turned and opened the door to her room. She watched as his guard followed him, the door closing with a click that meant it was locked.

The resolve she had managed to keep while he was present with her dissolved. She knew she was playing right into what he wanted, but marriage to Alonzo looked better than death. She thought about death for a moment, but that would only keep her from being a political pawn in her marriage. People would still die. *Philip* would still die.

The choice was before her.

CHAPTER TWENTY-FIVE

Ian sat with his father in the small room that they had been given. His head still reeled from all the news. He had yet to take in the riot at the square just the day before.

First, his father had snitched to Alonzo, and they now had free passage to three whole lordships when Alonzo came to full power and everything calmed down. It nearly overwhelmed him, but the riot had stilled him, shown him that perhaps their situation was a little more precarious than they had first expected. Maybe the Phoenix wasn't going to win? Maybe they had made the wrong choice?

Ian thought about it, unwilling to voice his concerns to his father, knowing full well that he would be scoffed at. He felt something close to remorse at his father's actions. He had never wanted things to go this far.

He stood and paced the floor, Henri watching his every step. It wasn't too late for him to go back, was it? If he could find an escape, could he still take it? Lucas and Wellington would still take him back, wouldn't they? But what if no one trusted him anymore? They had no reason to after the things he had done. But what if he could convince them that his father had done those things to him?

Ian was still only thinking of himself, but he was thinking about his choices, who he really was, and if he was being used as a pawn. The results he came up with hurt him. Something had switched within him. Perhaps it was the extremeness of the situation, perhaps he had actually begun to bond with those people, but something told him it wouldn't be the right thing to continue on this path. Something needed to change.

His heart raced, should he ask his father?

He needed to get out of the room he was in. He needed to be alone. He needed to clear his mind.

He left the room without a word, his father not even noticing as he left.

He paced the halls, meandering without meaning till he came upon an open door. He slowed, aware that he didn't want to be seen by anyone in authority. Voices could be heard within. One sounded like Avery, the other like Alonzo. He stopped and turned, willing to go another way, then heard his name spoken. He stopped, transfixed to the spot.

"If you chose to," the voice came distantly, "I can promise you that Henri and Ian will meet with death at my hand, and Philip will be spared. I will leave you with that."

Ian didn't even take in the words as he turned to go as far away from the door as possible.

He heard it open the rest of the way and then close, his heart beating in a way that he had never expected it to.

So he had turned traitor on the outlaws, and now the very men he had helped were going to betray him! He should never have trusted Alonzo. He should have known not to trust someone who had broken another's trust.

He turned and deposited himself in the alcove of a window, pulling the curtain around himself in the hopes that anyone passing by would not see him.

So now they wanted to kill him? He had just been thinking about how this was a terrible idea to begin with, so why not escape?

But, what about Avery and Philip? Alonzo was going to kill Philip and attempt to marry Avery. Should he try to save them?

No, it would be easier to escape without them. He needed to leave with the highest possibility of success. But he didn't know his way around the castle the way that Avery knew it. Should he try to get her?

He resolved on it. It wouldn't be that hard anyways.

He nodded, looking out the window at the dreary wet ground below him. It dampened his fervor, but he held onto the words he had heard, and his resolve stayed with him.

He had to tell his father, or maybe ... maybe he would let his father stay. Maybe he deserved what was about to be served to him? He had asked for it when he had betrayed the outlaws. He should follow through with his decision.

Besides, Avery would hardly come with him if Henri was with him. Things had already been strained between them.

He could handle everything on his own.

He turned back to his room to wait for the cover of darkness. His mind was made up. His plans were firm. Nothing could change his mind at this point.

The dark twilight outside deepened until it became night. Shadows flitted across the lawn, never staying in one place for a moment. Ian slipped out of his room, his cloak drawn around his shoulders with a free and easy hand.

He glided down the halls, twisting and turning till he came upon the door he had seen open before. No one stood guard over it and he reached for the handle, unlocked it, turned it, and pulled the door open. It turned on well-oiled hinges. No noise could be heard without or within.

He glanced inside the moonlit room. The pattern of the window was cast upon the ground in deep shadows and spills of blue gray light. Avery was sitting up at the window seat, her spirit still searching the surrounding country, unwilling to leave the freedom she now enjoyed to suffer the confining depths of sleep.

"I know why you're here," her voice came, unnatural and startling in the dark. "I will not give in."

Ian took a step further into the room. "I don't think you know why I'm here."

"Ian?" she turned her face from the window, surprised that her friend would be there. Or should she call him her enemy? She realized he was the one who was making her life so hard at that point. "I suppose you have come to gloat over me." She turned back to the window.

"No," he told looking around, not sure of where to begin. "I need you to navigate me."

"Where?" her aimless gaze continued to flip over the garden below her.

"Look at me," his urgent tone rose. "I need you to get me out of here, I need you to get me back to Farvel Forest."

"Really?" she turned to look at him in disbelief. "You turned yourself in. You gave him our secrets. How can I trust you?"

He tried to think, how could she trust him? How could she put her life into his hands?

"I overheard Alonzo's offer to you today," he began. "I figured we both want out of here so I've put together a plan."

"Are we going to rescue Philip?" she asked.

"I wasn't planning on it," he answered her as he looked down dejectedly. He knew what she would say next and he didn't like it.

"I won't leave unless we take him with us."

"Why? We should get out as soon as we can. Who knows when we'll have another chance?"

"You heard his threats as well as I did," she told him, her back straightened and looking down at him. "We are not safe, but neither is he. We cannot think only of ourselves."

Ian thought about it. "Alright," he gave in reluctantly. "Whatever."

He dashed to the door. "Come on," he growled at her. "This is suicide, but let's do it."

She followed him slowly, cautiously, something that he threw to the wind. But it worked for him. He could go around the castle and no one would question him. If she went around the castle, she would be captured and there would be other consequences.

She followed him for a while, left, right, right, left, down.

"You're going the wrong way," she interrupted at last. "We need to go left."

He turned and glared at her. "Alright, let's follow you then." He threw his arms down and stormed after her as she led him further into the dungeons.

If he wants to leave, he'd better be more cooperative, she thought to herself. *Escapes require teamwork, not just storming around. Escapes require caution, not emotion.*

She felt uneasy. Did he really mean it? Was he pulling her leg? Would they turn a corner only to be accosted by guards he had placed there?

She put her emotions off to the side as she led him further down. Finally, they came upon a heavy door. She tried opening it, but it stuck. She looked to him and he rolled his eyes. He muttered something under his breath and pushed past her rudely to heave himself against the door.

It caved beneath him and he was deposited on the other side of it.

"He should be right here," she pointed down the stairs that Ian had almost fallen down.

"You wait right here. I'll check," he barged past her and clambered down the stairs that led deep into the bowels of the earth. Smells and noises assaulted his senses, but he sighed and shrugged them away.

He stomped down the stairs, his attitude showing through in every motion he exhibited. When he reached the bottom, he kicked at a small rock that he could see in the faint light around him. It echoed and ricocheted off the walls till it came to halt with a simple thud.

"Who goes there?" Ian called out, stepping forward slowly.

A groan could be heard where the rock had come to its resting place.

"Who are you?"

"Avery ..." a faint whisper came. "Let me die, but don't..."

Ian almost turned around, resolving to tell Avery that no one was down there.

"Ian ..." he was stopped in his steps.

"Philip," he whispered. He couldn't ignore him now. "I'm here."

Ian glanced around the walls for a key, found it, placed it in the lock, turned it, and opened the door to the cell. Every part of him rebelled against his decisions.

"You came back for me?" Philip was in the far corner of his cell on the ground, his life seemingly gone from him.

Ian bent over the motionless form, examining the damage that only a few days had done to his former enemy.

Philip's back was shredded, skin and flesh combined together in a boiling mess under his torn shirt.

"It might be best if Avery doesn't see you like this." Ian took off his cloak and draped it over his shoulders. He knew Avery would be worried. She would not pay any attention to escaping if she knew Philip was in such terrible condition.

Philip accepted the cloak as though it had been a gift, not realizing the selfish desires behind the selfless action that Ian displayed.

"Buck up, boy," Ian helped Philip up as though he should not have had to do that. "Come on."

Philip pulled himself together, and grabbing Ian's offered hand with both of his, came to his feet.

He didn't say anything as Ian led the way up the stairs. Ian realized at once that Philip would not be able to run if and when things would come to that. He hid his realization and pulled on, ignoring the fact that their mission was doomed because of him.

They reach the top of the stairs, Avery helping them over the last few steps. She embraced her friend before she remembered the seriousness of their situation and led them back up the stairs.

She too realized that running would not be an option, but her eternal optimism made her hope that running wouldn't need to be an option.

Suddenly, she came upon a passage that she didn't know. The dungeons had never been her ideal place to explore, and she didn't know which way to go.

"What?" Ian cried out. "You don't know the way?!" he threw his hand in the air and turned to go back. "We might as well turn ourselves in right now."

Tears came up her eyes but she hid them in pretending to look at the passages closely.

"It's alright Avery," Philip assured her, he leaned against the walls around her, glad of the short break. "Just pick one."

She thought about it, but her memory could not bring either path into light.

"Just pick one!" Ian shouted. "It doesn't matter!"

She pounded her head against the wall, exasperated at her own stupidity. Why couldn't he just be quiet for a moment? Why couldn't he just be quiet?

A breath of air caressed her sweaty face.

"This way," her calm voice surprised her. "It's this way."

Ian moved immediately, nearly dragging Philip behind him.

"We can go slowly," she recommended.

They plowed on regardless of anything she could say. The path seemed unfamiliar, but that breath of air could only mean one thing. She made a few more turns, each time a breath of air guiding her to the path that she was to take.

It felt like they had been there forever. Each path seemed just like the last, and Avery was beginning to wonder how that one breath of air had made its way all the way up to them, for they seemed to be going down. Ian in his anger didn't see it, and Philip could hardly be expected to notice in his state, but Avery saw it clear as day and it scared her. What if you couldn't just follow the air and hope to reach the night outside?

They pushed on until it finally came to a dead end. Ian was angry. He had pinned every hope on them getting out, but they were now faced with certain death. "You've led us to a dead end," Ian growled. "I shouldn't have brought you along. We shouldn't have gone back for Philip. I should have just gone by myself. I should have left you to choose between two living deaths!"

He turned to sulk in the corner.

"Ian," a calm voice came from Philip. "That is not the way you treat anyone."

"And what do you know of how to treat people?" Ian scorned him over his shoulder. "You were never considered good enough to be introduced at court," he lied.

"I never had the time for it," Philip corrected him. "I never watched my mother as she slaved away to her death, but I could see the effect it had on my father." Strain could be heard in his voice, echoing over the cold stone around them. "He served her as she gave her life for others. No one should ever do that, no one should have allowed anyone to slave their life like that. You do not understand the pain that others go through," Philip pulled himself up. "The burdens that they bare because they do not want to share them with anyone else. If you do not want to help bear the burden of escape, I recommend that you leave now. I will be staying. I believe we can still get out of this with Avery's help."

Philip stood on his own, his words sinking into Ian's mind.

Avery turned from them, aware of the truth that Philip spoke, and yet also acknowledging that they would not be here if it hadn't been for Ian rescuing her from her prison.

She looked around the dead end, silence sinking in around her, beautiful silence. Her eyes scanned over the uneven stone, rough lumps covering every inch but a two foot by two-foot section on the ceiling. She brushed her hands over it, pushing against it to test its strength.

"This looks like it could be a trap door."

She stepped out of the way and Ian pushed his shoulder against it.

"It looks promising," his strained voice came at last. "Philip, lend a shoulder."

Philip dragged himself over and pushed on it, Avery helping in the last moments as the slab finally lifted with a heavy sigh.

"Ladies first," Philip took his hands, shaking with tiredness, and gave Avery a hand up.

She pulled herself out of the hole and reached down to help Philip up. Ian was next, he jumped and Philip and Avery helped him reach the top.

They surveyed their surroundings—a river on one side with a wood, on the other side was the castle Falkerstone.

"I know this place," she whispered to them.

Philip nodded, the river triggering reminders of things that had happened only a few weeks before.

"This is the place where I fell the last time I escaped Falkerstone," Avery whispered, her eyes scanning the place.

She saw the same trees that had been there before, the same river, the same grass. The last time she had seen them was in a feverish haze after she had escaped the castle and been shot in the arm. The trees faded into the quiet rain, that blessed rain. Shadows passed behind them. Avery sat on edge for a moment, and her fear was realized when a figure came out from behind them.

"Greetings," the figure called out in the common language and then the language of the nobles.

"Greetings," Avery replied to him in the common speech, she didn't need him knowing who they were.

As the figure neared, she noticed its long cloak, long gray beard, belted waist, shriveled face, and the fact that it was not armed. Nowhere on him could she find a visible weapon.

Philip stood up and took a few steps forward, ready to block any attempt the newcomer could make. "Who are you? Why are you here?"

"Why did you make it out of the tunnel?" the figure laughed. "Because of me, that's why. Allow me to introduce myself."

"We got out of the tunnel because of the lady," Philip's hard voice came back.

"Yes, and I was working through her."

"You have five seconds to start explaining yourself before you will find yourself in an unpleasant situation," Philip threatened, taking a step forward.

"Yes, I am Crovprix, the second wizard to ever be born. I was at the riot in the square just a few days ago. I helped with a little bit of magic and promised to help your group of outlaws. Tonight I looked in my book and did some deep thinking. Most of the time I can only stay in the present and see the past, but I tried as hard as I could to see the future, I knew something was going to happen tonight. I just didn't know what. I found out you would try to escape and it would fall through because you would not be able to find your way out of the labyrinth, so I came here and blew up a little wind to send down as my guide. Now," he turned to head back into the woods. "It's time to go back to your group."

Ian and Philip looked at Avery, her trusting eyes already following the stranger.

"Should we trust him?" the silent question was posed.

CHAPTER TWENTY-SIX

B ack in the camp the rain poured down in the motionless night. It dripped off the trees and fell on the sleeping men. Rain soaked their clothes, seeping in like the unstoppable tide. They shivered underneath their blankets, aware that their time was coming soon. The night guard sat on his log, his bow and arrow in readiness for any trouble, his hair dripping pools down his forehead. The woodland animals shook out their fur as they walked along, soon giving up trying to dry themselves and settling back into their burrows for the rest of the night. The clouds overhead glowed with the suppressed light of the moon, the drops of rain still falling refracting that light. The darkness around them made the cold rain more pronounced and hid any approaching groups from the guard. That is why Crovprix, Ian, Philip, and Avery were not seen until they were almost upon night guard.

Crovprix assured the guard of their identities, the others being too tired to speak for themselves, and they entered the camp.

Avery and Philip sighed, at last back with the others. It had been too long. Ian squirmed, already wishing he could be back in the castle. If only it hadn't been raining he might have stood it.

Philip nudged his father to wake him. They silently embraced and slipped into the woods to talk. Ian found a blanket and lay on the wet and muddy ground. He felt as though he no longer belonged there, and he was right. He had passed from this life. It could no longer be his.

Avery lay on the ground, not bothering to find anything to cover herself with and fell asleep in moments, already soaked through with the rain, having forgotten her cloak back in her room.

Philip's heart was as full as it could be. He didn't know the news about Vincent and fell silent as he heard. He told his father about everything that had happened—how he had been captured, how he had been taken, how he had seen Ian go to his father, how Avery and Ian had come and they had escaped, how they had been met with Crovprix—everything except for how he had been treated and when he was asked, he pulled his cloak further around himself and moved on.

Lord Lucas listened silently, unsure if he could even trust Ian anymore, but he pushed that to the side to tell his son everything that had passed since they had parted.

At last they finished. They embraced, aware that they had both thought they would never see the other again, and they went back to the camp.

Everything around them was silent and Philip thought about how lucky he was, how thankful he should be. Things had turned out all right. Things were going to get better.

Lucas gave his son a blanket and they hugged again before Philip went to lie down. He made his way through the maze of sleeping men. Avery caught his eyes, her shivering form already asleep and soaked.

Without a second thought he tucked his blanket in around her and turned back to find his pack. He found it and resolved to take care of his wounds before the others could wake and see them. He found an old shirt of his, ripped it, took a newer shirt, and turned away from camp.

He took off Ian's cloak and his shirt, and began wrapping his wounds. He wanted to cry out. It was unbearable. But everyone was asleep, unaware of the battle he fought with himself as he bandaged his wounds.

Philip finished at last, almost his whole body covered in the bandages. He pulled on his extra shirt and he went to lie down. His eyes closed, his breathing slowed, the rain stopped. Peace had come upon everyone in camp. Peace had come upon the kingdom. Sleep prevailed.

When everyone woke up the next morning, they hung their blankets on the branches of trees and moved on to breakfast, stepping around three sleeping forms that none of them recognized.

Lucas seemed to be in a wonderful mood, always noticing this or that about how beautiful the day was going to be, and mentioning to Crovprix several times that he was very thankful he had come to help them. Wellington seemed to echo his fervency, but with a little bit of worry.

The newcomers could make nothing of it, what could have happened? These men weren't happy just because they hardly got any refreshing sleep last night, or were they insane? Nothing seemed to make any sense.

Finally, when the figures stirred and woke, they found out. Stories were told, praise was given, and hugs between old friends. Philip, Avery, and Ian had come home, and they had been missed.

The heroes of the day were given food, men offered them dry clothes, they were praised, they were asked questions, they could hardly fit in a word edgewise without twenty others being thrown at them. Ian loved it. He told how he had chosen to leave and take the others with him, but after he had told it a few times he noticed that he no longer had an audience. Everyone was listening to Philip tell about how Avery had stood up under pressure, how her calm head had saved them all. No one wanted to listen to Ian talk about himself, but the unfiltered admiration of Philip brought them begging for him to tell more of their adventures.

Lucas watched the proceedings with much interest, commenting to himself how they had all changed.

Avery watched everyone, answering needs before they were spoken. She made sure Philip and Ian had food before she took her own, she thought through everything to make sure that they were as comfortable as possible. She no longer had to care for herself, make sure that no one figured out who she was, and now she could care for everyone else. She saw the pain that Philip felt. She knew he had been taxed beyond anything she could imagine, but her tact told her not to say anything about it. She had grown from the selfish girl who didn't care about her kingdom, who didn't care about convenience for any but herself, into a woman who saw other's needs before her own.

Philip had grown quieter, contemplative. His time alone had softened him, made him realize how lucky he was to have the things he had. He had grown to appreciate the beauty that had been taken away from him. He had realized the fleetness of it.

Ian had also changed, and Lucas couldn't at first tell what it was. He knew he should not trust the boy, but he didn't know why. Details had been left out of their stories. Philip was protecting him, and not for the right reasons. He made a note to talk to him about it later and then called everyone to order.

"Alright, if you don't mind," he turned to Avery, "I will give my speech in the common tongue." She nodded and he began. "Men from the country of Davia!" he did a quick mental count. "There are about a hundred of us now. We have come from all walks of life: lords, nobles, farmers, peasants, village folk, and men from the cities for only one purpose, to overthrow the Phoenix and establish one of our own in his place. But, if we are to realize our dream, we will need more people, many more. We have two fights before us: we need to take over the castle and then defend it from the power hungry Bucan Dynasty. I have been told Alonzo has been working for them this whole time." Gasps went through the crowd. "Once we take over the castle, they will come for us, knowing we are in a weak and perilous condition. We must stop them!" Lucas cried, his fist in the air. "We will stop them! Our fight will be heard!"

His cry resounded among the men, each one taking it and making it his own.

"My fight will be heard!" an old man shouted, his family had been taken away from him when the Phoenix had taken over.

"My fight will be heard!" a young man cried out, his wife killed, his home taken away.

Each cry had its own story behind it, each cry was plea for it to be heard, and they were.

"But," Lucas quieted them. "We do not have enough people to attack, we need more. I am not pushing any of you to accept this mission, but I want to send out groups to every village to gather everyone who will fight for us. You will be hunted, even killed. The Phoenix's grasp extends far from the castle, though we don't like to think it. I do not ask you to take this mission unless you want to. I understand if you do not wish to risk your life in this way. However, if you go, your name will go down in history, you will be remembered as the few who started the revolution. Your story will be told!"

The crowd erupted. No one held back. They were willing to risk their lives for their country.

Avery watched passively, remembering the time when she had refused to do the same for her country. Those feelings of hate had gone away. She realized that some things were bigger than herself. She couldn't just sit back and let everyone burn because she would burn with them.

Lucas stepped away, his job done. People flocked around him, begging to be sent out. He directed them to Wellington who distributed them into groups to send out to each village.

Darren fought his way to the front of the line, pushing past people in his hurry to help. "I have been on so many missions. Allow me to lead one now," he begged, pulling at Wellington's arm.

Wellington looked at him and gestured for three people to follow him, "You'll go south. I'll give you villages later." He turned back to assigning people as Darren turned to leave.

Avery watched as Philip waited in line. He reached the front and she watched as Philip posed a question. Wellington looked surprised and turned to look at Lucas. Lucas nodded and Wellington turned back to Philip. They conversed for a moment, but Philip pressed his position and came through in the end. He thanked Wellington and turned to pack up his things.

"Philip!" Avery called out to him, running to meet him halfway. "You can't go!"

Philip placed his hand on her shoulder. "I can and I must."

"But you're not strong, you need rest!"

"I'll have plenty of time to rest on the way there and back." He knelt down to stuff his things into his bag.

"There are other people who are willing to do this," she argued.

"You can't just sit back and say that someone else will do it. If you never take action yourself, no one will ever get anywhere and it will be your fault," he pointed at the line in front of Wellington. "Look at them, some of them are too old and shouldn't have to do this. I'm going because they deserve better, they deserve to sit back and relax but times have betrayed them. They shouldn't have to do this, so I'm doing it for them."

He stood up, his pack filled.

Avery glanced away to hide the tears that betrayed her. "You only just got back. I haven't seen you in days."

"Yes," he pulled her into a hug. "And when I come back we'll catch up on everything. I'll take it easy then. I'm only going away for a few days."

She hugged him tightly, the strange words caught in her throat. "Alright, I'll see you then."

Philip turned to join his small group. They were given horses because they were going further than some of the others.

She watched as Lucas said goodbye to his son, and she watched as they mounted and turned their horses' heads in the direction of the villages.

The last she saw of him was when he turned to look back at her, his hand raised in a salute.

She turned back, ignoring the other groups leaving. What was she going to do for the next eternity before they could make their next move?

Crovprix stood next to her, his arms crossed. "Lady," he addressed her in the common language. "You are disturbed."

"I am," she answered, aware he had managed to sneak up on her. "Things happen."

She left him, turning to Lucas. "Is there anything for me to do?" Despair saturated her voice, but Lucas had to turn her down.

"We don't need any help," he told her, watching her disappointed face fall. "I'll tell you if I find anything."

He left her, helping some of the groups saddle horses and load bags atop them. She shook out her skirt, resolving that she wouldn't just sit around doing nothing. She noticed that Ian stayed behind, selfishly using the same excuses Avery had used to try to keep Philip behind, but this time she didn't approve.

In less than an hour, the camp was empty of all the young men. Only the elderly, injured, Ian, Lucas, Wellington, and Avery were left—even Edward had gone. The life of the camp was gone too, leaving with the groups they pinned all their hopes on. Avery and Ian almost wished they had found a way to go along with one of the groups.

CHAPTER TWENTY-SEVEN

P hilip sat in the saddle watching the world go by. It felt like something had come to a close. He was becoming his own man, and it felt like he was leaving everything behind. He couldn't just think of himself anymore.

The countryside passed around him. He was bound for the country that his father had been lord over. He was going back home, back to where his mother had died, back to the place where his life had tumbled down around his ears on that one day in spring. He remembered that it had been so beautiful, so reassuring that nothing could go wrong.

Time passed as they rode by day and slept by night. They were on the road for three days before they reached the village Philip would never forget. He traced the roads through the city till he reached the center of town. His gaze went to the well where the Phoenix man had called him and his dad outlaws. How could he forget it? And here they were again, blending into the crowd.

They grouped together—everything had been rehearsed, everyone knew their part, everyone was nervous.

Philip stood up on the well, making sure he didn't disrupt the women gathered there. He raised his hand.

"People under the former lordship of Lord Lucas the Just of Southland, listen to me!" the crowd quieted. "If you remember, but a few weeks ago the Phoenix Followers stood in this very spot and announced your lord and his son as outlaws. Just a few days ago, the news that the Phoenix is working for Bucan has come to light." Gasps filled the crowd. "The Phoenix was having a demonstration of power, an execution of blameless men, when our friends and families revolted. Your fellow countrymen could no longer stand the oppression, and they fought for their freedom! Now, we are asking that you join us in defending our country from the terror of the Phoenix. Let's take back what is ours!"

"Our kingdom has been torn down by the Phoenix, 'From the ashes of the old shall he rise!'" one of his fellow outlaws called out. "'Like the Phoenix of old ...'"

"'The time for new has come,'" another called out. "'From the old ashes of the kingdom shall a ruler rise ...'"

Philip raised his hand for silence. "Your nobles have been outlawed, and they are hunted down by the Phoenix. Lord Alonzo—for that is who claims to be the Phoenix—kills nobles, and yet is one himself. He is a hypocrite! We have been called lawless, and yet the true Phoenix is lawless. I urge you to join us in taking back our kingdom. We are weak alone, but together we are strong!"

The crowd roared, though many men remained unsure. While some men took leave of their wives, kissed children goodbye, went back to their homes to gather supplies immediately, most slowly took their leave to go back to their homes to think about it.

Philip was done. His job was complete. He jumped down from his pedestal and turned to leave. Hands reached out from all around him. People thanked him as their savior, someone even went so far as to call him the Phoenix, but Philip silenced the outcry with a severe look.

Philip led the men from the center, trying to remember the way to his father's friend's house for he had promised to visit and he wasn't going to let his father down.

He knocked on the door, certain that he had come to the right place, but no one greeted him. His heart quavered. Perhaps he wasn't home? Or perhaps something worse had happened?

He went down the street to the inn where he had seen the Phoenix drinking. He went inside and sat down on a bar stool.

"Innkeeper?" he called out to the person behind the counter. "Do you know what happened to Murray? The man who lived just down the street?"

The innkeeper sighed, set down the cup he had been drying and leaned on the counter. "Aye, I know what happened to the man. Why?"

"I need to know," Philip kept his voice steady.

"Well, if you don't mind the Phoenix trying to capture you, then I might as well tell you," the innkeeper nodded at his friends. "The man harbored some enemies of the Phoenix and they found out. I should have told the man to stop after the first time, but after that, he was hooked. I could do nothing to convince him to give it up, and when the Phoenix found out? He was taken to the village prison. He might still be there; he might be gone. I don't know."

Philip thanked the man, left him a tip, and walked out the doors.

His men followed him without a word. They didn't care much about this secondary mission, but they didn't want to ask for leave because they knew they would get it and they didn't want to feel bad about leaving their leader alone.

They found the village prison without trouble. The dark house front that greeted them was foreboding, but they entered anyway.

Philip looked around. The law keeper or sheriff sat in the corner, his Phoenix feather clearly visible his hat at the door.

Philip approached him. "Dear sir, would you be so kind as to allow me to see my father's old friend?"

The man looked up, startled from his book. "Who are you and who are you here to see?"

"My name is Philip and I am here to see Murray, my father's old friend."

"Murray ..." the man stood up and turned to his grubby desk, flipping through the book that lay there. "I believe he was transferred to a town to the east and executed a few days ago. You have my deepest sympathy." The man looked up and turned to sit in the corner again. "You only missed him by a few days!"

Philip seethed at the man. His cocky attitude rubbed him the wrong way, and it wasn't just because he was from the Phoenix.

"Who else is in there?" Philip asked, hiding his voice.

"A few men who were found in your friend's house. A few people who were suspicious. Why?" the man finally began to take his job seriously.

"You don't have any murderers? What about thieves?" Philip was appalled. Was crime allowed to prosper while this man locked up innocent people?

"I'm afraid I didn't catch your name?" the man changed the topic.

"Frederick," Philip lied, only now realizing the mistake he had made in his haste.

"That's not what I heard you say the first time. Are you the son of the former lord? Philip?" the man was about to have his biggest break and he knew it, but what about these other men?

"Yes," Philip answered at last. "My name is Philip, and I am the son of Lucas the Just, Lord of Southland. You are relieved of your duty. I will appoint someone to take your place."

The man almost laughed, but he hadn't expected to be relieved of his duty.

"Frederick," Philip turned to the man who was actually called by that name. "I appoint you as sheriff of Southland, kneel." Frederick knelt and Philip drew his sword and lay it on the man's shoulders. "I appoint you sheriff of Southland. I challenge you to uphold the laws of this country and enforce them to the best of your ability. Rise," Frederick rose. "You are to take up your position immediately."

Frederick nodded as he turned to the Phoenix Follower who had been watching in surprise. "I place you, the former sheriff, under arrest for not fulfilling your duties to the best of your abilities, for murdering innocent men, imprisoning innocent men, and being an accomplice to the impostor known as Alonzo the Phoenix."

The man didn't know what to do. Was this all a practical joke? His mind was made up in a moment when the other men took the keys and escorted him to his own cell.

"You know what you have to do," Philip turned to Frederick. "Check the records and release any innocent men. Make sure that any complaints of real crime are addressed. I trust your decisions."

Philip turned and left his men. They all stayed behind to help Frederick in his endeavors to bring back justice.

I failed him. Philip sat down in the square on the well. *I came too late to save him. I didn't even know he was going to die.*

Philip threw his head in his hands and sat in contemplation. There was nothing left but to avenge him and move on. He would never forget the man who had saved their lives so they could set everything in motion. He hadn't just saved them, he had gone on to save others. Tt was up to Philip to continue that legacy, to make sure that his death had not been in vain.

And isn't that what we all want?

CHAPTER TWENTY-EIGHT

They finished their mission, the people around them seemingly recalled to life. They went from their normal lives, their mundane tasks, the simple joys, to a much greater purpose, to something beyond themselves. It was wonderful to watch, but Philip turned his heart from them, wishing with his whole heart that this lot had never come to him. If the Phoenix had never come he would not have been thrust into this life, this life he was still not ready for. He would not have met with all this terror, this pain, this loss. But, he would never have met the many new friends he now had. He would never have met Avery.

He might wish that everything was the way it had been, but he realized that life would be pointless without it. He realized he would not be the same, and that it was all right.

He turned from the village, leaving behind a few men he had brought, but bringing with him more than he had ever imagined. He led them back on the three-day journey to the camp, past the castle in broad daylight, always remembering what had happened the first time he had been there. Every time he saw the river, his mind brought back memories. He would never forget the strange look of that pale face and black hair, no matter how hard he tried to push it from his mind.

They reached the camp. It had been seven days since he had been there, and his group was the last to come through.

Hundreds of men were gathered there now. He plowed through the many who lay on the ground, sat, played, and talked. He searched for Avery. Where was his father? Where were they?

He called out, but no one answered him, strange faces looking up at him as though he were crazy. He ignored them, finally spotting his father.

"Father, I found Murray."

"That's fantastic. Where is he?" Lucas gave his son a hug.

"He has been taking in outlaws like us, and giving them shelter just like he gave us shelter," Philip explained as Lucas began to realize what those words meant.

"Where is he?" Lucas took Philip by both arms.

"He was found out and killed," Philip answered, not looking in his father's eyes.

Lucas turned away. "He died defending what he stood for," he reassured Philip. "Avery is over there," he told him. "I'll talk with you later."

Philip turned, aware he was no longer wanted. He followed where his father had gestured.

Avery knelt on the ground, an old man lying there, his cold hands in hers.

"You did what you could," she smiled at him. "No one could have asked for more."

Philip stood far off, aware he was not invited into the conversation.

The man murmured something, and she had to lean down to catch his words.

She smiled and brushed her short hair out of her eyes.

Placing his hand on his blanket she stood up. "Alright, I'll leave."

She made her way through the groups of men around her until she reached Philip.

"What was he saying?" he asked her when she reached him.

"He was telling me about the skirmish he had led just yesterday," she answered. "The Phoenix Followers occupied his village and when our men showed up, he brought the villagers to arms."

"I see you have made yourself busy while I was gone," Philip changed the subject. He also noted that her hair was growing longer and her speech was coming more naturally, but he didn't say it out loud.

"There isn't much else to do," she replied. "These men have been coming in for days. You're the last group to come in so we'll probably make an attack in the next few days." Philip nodded as Avery continued. "The time is ready to make a move. Crovprix has been talking with Lucas and Wellington about strategies. It sounds like they are going to use the tunnel we used to escape from the castle."

Philip changed the subject. "Is Ian still here?"

"Yes," she answered him.

"How is he? I hope he's been recovering,"

"He has," Avery said matter of factly. "Beyond a doubt. He's up to his old tricks and everything,"

"I'm glad. When he didn't go out with one of the groups I was worried about him," Philip lied.

"He was just being selfish," Avery told him, knowing full well that Philip was lying.

Philip didn't know how to respond, but he had known the answer before he had asked.

They stood there silently, watching the people around them. It was like old times again, but there was nothing left to say.

Lucas watched them from where he sat, his head in his hands. Murray was dead. It was going to happen sometime, but he had never expected it so soon. Murray had been the single tie that had kept him sane in school. It was almost impossible that they had fallen apart after they finished and gone down their separate roads in life, but it had happened and he would regret it for the rest of his life. He pushed his own thoughts to the side and carried on. Life still needed him for whatever purpose it had left.

Lucas summoned Wellington, Crovprix, Edward, Grurhoum, and Darren to him.

"Our final party just came in," he told them. "It's time to make our next move."

"I've checked. We can fit many people into the tunnel," Crovprix informed him. "It will be ideal if we can get a group to distract at the front gate, but we should be able to make it anyway."

Lucas thanked him and turned to Wellington. "Have you informed the men?"

"I have, although I still have to get to the last group that just came in," Wellington explained.

"How are the men?" Lucas turned to Darren.

"We have a few old men who we cannot turn away, but we'll manage."

"I put you in charge of the men, Darren. Keep tabs on them. Tell me if anything goes wrong." He turned to the dwarf. "You are not obligated to stay here any longer unless you would like to. You have helped us more than you could ever imagine. You are free to go,"

Grurhoum closed his eyes. "I have no place to go. I cannot make it to my cousin's kingdom under the mountain by myself. It is far to the north and there are people between us who would wish to kill me. I will stay for the moment."

Lucas thanked him and moved on. "Then we attack tomorrow night. You are dismissed."

CHAPTER TWENTY-NINE

P hilip waited behind the trees, his breath slow and steady. The castle was cloaked in darkness except for the few windows that had candles in them. He realized their escape must have been noticed. He wondered how it had gone over and why no one had done anything about it.

The moon came up, and he could see the other men around him also waiting for the signal. He caught Avery's eye and gave her a smile, her green and brown dress blending into the foliage around her. He remembered the past few days he had spent with her. They had done some sword fighting and target practice. He wouldn't trade in those days for anything.

The signal came from the almost invisible figure out in the field. Philip was to go first, gliding out into the open and then down the tunnel he had escaped from little more than a week before. The cold stone welcomed his rough hands as he slid down, hitting the ground with a thud. The signal came again and another person entered the tunnel. They kept coming until the tunnel was crowded. Finally Wellington and Lucas came. Darren was with Edward at the front gate distracting the castle.

Philip led the way as Avery caught up to him and everyone followed them deeper into the ground.

Everyone's nerves were on edge, but none of them were on edge like Lucas's and Wellington's. They had done this before and met with disaster. They had been captured with no hope of release, and now they were doing it again. This time, the result had to be different.

Their hands caressed the walls as they passed. Avery and Philip led the way to where they knew the stairs would be. They traced their way through the mazes beneath the ground, hands on the hilts of swords, bows and arrows in position to kill.

Philip found the stairs that would lead them to the same level as the rest of the castle, and he raised his hand. His hand reached out to the door handle, making sure that when it swung open, Avery would be protected by its thick bulk.

He nodded to his men and turned the knob. The door swung open and he stepped into the dim light beyond. Everyone poured out of the door. No one was in sight.

Lucas called out in a whisper, separating his men into groups, Wellington heading the bigger one, he the smaller. Philip and Avery followed Lucas, mazing their way to where the throne room would be. The few guards they met were disposed of quietly. They came upon the big doors, the two guards beside them already sinking to the ground with arrows still quivering in them.

It felt almost like a dream. They would wake up in a few moments, turn over, sigh, and fall asleep again. But it didn't end and the doors opened.

Alonzo and Arlington stood at the front of the room, turning at their noisy entrance.

They drew their swords, preparing to fight back, but they were no match and were quickly cast down but not killed. They would face trial for their treason.

Everyone in the room knelt as the only heir left to the throne sat on it, her pale face paler than ever in the flickering candlelight, her dark hair reflecting that same light.

She looked out over the surreal moment. Everything was right with the world again. Things were missing, but this was the end. They had done it.

"Your Majesty," Lucas stood and bowed.

Her heart sank. How could this be the end? This was only the beginning. Now she must rule this country. It wasn't just taking it back She had responsibility now.

"Lucas the Just of Southland," her calm voice cast itself over the room. "I restore you to your titles. Your land is yours again, your manors are yours, and you shall receive due commendation."

"Thank you," Lucas bowed again. "But we have more things to think about than that."

"I agree. I give you permission to cleanse this palace of the so-called Phoenix. I allow you to use every method you deem fit."

Lucas turned. That was all he needed. He gestured for his men to follow him, leaving some behind to guard the new ruler.

They left, dragging Alonzo and Arlington behind them. She breathed a sigh of relief as they disappeared. She knew she would have to deal with them at another point in time, but she was glad to see them go.

She looked at the men left behind. Philip was gone, but that didn't matter. What was she to do?

The men glanced at each other, surprised by the turn of events, but not worried by them.

Avery left her throne to circuit the room. The tapestries, the pillars, they were all there.

"Follow me," she turned to leave, but the men did not follow.

"Your Majesty, it is not advisable for you to leave the protection of this room."

Her chin lifted just a hair. "You are to follow me."

They followed her, opening doors before she reached them, killing guards before they noticed them. She made her way to the front of the castle, the front gate.

She brought her men to a halt just around the corner of it, ordered them to be quiet and then directed them to step out.

Darren had been attacking the front of the castle to distract the Phoenix from the group sneaking in from the tunnel, and now many men had gathered at the gate to defend it, or mostly just watch the pitiful attempts that Darren made.

Avery's guard attacked the men who had gathered, swift and silent. Arrows flew, and swords clashed. The battle was almost over before it started. Avery sat back and watched as her men tore the guards apart, and then oversaw as the portcullis was lifted to the bewilderment of Darren and his group.

Her men called out to them and they came through, joining her in the hall.

"See?" she turned to the man who had challenged her before. "Now we go back and wait."

She turned and led them back to the throne room, grinning from ear to ear. When she reached it, the other groups had already gathered there.

"You left, your majesty," Lucas rebuked her.

"You forgot about Darren's group," she reminded him.

"I did, though he could have waited and need not have been gotten at the expense of your safety," he reminded her.

She thanked him for his concern, and he led her to the throne where she sat down, searching the men for Philip's face. She found him, bent over his arm. He had been injured but didn't want her to know.

"Thank you," she addressed the men gathered. "Davia thanks you. You have done your country proud, and there is nothing more worthwhile than that."

"Men," Lucas spoke up. "I will be setting up a guard for tonight. It will be double what it would normally be just in case we have missed anyone in the purge. I expect you to volunteer if you are able. Otherwise, you are dismissed. I am very proud of you."

The men gathered around him for further assignments, and she watched as Ian left with a group of old men. He was not going to stand watch unless he was ordered to. She found Philip already in line for an assignment, though his injury ruled him out.

Avery was given a guard of ten men and was escorted to a room that Lucas had decided would be suitable. It was close to the throne room he was setting up as their headquarters. When she saw it, she smiled. It was her old room. Her dresses were there just the way she had left them. The bed, the window, everything just as she remembered. She was home again.

CHAPTER THIRTY

Dawn came sooner than anyone expected as everyone convened in the throne room where a few of the men brought in a meager breakfast they had prepared. Tables from the great hall had been brought in, and everyone was seated at their respective tables. Avery was offered the best of things, but her conscience advised her against taking the better things when her men needed them as much as she. After breakfast, Lucas, Wellington, Edward, the wizard, the dwarf, and Darren pulled Avery into a conference.

"Alright," Lucas called them to order. "We have taken the castle. Our next step is to fortify the castle against invasion from Bucan, and I believe the queen should address her people."

Avery looked up, the new title rolled off his tongue so strangely and she hadn't realized he meant her.

"But," she began to object. "What if they think I'm too related to the king to be thought of as 'change in the bloodline of rulers'?"

Wellington sighed. "It's true, I have heard some of the men whispering among themselves that she is not 'change.' They think the throne is up for grabs and that any of them worthy enough can just up and take it. It might be best if you addressed the crowd as the leader."

Lucas sighed. "Why all the politics?! Why can't we just ..."

They waited for him, but he shook his head and Darren moved on. "Someone needs to address the people, and at the moment it looks like Lucas and Wellington are the two to do it. I'll organize our men into squads to fortify the castle while you are doing that. Edward can help me." He got an affirmative nod from Edward.

Crovprix and Grurhoum only listened. They could understand everything being said, but they had no part in it. It was their job to offer their services when needed. That was all.

"I have a few spells that might help," Crovprix interjected, sighing. His face looking worn, tired as though the magic lifeblood within him was sapping away.

"What's wrong, Crovprix?" Avery asked.

"Spells take energy, that's all. I've cast several these past few days, but I can cast a few more before I have to rest," he informed her. "I'll fortify the walls to be extra strong, I don't expect them to come with war machines, but they might be that desperate. I'll also cast a few over the works here and there. They won't be noticed but they will be powerful. They had achieved their goal but we just stole this kingdom back and they're not going to be happy about that. If they fail now after having secured the kingdom once, they will never be able to look another kingdom in the eye ever again. They will stop at nothing to get Davia back."

Everyone thanked him for the offered service and assured him that he could take a rest before he did them, but he smiled at them knowingly and told them he was fine.

They broke up, everyone heading out to do the jobs they had taken upon themselves.

Darren and Edward called their men together, Philip following them to help out as best he could with his arm now wrapped up.

When Avery's mind was not thinking about Philip, it turned to Ian. What had happened to his father?

"Ian," she asked at last. "Where is your father? I take it that last night did not favor him?"

"It did not," he told her. "My father has yet to be found."

He did not seem surprised by the information, almost as though he knew something had happened to him.

"Do you think Alonzo dispensed of him?" she asked.

"I overheard him talking with you, and I do believe that something of the kind happened," he answered her, looking away. She did not respond.

She had orders to stay near the throne room at all times in case a matter came up, and so she skimmed the hallways outside. She had on a new dress. She was getting used to wearing dresses again. She opened a door and entered a room, her men following her. Straight to the window she went, following sounds of people. She looked out over the courtyard below. People were gathered to listen to Lucas and Wellington's speech. She sat down on the window seat and listened, almost taking notes for when she would be accepted into their place.

"People of Davia!" Lucas called out, his hand upraised. "As you have noticed, many events have been going on in the kingdom these past few days." The people below him murmured. "A week ago, Alonzo, the so-called Phoenix, attempted to execute your former lords. You revolted, your voice was heard, you made your opinion known, and now, our dream has been realized. The impostor known as Alonzo has been overthrown and cast down. It is time for us to rebuild this kingdom 'from the ashes of the old,'" he chanted. "'Like the Phoenix of old, the time for new has come. From the old ashes of the kingdom shall a ruler rise. He shall be known as the weak, but shall be made strong. He shall be known as someone, but in truth is another. He shall be hunted by hypocrites—the ones he came to save. With the lawless he will dwell, and one of them he shall be. The time has come for change, change in the bloodline of rulers.'" he paused as the crowd cheered, recognizing the words of the old prophecy. "We have bonded together, and now it is time to rebuild this kingdom with the help of the true Phoenix," the crowd held their breath, catching every word that dropped from his mouth. "Our council is considering several candidates," he lied. "However the one we are considering the most, seems to be too close to the bloodline of rulers to suffice the prophecy. We are in council with a wizard ..."

The crowd erupted in whispers as Lucas tried to quiet them. They had heard the old story about the wizards. How could they trust them?

"The wizard is being helpful in this entire endeavor. But I come at last to what really must be said: Alonzo was deep in the company of Bucan, even going so far as planning on turning Davia over to them when he was done. This means that when they find out that we have retaken the castle, they will surely attack. They will be furious," he spoke the words passionately, Bucan would not retake Davia if he had anything to say about it. "They will not take no for an answer. They are power-hungry and violent. But we cannot give in. We have come so far already; surrender is not an option! We will bond together. We will take them on together!"

The crowd roared and Lucas had to hold his hand up again to silence them. The energy was palpable. The crowd was on fire.

"I offer you the protection of the castle. Bring food, bring water, prepare for a siege. If you are able to fight and have not yet joined our forces, I encourage you to come forth now! Your country is worth fighting for. Your families are worth fighting for. If we lose now for the want of one man, will you ever be able to forgive yourself?"

Many men came forward to answer his call, and they were greeted with cheers from the crowd.

Lilliana watched the proceedings, for the first time realizing what the events really meant. If they lost now, they could never go back. It was go forward or die inside. Sterling could only fight for what he loved, her. If he didn't do that, they could never be together. She would never ask him to not fight for her, or for her country—their country. She turned, he would fight. There was nothing more to it.

"We must prepare!" Lucas cried out over the loud roaring of the crowd.

Avery turned from her windowsill and left the room. There was nothing more.

CHAPTER THIRTY-ONE

P
eople gathered into the castle like bees in a hive. The lords tried to make as much room as possible, but when people began to flock in from other villages, Lucas had to turn them away.

Avery and Philip helped settle people. There wasn't much else for them to do. The other outlaws were out fortifying the castle and bringing more people in. While the injury Philip had received was not bad, they still considered him too injured to help.

He stood with Avery at the gate, taking the families that came and putting them in the rooms they knew to be open, and then coming back to the gate to do it all over again.

When the castle was filled, they wandered the halls making sure everyone was all right.

A tightness hung in the air. They were there in the safe castle, but they knew it wouldn't be for forever. Lucas had let them know on no uncertain terms that Bucan would come for them and the people who flooded to the castle held no hope.

Philip and Avery tried to sooth their uneasiness. People hardly asked them who they were, but their influence was greatly felt as they dashed through the halls like busy bees, fetching things or taking messages.

As they took trip after trip through different parts of the castle they would run into Crovprix, chanting over some part of the wall or some supplies. They passed him silently, trying not to worry his haggard face more than they had to.

A week passed as the tension grew stronger. People no longer spoke loudly in the hallways exchanging news from different parts of the kingdom. Now they spoke in hushed whispers, noting that Lucas had not chosen a new Phoenix. The two lords were clear leaders, but they had been promised a Phoenix. The whispers echoed the thoughts on their hearts that maybe

Alonzo had been the real Phoenix, and Lucas and Wellington were just using the situation to gain power.

The common people complained openly to Philip and Avery, prodding them for answers to their questions.

Avery just shook her head, her face like stone. "Lucas and Wellington are honorable men. Getting a new Phoenix is not at the top of their list. We must first make sure we are ready for Bucan when they come."

"They're just putting it off so we will forget and let them rule," a woman told her. "They're not a change in the royal bloodline. We can't trust them any more than Alonzo."

"The two lords are thinking about many candidates," Philip assured them. "Once the war is taken care of they will make a decision."

"Who put them in charge anyways?" another man asked. "I don't remember saying I wanted him to choose for me."

"Lucas and Wellington are the only reason you're here today," Philip reminded him. "Who else would you have?"

"They're not the only reason," Avery spoke slowly, still having troubles picking her words. "Crovprix, Grurhoum, Darren and many other have poured themselves into this effort."

"What about you?" the woman spoke up again addressing Philip. "You're obviously a big person around here, why haven't they considered you?"

"If you don't think Lucas and Wellington are change enough then neither am I or Avery," Philip gathered his things, turning to leave.

"I wouldn't mind," the man interrupted again. "Having a queen on the throne would be enough change for me. The bloodline has always passed through the kings. Changing the law to allow a queen would be a change in the bloodline of rules."

The people were willing to break their old traditions and laws for her.

Philip looked at Avery in surprise. He had never guessed the effect her presence had on the people, and it now made sense why his father had insisted she take up this job. Even if she didn't see it, the people were slowly accepting her. Many of them would not think to question their old laws and traditions, but even if only a few of them realized her potential as a ruler it would be enough.

Finally, one last group of people came, but this time they had real news of war. Bucan had started to invade.

Lucas was sitting at the morning meal when he heard. His face grew taut and he turned to his advisors, slipping from the throne room into another chamber to speak in peace.

"They have come," he announced to the men.

Avery stood in a corner, knowing she had been brought because she was the ruler, but yet unsure of what to do.

The men bickered: should they stay and hold siege? Or should they go out and meet their enemies in battle first?

No one could agree, and Lucas stood in the back, watching the results of his words.

Finally, he spoke up. "Avery should decide," the room went quiet.

"I am not a general," she spoke in confusion. "I don't know anything about strategy. I should not have this responsibility."

"You need to have this responsibility," Lucas answered her. "I have heard a few good things about you from the people here. They need to accept you, and they will never do that if you sit back passively while others do things for you."

Everyone nodded. "You need to make this decision."

She thought, unsure of which would make things easier to win. "Go out to meet them," she answered. "Let's keep the battle as far away from the people as we can until it is necessary," she paused. "As ruler I would go with you, but I would need prepare to go with you, and I would need a sword made. Perhaps I should stay," she looked over at Philip. "Someone needs to stay behind for the people, and like you said, the people are beginning to accept me. Now might be the best time for me to take the next step."

Lucas cleared his throat and looked at Wellington. "I don't think that would be the best decision either."

She sighed. So, somethings she could decide, but others she couldn't?

"It might be best if the people did not see you as the fighting type," Wellington cleared throat again. "After this they'll have had enough of war for the rest of their lives."

"But if they see her sacrifice, they will realize she is the best for the job," Lucas argued.

"But this will be a chance for me to rule without you here to protect me and do it for me. This will be the time when they get used to me," Avery urged him. "You once told me that as someone who fights for their country, you must give up your own desires and replace them with your kingdom's."

"I have watched you," Lucas began, relenting. "You have started down that path. I would not wish to see you depart from it so soon."

Avery nodded. This was beyond her. She had promised to put her country first, and now it was time to sacrifice her own wishes for the good of her country.

"Thank you," she answered. She would stay, she would find some way to make it bearable, but she would stay. She had grown used to the rush of adventure the last few weeks and the prospect of waiting around in the castle while the others fought for their freedom sounded tame to her.

She left and Lucas followed her, giving her instructions that she promptly ignored.

They left the next day. She watched as Philip followed his father Lucas and Wellington out into the field of battle. Ian followed behind, and Edward skirted the outside of the army.

She was surprised at how many people they had managed to gather, how many people had offered to give up their lives to the greater good, and here she was, still rebelling against having to stay behind and make her sacrifice in her own way.

Her heart would have followed them, but it had to stay behind and take care of her kingdom. The army moved quickly, gaining the ground they had lost while they prepared to take the battle outside of the walls of the castle. They traveled past Farvel Forest, and by the end of the day they were on familiar ground, at least for the group that had already gone to Bucan.

Edward remembered every step of the way even though the last time he had traveled it he had hardly taken anything in. He remembered pain that he had buried deep inside him and the thirst for revenge grew. He would avenge his brother's death or die in the process.

Crovprix could not be convinced to stay behind though he was very tired. He watched Edward with a heavy heart, but knew that there was nothing he could do to unseal the fate that awaited him.

Grurhoum followed from a distance. He realized too late that this fight was not truly his, but fate seemed to drive him forward. It was too late for him to turn back.

Lucas could only think of his army. The landscape that passed them by fell on blind eyes. He was leading them to certain death. How could he reconcile that to himself?

The woods around them passed without their due recognition. The sun fell without notice and the temperatures dropped without anyone batting an eyelash. These people were on a mission, and nothing could deter them from their purpose.

They finally came to a halt, set out guards, and took rest, but the night passed impatiently. They packed up and finally reached the peak. They looked down, the army they expected stretched out far below them, and Lucas called out to his men to set up camp again. He mechanically scanned their forces, but he could deduct nothing from them. They too had set up camp, almost as though they had expected to be come upon at this exact place.

Rows of tents lined up in front of them. Lucas mounted his horse. He looked out over his own army before summoning some men to him and descended the hill.

In his hands lay a leafy branch of peace he had plucked from the forest, but he despised it. He wished to meet them in full out battle to punish them for what they had done to their country.

He entered the camp below him, his men's hearts in their mouths as they waited to be killed, but the leafy branch of peace assured that it never happened. Lucas pulled up to a large tent, consulted with the guards outside the entrance, and entered, bidding his men to stand guard outside.

Lucas entered the tent and watched as a man stood up. They bowed and the guard announced Lord Lucas to the man.

"Lord Lucas," the other man began, cutting right to the point.

He spoke the language of Bucan and the nobles with a strange accent making it hard for Lucas to discern some of the words.

"I offer you many things if you do not attack."

"Sir," Lucas sounded appalled. "I have not come here to hear your offer; I have come to ask you to retract your hold on Davia or suffer the consequences."

"Ah," the man sighed, turning to lean over a table. "I'm afraid that the odds of your winning are very low. I have plans and I have orders from our king."

"Then I'm afraid that you will have the pleasure of surrendering while your men fall like stones around you," Lucas forebode.

"I think that when the morning of tomorrow comes, you will find the opposite will happen," the general informed him.

"Tomorrow it is then," Lucas pulled himself up to his full height.

"So be it," the man pointed to the door. "Be gone."

Lucas scorned him as he left and mounted his horse in a swift movement.

He turned his horse back to the hill, his men following closely behind him. They reach the camp and it was almost set up. He cried out over the noise of his men, "We fight tomorrow! It has been decided. So be it."

CHAPTER THIRTY-TWO

The morning came and the men prepared. Some knew they would not come back from this—their ailments already deciding their fate. Others had things to live for and could not imagine not going back to the same life they had led before. Stirling knew better. He had already seen the change this war would bring upon them, but he was not afraid of it. Everyone else would change and he knew it. If he were the only one to stay the same, he would soon be lost and left behind.

Philip followed his father to the front of the lines, his injured arm bound beneath the heavy chain mail that covered him, and his knee faltering as he mounted his horse. He bit back the thoughts that told him he would fail, the thoughts that told him that this would be the last thing he would do.

Lucas held back the same thoughts for his son. He wanted to tell him to go back. He wanted to save him, but he could not allow his son to sit back while older men fought to protect him. He offered up a prayer for him, for everyone, and signaled for the drummers and trumpets to sound the attack.

Edward pushed his way to the front of the lines, fighting the men who tried to hold him back from his revenge.

The battle cry was picked up giving chills to everyone that heard it. The two moving lines clashed together—arrows flying, swords clanging, horses sighing, metal clashing together—noise surrounded everywhere. Almost immediately the low moan of death could be heard and then the slow song of the dead as men turned from their purpose to mourn for the fallen.

Edward pushed on, killing everyone who came upon him. He attacked men who were already fighting others, but soon he fell. Crovprix watched as the strong man fell beneath the blade.

This was not his first battle, but it was the first one that he felt prepared for. Crovprix Nightcrest stood upon the top of the hill, muttering slow chants under his breath. He was out of practice for this level of magic and the spells he uttered took more strength from him than they should have. But he continued to put his energy into the spells that he whispered.

Victories were won and lost every second.

Philip fought with every ounce of his strength. His goal changed from saving his country to staying alive enough to return from this battle. Davia seemed to be losing and Bucan was going to win. But Crovprix would not allow that to happen, falling to his knees as his spells came faster and sapped more of his life away.

Davia regrouped and retaliated. The day might be won. Bucan pulled back, unsure of where Davia was getting so much strength.

Crovprix uttered one last spell and knelt there unmoving, his work complete.

The sky turned dark, the clouds poured down rain. Lightning shot down from the clouds and the enemy's camp burst into flames. The ground shook, people trembled. Bucan fell when Crovprix smiled. Standing where he was overlooking the battlefield he knew they had won.

Crovprix knelt where he was for several hours, not having the energy to move. The dead were already being lifted and burned, the smell of their bodies tainting the now night air. But more importantly, the dead were being carried away to make access to the injured, the living, the people who still had hope within them.

Crovprix picked himself up, his tired gait leading him down the hill and away from rest. He staggered down the hill, stepping around the dead, and offering a word of hope to the living who made their sad way through their fallen friends. He murmured the death song under his breath, offering up prayers for the men who had no one to sing it for them.

His eyes fell upon two men lifting up a motionless body. It was short, almost childlike. His heart wrenched within him. The boy would never go back to his mother. He could not have been older than twelve. He turned his eyes away.

He continued down the hill, watching Philip caress the hand of his fallen father, Wellington lying on the ground only a few feet away.

Crovprix could take it no longer. He searched for a fallen man who could still breath and have hope.

He stumbled upon Grurhoum. His hand covered the wound on his head, the weapon that had inflicted the blow was nowhere to be seen. Grurhoum's unseeing eyes looked up at Crovprix as the wizard knelt beside the dwarf.

Crovprix took his withered, old hands, held them over the wound and began to chant. His energy passed from him on the last words, but the glazed look on his eyes disappeared and the wound closed. Grurhoum fell into a deep sleep, his head falling to rest atop the wizard's shoulder.

The death around them was only broken by the weeps of the living. They had won, but the cost had been too great. They could never be the way they were.

Avery waited in the castle, watching as the sky had grown dark with thunder and lighting. She could feel the ground shake from where she was and her heart turned within her, sure that things had gone wrong somewhere. She reassured her people but had no such reassurance herself.

Avery looked out over the city from her position on the castle walls. An army of men stretched out before her, gathered under a red and orange banner. The storm still raging.

She saw clearly the plan Bucan had put into action. They had taken a chance and split up their forces. Some of them would engage Lucas and Wellington out on the battlefield while the rest would take up an attack on the castle. They were simultaneously retaking Falkerstone and keeping the rest of her forces from reaching the castle without another fight.

She dashed back into the castle, calling for the few men who had remained to join her.

She sent for two messengers, already preparing a scroll one of them would take.

She handed the scroll to the first messenger who arrived. On the scroll was a quick description of what Avery guessed was going on and a plea for help. She ordered him to leave from the back gate and take the scroll to Lucas and Wellington as soon as possible.

She did not have to remind him of the importance of his mission.

The messenger bowed and took the scroll, dashing away to prepare for his trip.

The second messenger arrived only seconds afterword.

Avery instructed him to roam the halls for anyone who could fight and dismissed him.

By then the few soldiers and guards who had been left with her had gathered.

She addressed them sternly, ordering them to line the outside wall as best they could. She reminded them that haste was necessary, in only an hour the army would be within an arrow's shot and they would be doomed.

The soldiers and guards sprang into action, enlisting the help of the men the second messenger had gathered.

Avery climbed a tower to overlook everything.

She watched as the guards quickly filled in the wall. It was far sparser than she wanted, but there was nothing she could do about it. There was no one else to pull.

She turned her gaze toward Bucan but could see nothing. Even the messenger was gone.

She noticed the army had pulled around the back. It was possible the messenger had not made it out in time, but she didn't allow herself to think it. Every hope rested on him.

She dashed back down the stairs to take up her position on the wall, waiting for the onslaught she knew would be coming.

She reached the outside wall and waited for what seemed like hours.

The Bucan army marched right up to the wall and then stopped. They didn't do anything immediately discernible, but the men on the wall waited patiently.

Deep within the castle Avery knew the women and children would be on edge. None of them had been out to the wall and knew the real state their protection was in. Avery was thankful they didn't. They would have taken one look and begged to surrender immediately.

She sat, not sure what she was waiting for.

Would Lucas and the rest of the army come back? Or would Bucan strike first?

Night fell and the army grew tense with expectation. She could see the strategy Bucan was taking by making them wait. Each moment of silence, each moment they stretched out, only made the anticipation grow till it was almost too much to bear.

Suddenly the tension broke and the rain of arrows came.

Avery called the attack and they returned the volley.

Everyone could breathe now and their heads were clear. They were finally able to take action.

The hours passed in pain, her old wounds reopening with the heavy lifting she did around the castle, reopening the pain that she felt in her heart, reopening the pain that told her everything was over.

She hid her pain, waiting for the messenger she had sent to bring back his fruits, for better or for worse, but the messenger never came.

Life felt empty to her—there was no joy in caring for her people or calling out the attacks. She resented them every moment that she spent with them.

CHAPTER THIRTY-THREE

Day broke and the fighting stopped.

Avery took the chance to escape back to the top of the highest tower. She looked everywhere, scanning for any sign of the returning army.

The storm from the night before seemed to have dissipated and though the roads had been wetted down, she could see the dust rising from the path that she knew the army would take. Her heart rose in anticipation though there was no way to tell if it was Bucan continuing their invasion or Davia returning victorious. Whether it was for her death or for her life, she did not know.

She dashed down the stairs of the tower, her cloak flowing out behind her to protect her from the cold wind that blew at the top of the tower. She dashed through the crowded halls, people watching her, knowing instantly that something more had happened.

She mounted the stairs to the castle wall, looking out over the Bucan army. They seemed not to notice the approaching army and she prayed it was a good sign. They must not be expecting anyone.

She waited in silent anticipation, the two armies standing face to face, seeing who would budge first.

Suddenly the army emerged from Farvel Forest and Bucan took notice of them.

They came to a halt, the glint of shining armor overcoming the great cloud of dust that advanced toward the castle. Her heart stopped. This was the moment she had been waiting for, living for, dying for. The cloud became shapes, the shapes faces, the faces people.

Avery still couldn't see who it was, but she didn't care. She called for her men to attack.

The Bucan army seemed confused. Arrows flew at the from above, and from the forest they were being attacked by another force.

Avery watched as the two armies melded together and called a ceasefire, afraid that they would shoot their own army.

She watched for several minutes, the two armies so evenly matched that she couldn't decide which side was winning.

Avery made up her mind, calling for every other man to leave his position to go down to the gate. She was about to tip the battle in their favor.

She opened the gates to the castle, her men pouring out onto the battlefield.

With the door now open there was nothing between her and the battle just outside the gate.

She grabbed up a sword before taking up her stance with a group of other to defend the gate.

But no one came. The battle had tipped in their favor and the Bucan army was slowly retreating.

A few battle-crazed men attacked the gate, but she and her group easily deflected them and in a few minutes the Bucan army was surrendering.

Avery stood in the middle of the gate watching them surrender and she smiled.

Slowly from out of the confusion a group emerged.

The men dismounted from their horses and fell at her feet, victory and defeat showed through in their eyes, and she noticed that the returning group was far smaller than the one that had set out. Several stretchers dragged behind them.

"Rise," her voice caught in her throat.

Philip brought her hand to his lips in reverence before he spoke.

"My lady, your highness. We have brought you the victory you deserve. I pray that it has not come at too much cost to your country." His eyes did not meet hers and she felt lost.

"Did you get the messenger I sent?" she asked.

"No, your highness," Philip answered her. "We did not know that Bucan was attacking until we emerged from the woods."

"Where is Lucas? Where is Wellington?" she asked, taking his hand and leading the returning party into the castle.

The rest of the army waited outside, taking care of the surrendering army.

"I want to see them."

"They did not come out of the first battle," Philip turned his head away.

"I'm sorry." She looked away, the pain showing through her eyes.

She felt like she should say something about how they wouldn't have had it any other way, that they died defending what they stood for. But those words felt empty and she knew that they meant nothing.

There was no one left to take the country from her. It was hers now if she chose to take it.

They entered the castle and the people gathered around them to welcome the returning victors. The people hardly noticed the heavy blanket of despair that covered each person from the party.

They paraded to the throne room, the people falling in step behind them. Philip, still holding Avery's hand in his, led her to the throne. The common people watched, confused as she sat on the throne and the returning army knelt in front of her, but they did not oppose it. In a moment, everyone was on bended knee. She was queen. They accepted her. She accepted them.

The ancient tapestries around the throne room wavered in the moving air and the people already mentally added another one to the history: the story of the true Phoenix.

Ashes would lie on the ground and everything would be desolate and hopeless. But the mighty bird would rise above the bleak world, its beautiful feathers shining bright in the hope that it shed upon others. Each stitch would be made with care, with the love and hope that the people were given now.

The injured were carried in, each one remembering his brothers in his time of need. Avery dismissed the gathering throng, only asking for those well versed in medicine to stay. Many people stayed and the throne room was quickly changed from matters of state to matters of the people. Beds and tables were moved in. People flocked to and fro, each trying to make the others better.

Grurhoum carried an almost-lifeless body through the masses, searching for a place to lay it down. His eyes turned surprised, as though he were seeing everything for the first time. Someone shouted to him to help lift another body and he hastened to obey, his body remembering the many times he had been punished by men when he had not answered quick enough. He felt attached to the lifeless form, but he didn't know why. Why would he want to save a human who enslaved his race? Weren't they all the same?

He lay the body down on a blanket, huddling close to it to avoid being seen. Where were all the other slaves? Why weren't they doing these things instead of the humans?

A dark-haired lady knelt beside him, speaking to him without the shame that was due.

"What happened to him, Grurhoum?" her pale face seemed familiar against the dark hair but something was missing.

Grurhoum shook his head, feeling a small bruise that had formed there. "I do not know," he answered.

Avery looked down at the wizard, watching his eyelids flutter as he slowly woke. "His energy has been so drained because of the spells."

Grurhoum nodded.

Spells? he asked himself, confusion covering his face. What was happening? What had gone wrong?

The wizard's eyes opened and he smiled. "Ah, Avery," his voice sounded as though it had come from beyond the grave, but it still hinted at life.

"Crovprix, what happened?" the lady asked.

"Casting spells takes energy," he stretched and sat up. "I saved the army with only a little of my energy left, but then I saw Grurhoum," he paused a moment, waxing philosophical. "The thoughts of man and their futures are hidden to me, but I have a book that outlines our past history. Since the past writes the future it is not hard to see the patterns emerging. I saved Grurhoum's life because I know it is important and I used up the last of my energy," he answered simply.

Recognition dawned on the dwarf, but things still seemed to be missing. The wizard locked eyes with him, his gray eyes sinking deep into his memory, deep into the unfathomable depths that would not be explored for years.

"I see," Crovprix sighed, noticing the faint bruise on Grurhoum's head. "I found you almost dead with a large wound on your head. I see that I did not fix it entirely."

"How come I can't remember anything?" Grurhoum asked.

"Because I focused on the wound and not the deeper damage," Crovprix sighed, he knew of no spell to reverse the damage he had done.

Avery looked away, tears filling her eyes, but the dwarf looked at them confused.

Crovprix made a quick decision. His life was so low that he would not regain enough of it for many years. How was he going to undo the harm he had inflicted?

"I must stay here for a few more years," Crovprix finally spoke. "I know I must eventually travel east again, but I can try reversing what I've done."

He did not need to look into the future to know what it held for him. He could see that it would take him years to regain his strength.

Something Grurhoum had once told him lay on his mind. The dwarves had already begun taking their mountain back again and he was needed there. He knew it would be years before it would be time for Grurhoum to return there, but he knew it would eventually happen.

Suddenly his mind took him more west than he had expected: he saw a kingdom without a king, a princess running away to the east, to dragons, to adventure, to him.

"It may be years, but I shall continue my journey east. I have many things that must be taken care of before I go, I will take you Grurhoum, and then return you to your cousin's kingdom."

Grurhoum thanked him, his wiped mind thinking that he was being given his freedom for the first time. He looked at the world around him with new eyes, eyes that told him he was about to take his part in it. He was about to own a piece of it too.

Crovprix could feel a new power that he held within himself now that he had brought himself to the brink. He knew had not become a part of this for nothing. He would need many years to practice his new-found abilities, to perfect them for the times that he knew would be coming, but now was not that time.

CHAPTER THIRTY-FOUR

T he castle emptied. The common people moved back to their residences, thankful they had been defended and could go back to them. Lords, sirs, dukes, and other nobility came to the castle city for guidance and found it. Their titles were restored, and men who had made themselves worthy took the place of the men who had fallen, their legacy living on through them.

Philip became a regular at the castle. His father's old estate had been restored to him, but he could never find any respite there and spent much of his time waiting on Queen Avery. His manners softened and they became even closer friends than they had ever been before.

A year passed and with their hard work, things were slowly put back to right. The kingdom pulled together to celebrate the anniversary of the overcoming of the false Phoenix. The people in the cities and villages celebrated while up at the castle the few survivors of the group of outlaws gathered.

The royalty, new and old, gathered for a ball.

Avery hardly remembered the last time that she had prepared for a ball. That time she had resented every moment. But now on her own terms and with its own special anniversary, it was something she could look forward to.

The lights were lit, the music started, and she was brought in on the hand of her closest friend and advisor, Lord Philip the Valiant, of Southland.

The first dance was called and he took it, kissing her hand as he led her to the floor.

So many things had changed. Almost all the nobles now spoke the common language. Whether it was because they were disgusted with the origins of the language of the nobles, or because they had been commoners who had shown great courage and been promoted to vacant positions.

They danced the waltz. The whirling faces around them blurred together to fill in for the many faces who were missing from the crowd. Their lost presence felt like an aching pain. Philip looked up many times to search for his father, but his face was no longer there. Avery looked up to find Wellington to advise her, but he was no longer with them. Even the wizard and dwarf were gone to the west to await another princess.

But even with the missing people, the hall was not empty. Many friends had been made in that year. Many new lords were present and the fact that they had earned their positions only made them dearer to their country.

But not everyone was gone. Darren stood in the place of Alonzo, heading his holdings and money. Sterling and his wife, Lilliana, watched them from the audience.

The dance ended and Philip led Avery back to her throne. He sat down beside her, assuming his position as her head advisor. They watched the people dance for a while before Avery leaned down to him, asking him to bring her around the room.

They stood, arm in arm and took the rounds of the room, people bowing before them as she curtsied back at them.

Many of the people she had not seen since giving them their positions. She smiled to see how they seemed to have prospered. There were so many new faces around her and she felt proud, knowing they were here because they had earned it.

Philip pulled her off to the side, opening a door and slipping out into the empty garden. The stars above them danced in their slow courses and the moon looked down at them with familiarity. They sat down on a bench beneath a tree, the branches hiding them from the windows of the castle. Avery leaned her head against his strong shoulder, trying to imagine life without him—life without his gentle guidance, without his company, without his strong shoulder to lean on.

Philip looked down at her, his affection growing greater by the moment. "Avery," he whispered. "I love you."

Those simple words went straight to her heart, sending pangs all through her. "I love you too."

Philip moved her head so he could look at her. "I," his voice caught just looking at her. "I want to share the rest of my life with you, will you share the rest of your life with me?"

Avery gasped, looking up into those eyes. "Philip, I do."

He pulled her into an enormous embrace, tears falling shamelessly from both of their eyes. He wrapped his arms around her. They journeyed the garden in each other's arms, the cool night air caressing the trees around them.

Avery pulled away from him for a moment.

"What is it?" Philip asked, his calm voice casting its spell over her.

"I never thought this day would come," she answered. "And I would never have expected something like this when I first saw you."

"It's true," he kissed the top of her head. "And nothing can separate us now."

They cast their gaze over to the castle, aware that they must go back soon but not wanting to. They had to go because another dance was being called.

They slowly ambled back to the castle, the cool night air caressing their bright and happy faces. They entered the castle again, their entrance instantly making an impression on those around them. Everyone wondered why the queen looked so happy. They had never seen her face look like this when she was leading her country. They noticed the intense care that Philip seemed to bestow upon her, but nothing stood out to them. He was always like that.

Philip bowed to her and she smiled that radiant beautiful smile he would enjoy for the rest of his life. They picked up the dance with fluid motion, the center of the attention of every couple on the room.

Philip looked into his future wife's eyes and did not lament the past. Everything had happened for a reason and he would not exchange any part of it for more happiness. He was as content as he could be.

EPILOGUE

P eace was never restored between the kingdom of Davia and the Bucan dynasty. For many years, the two countries remained on edge until war broke out again. Davia pulled through in the end and still holds sway over Bucan to this day.

Grurhoum and Crovprix went west in disguise to a small village by the sea to get rid of the witch population, but Crovprix was there for the sole purpose of advancing the building of ships to visit the countries to the west and practicing his new-found magic. Grurhoum Greatbrow never regained his memory and to this day he believes the wizard saved him from his slavery. They met up with a strange traveler from the west many years later, and Grurhoum made the journey to his cousin's kingdom under the mountain to lead his people to freedom.

Alonzo and Arlington met the fates that they deserved. Alonzo was led to the block by the order of Lord Philip the Valiant a few months after the attack from Bucan. Arlington was found strung up by his tunic in his cell a few hours later.

The country itself healed its wounds as best it could, but the valley where the battle was fought would never be the same. The ashes of the bodies blew away and the sun shone there, but the ground still held the magic that had been used, and nothing grew there till the end of time. When all remembrance of the battle was forgotten, people would walk through the valley with bated breath. The unnatural silence and death made itself pass deep into legend. Many said the place was haunted with ghosts, and truth be told, it was. It was haunted with the ghosts of the people who had died there, hoping they could change the past and forget the massacre that had taken place.

King Philip and Queen Avery lived on after they were married and had several children to carry on the lineage of the Phoenix. They helped the dwarfs as much as they could and reinforced the strong culture that had been lost when Davia had strayed into the paths of other nations.

The sun fell upon their story and the light that they cast faded. Their story came to a close and they were laid to rest with the many people who had died to let them live. The dawn of another age began and memories passed into darkness. Much had changed, for better or worse.

Life and death, happiness and sadness, beginnings and ends, peace and war, birth and death: it was the time to celebrate them all and there was no going back.

ABOUT THE AUTHOR

Erika is an enthusiastic young author from the Cleveland area. Spiced with an active imagination and fueled with real-life camping, hiking, and climbing adventures, she creates worlds that draw you into the action and adventure of her books.
She enjoys working on camp staff during her summers where she collects enough stories and memories to last a lifetime.

Find out more about Erika at www.teragram.ink

www.ingramcontent.com/pod-product-compliance
Lightning Source LLC
Chambersburg PA
CBHW032006170626
46807CB00006B/2674